Merry Chris...

THE SIX O'CLOCK RULE

BRUCE THOMASON

Cover Design by Summer Morris

Published and distributed by:
High-Pitched Hum Publishing
321 15th Street North
Jacksonville Beach, Florida 32250

   Contact High-Pitched Hum Publishing at the following website:
www.highpitchedhum.net

ACKNOWLEDGEMENTS

I am forever grateful and indebted to those who contributed their time and considerable talents to the creation of *The Six O'clock Rule.*

To Jen Zdunkiewicz: Your editing skills were once again on display, and your sharp wit was something I enjoyed immensely.

To Mary Sikora: The first time I read your e-mail telling me not to be afraid to "kill the babies," I told Jackie I thought our Ohio friend had lost her mind. But you were right, of course. I was so attached to my words that I found it almost impossible to cut anything. However, with much encouragement from you, Master Editor, and my loving wife, I learned that less can definitely be more. Hopefully, I killed enough babies to make *The Six O'clock Rule* a taut yet tantalizing read.

And to the love of my life, my wife, Jackie: I've been told the mark of a successful book is the number of units sold. To me, whether we sell one or ten thousand, *The Six O'clock Rule* is a success because of you. Throughout this process, you were always there for me, encouraging, praising, persuading, and occasionally offering criticism (constructively, of course). When you had an opinion, you defended it fiercely. More often than not, you were right. For all that, and for everything you do to make my life such a joy, I love you and thank you.

<u>Excerpt from Police Department Policy Manual</u>

03-16: DEFINITION: THE SIX O'CLOCK RULE

Prior to taking any action, both professionally as well as personally, all employees should consider the following: If your action becomes the lead story on the six o'clock news,
- Will you be proud?
- Will your police department and your community be proud?
- Will your family and friends be proud?

Interpretation of the Rule by a field training officer to his rookie partner:

"If you're thinking of doing something that might make you look like a dumbass on the six o'clock news, here's a tip. Don't."

Chapter 1

It was almost midnight as Clay Randall low-crawled through sea oats covering the sand dunes. A major drug deal was about to go down under the fishing pier, and Clay was part of the takedown team. Their target, Dante Brown, was a violent drug dealer known to carry a pistol. The twelve-gauge shotgun Clay packed gave him a tactical advantage and a level of comfort he didn't feel with his handgun.

At thirty-seven years old, Clay could pass for a much younger man. Happily married to Dana Cappella Randall, he was the proud and loving father of Catarina LeeAnn, or Cat, as she was called. The precocious three-year-old had both her parents, but especially her daddy, wrapped firmly around her little finger.

Clay was the youngest division commander in the history of the Jacksonville Beach Police Department. Normally, commanders spent their days reviewing paperwork, monitoring budgets, and overseeing the actions of their personnel from afar. But not Clay. When he heard a robbery or other major crime dispatched, he would race from his office, responding at high speed to back up his officers. And when one of his detectives served a search warrant, Clay was there to provide support.

Tonight, he had insisted on being part of the takedown team of detectives when told the drug dealer they were after was Dante Brown. Three people, including a seventeen-year-old high school cheerleader, had died after injecting a lethal mix of cocaine and heroin known as a speedball.

For Clay, taking Brown off the street was personal. Until a few months before, Michele Wilson had seemed to have everything going for her. An academic scholarship to Florida awaited her upon graduation from Fletcher High. Head cheerleader, Michele was well liked by everyone. However, a disastrous breakup with her boyfriend sent her on a downward spiral of depression that eventually led the teenager to fall in with a group of kids experimenting with drugs. Her grades dropped, and she began skipping school to hang out with her new circle of friends. Her grandfather, Police Chief Mike Wilson, asked Clay, a family friend since she was a child, to talk to her. But she wouldn't listen. A week later, she was dead.

As the pastor ended her graveside service, Chief Wilson pulled Clay to the side. Speaking quietly but intensely, his eyes filled with tears, the chief told Clay to find the man responsible for selling the drugs to his granddaughter and make sure he never got the opportunity to kill another child.

The detectives put their informants on notice that they wanted the name of the guy dealing speedballs. And they wanted him now. Within a week, tips began coming in about a dealer named Dante Brown who had just moved into the area from Atlanta. Detectives pursued the information, and the operation tonight would be the culmination of their exhaustive investigation.

"Ty," Clay spoke softly into his radio, "I'm in the sea oats south of the pier about forty yards. Any sign of Brown?"

"Not yet," said Sergeant Ty Honchen, supervisor of the drug unit known as the Community Response Team, or CRT.

"You have eyes on Danny?" Clay asked, referring to the undercover detective, Danny Malone.

"Roger that, boss," Ty said. "Malone's waiting under the pier. Soon as he makes the deal, Dante Brown is goin' down."

"Danny, you copy? Any sign of him yet?" Clay asked.

"I copy, Commander. Nothing yet."

"Where's Jeremy?" Clay asked.

"I'm just north of the pier, Commander. I'll have a clear view of the exchange," Jeremy Rivers responded. The veteran detective, known as "Three" to his fellow officers, was nicknamed after the old Three Rivers Stadium his beloved Pittsburgh Steelers called home for decades. "When Danny gives the signal, we'll jump on Brown like a Steeler linebacker on a Jaguar fumble," Rivers said.

"Three," Detective Rafe Santos responded, "Does everything in your world revolve around Steelers football?"

"Nah, just the important parts," he answered.

"Cool it, guys," Clay interrupted. "Let's remember why we're here. Keep your head in the game."

"Brown just pulled into the parking lot in his white Mercedes. I'll advise as soon as he heads your way," Rafe said.

"Okay, guys, it's show time," Ty said. "Santos, check him close. See if you can spot a gun."

"I'm on him, Sarge," Rafe said.

The detectives waited nervously for Rafe to report, aware of Brown's penchant for ripping off his customers.

"He just took a black bag out of the trunk," Rafe said. "It looks kinda like a laptop case. I can't tell if he's got a gun in the bag or somewhere on him . . . okay, he's heading Danny's way. He'll hit the beach on the north side of the pier."

"Three, stay down," Ty said. "Brown will pass close by you. Danny, activate your wire so we can hear the deal. Everybody else, keep a sharp eye out, and be ready to move."

Danny Malone leaned casually against a pier support, his right hand gripping a subcompact pistol in his pocket. Watching the drug dealer approach, he called out, "Yo, Dante, whassup?"

Brown glared at the detective. "You ain't black, Duncan, so don't be talkin' no honky ass street with me," he said, using Danny's undercover name. "Let's just take care of business. You got my money?"

"Right here," Danny said, opening a paper bag at his feet. He tilted it to show five thousand dollars in bundles of twenties, each held together with rubber bands. Brown moved closer, lifting the bag and riffling through each stack of bills. Satisfied, he dropped the computer bag on the sand.

"Here's the stuff," he said, unzipping and reaching inside the bag.

Danny tensed, his hand tightening on his gun. Brown pulled out a clear plastic bag containing two smaller bags, each full of white powder. Looking in all directions for anything suspicious, Brown seemed satisfied, tossing the bag to the undercover detective.

Danny caught it one-handed and dropped to his knees in the sand, pulling cocaine and heroin field testing kits and a small mirror from his pocket. Tearing the cocaine test kit open, he removed a plastic tube and a strip of collection paper.

As Brown watched, Danny opened a corner of the bag marked with a "C" and slipped out a tiny amount of the white powder on the edge of a penknife. Balancing the knife on the mirror, he peeled away the protective covering from the collection paper and touched it gently to the powder, being careful to avoid contaminating the paper with the knife blade or his fingers.

Placing the collection paper back on the mirror, Danny picked up the plastic tube and squeezed gently so that the glass ampoule inside broke open, releasing a liquid. He then shook the tube for several seconds to mix the contents before removing the cap and applying a few drops to the powder residue. Almost instantly, the residue turned a bright, bluish-green color, a signal the powder was cocaine. Using the heroin test kit on the powder in the other bag, Danny got a second positive result.

"Awright, man, you satisfied?" Brown demanded impatiently.

"Yeah, I'm good. Hey, man, I gotta do this, you know? I trust you, but my boss, he don't trust nobody. He'd bust a cap in my ass if I brought back some dope that wasn't righteous. You know what I'm saying?"

"Yeah, well that ain't my problem," Brown said as he stuffed the cash into his bag.

Danny stood up. "As always, man, nice doin' business with you," he said, the phrase that served as a signal for the takedown team.

"Yeah, right," Brown responded, turning to head back the way he had come.

Suddenly, Three Rivers came bounding through the sea oats, gun in hand, yelling, "Police! Get on the ground!"

As the detectives raced toward Brown, he spun and charged full speed at Danny, who was just drawing his pistol. Dropping his right shoulder, Brown slammed into Danny sending him sprawling onto his back. The drug dealer ran south, heading straight toward Clay's hiding place, the computer bag filled with cash banging against his leg. He fired his pistol twice over his shoulder to slow his pursuers.

Clay knew he was facing a man who wouldn't hesitate to kill him if he had the chance. When Brown got within forty feet, Clay flipped on the flashlight mounted to the shotgun, targeting the man's face to blind and disorient him. He screamed, "DROP THE GUN!"

Without aiming, Brown snapped off a shot at the source of the light. The round struck the flashlight lens, jamming the weapon into Clay's shoulder. His trigger finger involuntarily jerked, sending double-ought buckshot harmlessly over Brown's head into the surf.

But Clay was not so lucky. A piece of bullet shrapnel from Brown's shot deflected off the flashlight, striking him in the neck and buckling his knees.

Dazed, he keyed his radio mic, "I'M HIT! HE'S HEADED BACK AT YOU!"

Continuing to shoot at the detectives running toward him, Brown suddenly veered toward the sea oats, his headlong flight slower as loose sand pulled at his shoes. Breathing in ragged gasps, he made it almost to the Boardwalk when he heard a shout behind him.

"Drop the gun, Brown!" Danny yelled.

The drug dealer stopped, his weapon pointed at the ground.

"I said drop it, asshole!" Danny commanded.

Brown looked over his shoulder at Danny, hate filling his eyes. "Fuck you!" he screamed, spinning around as he brought his gun up. Before he could fire, Danny pumped five rounds into his body, center mass, and the drug dealer pitched backward, dead before he hit the sand.

Chapter 2

No one moved, as if someone had hit the PAUSE button in the middle of an action movie. Danny was still in a shooting stance, knees slightly bent, arms extended, both hands gripping his pistol as it pointed at the empty space where Brown had so recently stood. Ty, Rafe, and Three stood behind Danny.

Clay staggered up, blood dripping down the front of his shirt. "Danny, you okay?" he yelled.

Danny shook his head as if awakening from a dream. Brown was sprawled on his back in the sand, arms thrown out to the sides. Although his hand still held the pistol, it was clear the drug dealer had shot at his last cop.

"Danny!" Clay said, grabbing his arm and shaking him. "Hey, man! Talk to me! Tell me you're okay!"

Dragging his eyes away from the body, Danny said shakily, "Yeah, I, I'm okay." Seeing the blood, he exclaimed, "Whoa, Clay, you're bleeding!"

The other detectives started talking over each other, telling Clay to sit down, lie down, go to the emergency room.

"Guys, I'm fine," Clay said. "It's just a scratch."

"That's no scratch, boss," Three said. "You need to go to the ER."

"Not yet, Rivers," Clay growled. "Our first priority is to get the scene under control. Has anyone notified dispatch?"

"Yeah, they're sending Rescue," Ty said. "And they're also calling the on-call state attorney, Chief Wilson, the ME, and a couple of evidence techs."

Clay turned to Danny, sensing his emotional turmoil. Touching his arm, he said, "Bro, you did what you had to do. Nobody forced this guy to start shooting. But once he did, you had no choice. He was gonna keep shooting until one of us took him down or he got away."

"I, I guess you're right, Clay. It feels weird, you know? I've been a cop for ten years, and I've never shot my gun except at the range. Until now."

"I'm with you, man. No cop feels good about something like this. Now come on. Let's get you out of here. Give Ty your gun, and you take my backup until we get you a replacement," Clay said.

Danny stared at the weapon in his commander's hand, then down at his own pistol. "Why do I have to give up my gun?" he asked.

"It's for the internal investigation, Danny," Clay said.

"But why does IA have to get involved? You said it was a good shoot," Danny objected. Turning to the other detectives, he pleaded, "Guys, you all saw it! I didn't have a choice! If I hadn't shot first, he would have killed me . . . or maybe one of you!"

Clay put his hands on Danny's shoulders, forcing him to look directly at him. "Calm down! I *did* say it was a good shoot. You're so wired up you're not thinking straight. You know we do an internal on every shooting. That's department policy. But that doesn't mean you screwed up. You didn't do anything wrong, so chill out," he said, taking the gun from Danny's limp fingers and handing it to Ty.

"Here, take mine," Clay said, pressing his weapon into Danny's hand. "And stop worrying. Now let's go to the ER."

"Why do I need to go to the ER? I'm not hurt."

"No, but I am. And if the doc gets too aggressive digging around on my neck, I want you there for backup," Clay said, trying to lighten the mood.

"Okay," Danny said softly, taking Clay's pistol and strapping the holster around his ankle.

Ty looked closely at Clay, noticing he was getting whiter by the second. "No more delays, Commander. We're getting you to the hospital. That wound needs tending to right now!" Seeing the rescue unit arrive, he said, "Stay here, Clay. I'll have them bring the stretcher to you."

Clay glared at him. "He didn't shoot me in the damn leg, Ty. I can walk," he said, striding toward the rescue unit, shoulders back and head erect.

Chapter 3

A week later, the Randall's expansive terrace facing the ocean echoed with talk and laughter. Their four thousand square foot, three-story Florida beach house overlooked the unchanging yet ever-restless green waters of the Atlantic Ocean. With a combined income exceeding half a million dollars, they lived very well, thanks primarily to Dana's exceptional talent and success as an artist.

Clay presided over the grill, basting and turning the meat in time to an eclectic mix of country, hip hop, and alternative rock booming from the speakers located at strategic points around the terrace.

Beer in hand, Ty Honchen came up to Clay, laughing, "Son, I swear, from across the way, those stitches looked like a damn centipede crawling up the side of your neck."

Clay grinned, "I wish it *was* a bug instead of stitches. I forget sometimes and turn my head too quick. Let me tell you, it hurts like hell when that happens."

"How's Dana handling you getting shot?"

"Oh, man, she's still freaked. She told me this afternoon we ought to cancel the party. She said I'm still too weak. I said to pour me a double shot and lean me against the bar. Then if she sees any whiskey leaking through the stitches, just break out the hot glue gun and seal 'er up!"

"I can just see that," Ty said, laughing as he headed off to the bar for another round.

As driving rhythms blasted from the speakers, the center of the terrace became crowded with people swaying to the hypnotic beat and repetitive phrases. Leaning against the bar, Patrol Officer Bobby Hawkins took a pull from a quart bottle of tequila, chasing it with a deep drag off a hand-rolled Cuban cigar. Only son of a wealthy family in Ponte Vedra Beach, he had never worked hard for anything. As a result, he had grown up with an acute lack of self-discipline and drive.

In college, he partied hard and studied little, eventually dropping out. For a while, he drifted aimlessly, living off his parents' money, spending his days surfing and bedding young women attracted to his good looks and wealth. Finally, Bobby's father lost patience. He gave his son an ultimatum, join the family construction business starting at the bottom or go out and find a job on his own. To Bobby's way of thinking, manual labor was simply unacceptable for a man of his breeding. He told his dad he would think about the offer.

As Bobby drove slowly along First Street in Jacksonville Beach a week later, he saw a group of gorgeous young women surrounding a police officer outside a nightclub. They were laughing and smiling at the cop, who was obviously enjoying the attention. At that moment, Bobby realized police work was his destiny. After all, how hard could it be? Write a few tickets, put people in jail that pissed him off, and have his choice of good-looking women hanging all over him because of the uniform. It was a no-brainer.

After numerous arguments with his parents over what they believed to be a dangerous, dead-end career, Bobby signed up for the police academy. He barely passed, graduating last in the recruit class. Then, through some political arm twisting by his disappointed but resigned father, Bobby Hawkins became a Jacksonville Beach police officer.

To his dismay, he found his perceptions of police work seriously skewed. It was hard and frequently dirty work, exactly what he wanted to avoid. The paperwork was mind numbing, the hours sucked, and nobody cut him any slack in spite of his wealthy pedigree.

Rather than quit and face his father's wrath, he persevered, eventually transferring from patrol to detectives, an assignment he figured had more glamour and involved less physical labor. When that also didn't live up to his low expectations, he became the department's public information officer. Failing to show any talent as a PIO, the chief sent Bobby back to patrol, where he languished on the midnight shift.

His lack of personal discipline, character, and emotional maturity, coupled with a family tendency toward alcoholism, virtually guaranteed he would succumb to the bottle. That came with its own set of problems for Bobby, who, when deeply under the influence, lost the vital connection between his brain and his mouth.

Tonight was proving to be no exception. From his vantage point at the bar, drink always close at hand, he watched the dancers. More specifically, he eyed the women. Whether married, in a committed relationship, or a fellow cop's date, he didn't care. They were all potential conquests.

One woman in particular drew his attention. Dressed in tight-fitting pants and a top that showcased her well-toned body, Fontana Jones was a veteran detective who had been with the department several years longer than Bobby. Tana, as she was known, was an attractive African-American woman who had recently divorced. She held a black belt in Tae Kwon Do, a discipline that had come in handy on several occasions working the street.

Speaking in a slurred voice that betrayed his level of intoxication, Bobby gushed, "Wow, Tana! You were like freakin' aw-shum! When you did that flippy, turny thing, it looked like you were gonna bust right outta your tee shirt. I gotta tell ya, I was waitin' and hopin' for that to happen so I could be like your livin' bra. Am I right? Am I right?"

Tana stared at Bobby with a look of contempt. "I couldn't have heard you right," she said, crowding him against the bar.

Intimidated by her aggressive attitude, he nervously replied, "Hey, uh, you were like tanfastic . . . uh, I mean fantastic."

"Hawkins," Tana said, "you are without a doubt the biggest asshole ever spawned."

"What? What did I do?" he whined.

"What did I do?" Tana mimicked. "What you did was diss me, a fellow cop, somebody you might need to back you up when some guy's whipping your butt."

Bobby frowned, "C'mon Tana, what did I do to diss you?"

"You must be stupid as well as drunk," she said. "You want to be my living bra? What kind of sexist crap is that?"

"Aw, Tana, can't you take a joke?"

"Sure, I can take a joke. But then jokes can go both ways. Some of your ex-girlfriends claim your penis is so tiny you need tweezers to get it outta your pants when you take a leak," she said, continuing to glare at Bobby.

"That's bullshit!" he yelled, his face turning red as several people started laughing.

"What's the matter, Hawkins? Can't take a joke?" Tana said sarcastically.

"You bitch!" he yelled, taking an unsteady step toward her.

Tending the grill, a shot of whiskey close at hand, Clay had a chicken breast in mid-flip when he became aware of the ruckus. Abandoning the pit, he hurried across the terrace and stepped between them.

"Hey, guys, it's a party," he said, trying to defuse the escalating situation. "Chill, okay?"

"I'm cool," Tana said, the anger in her voice belying the words. "Tell him to chill."

"Tana, you're just too sensitive," Bobby objected.

Before she could react, Clay held up his hand. "I'll handle this, Tana." Looking at Bobby, he said in a low voice, "Back off, Hawkins. You're acting like a jerk as usual."

"What're you talkin' about?" Bobby protested, swaying so badly he almost fell.

"Dana is the only reason you're here tonight," Clay said. "She thinks of you as a friend, although I don't understand why. I figured you'd get drunk and end up acting like a fool. Sure enough, you did, so it's time for you to leave. Just stay right there while I find somebody to drive you home."

His voice slurred, Bobby growled, "I don't need no stinkin' desugrated driver, Commander!"

"That's *designated driver*, and yes, you do, *Officer* Hawkins. That is, unless you want to go downtown on a DUI charge." Stepping closer, Clay said, "Now listen up, Bobby. If you don't get control of your drinking, you're going to find yourself in serious trouble with the department."

"Oh, yeah," Bobby snarled, "better lishen to the golden boy. Married Dana Capella after stealing her away from me. Lives in a fancy million-dollar house. Gets hisself promoted by kissin' ass. You're right. I better listen to the Commander."

Anger flashed in Clay's eyes. "Tell you what, Hawkins. I know you talk behind my back, claiming I was lucky to get where I am. That's damn funny coming from a lazy bastard that spends more time getting out of work than it takes to just do it. And by the way, I didn't steal Dana from you. She dumped your sorry ass. So here's the deal. If I ever hear of you shooting off your mouth making personal attacks against me or anyone else in the department, you're gone. Fired! You got it?" Breathing hard, hands balled into fists, Clay felt a hand on his shoulder and turned to see Dana beside him.

"Clay's right, Bobby," Dana said, frowning. "He warned me you would get drunk and do something stupid. I told him I thought you had matured, but obviously I was wrong."

Hawkins looked down, unable to meet the eyes of the woman he still believed would love him if only Clay Randall were out of the way. "Dana, I, uh, I didn't do anything. I was just clownin' around with Tana, and it's like she got pissed for no reason."

"I heard what you said, Bobby," Dana said evenly. "Tana had every right to be angry with you. Now you need to leave."

"Aw c'mon, Dana. I'll be cool," he pleaded.

"No. Go home, Bobby," she said firmly.

Spotting Ty Honchen and Three Rivers, Clay waved them over. "Ty, can you and Three get Hawkins and his car home?"

"You got it, Clay," Ty said, turning to stare at Hawkins.

Bobby looked away from Ty. He was nervous around the short but physically powerful sergeant, having been on the receiving end of his wrath on more than one occasion.

"Okay, Hawkins," Ty said. "Let's see how well you can multitask. Breathe and walk to my car at the same time."

Spinning on his heel without waiting for a response, Ty headed for the door with Bobby meekly following behind.

Chapter 4

Ty was surprised that Bobby had not said a word since shortly after climbing into the passenger seat of his car. Surprised, that is, until he glanced over and saw he had passed out, saliva dribbling from the corner of his mouth as his head lolled against the window.

Good, he thought. *That saves me from having to kick his ass just on general principles.*

Turning west onto Beach Boulevard, Ty was passing the Beach Plaza shopping center when he saw a man grab a woman's arm and pull her toward a red pickup truck. Without hesitation, he whipped into the lot with Three Rivers close behind.

"Police officers! Let her go!" Honchen shouted.

The man stopped, looking over his shoulder as the officers approached, his hand still firmly gripping the woman's arm.

Squinting, Ty said, "I'll be damned! It's Roy Connor!"

The man, a former Jacksonville Beach cop, carried almost two hundred and sixty pounds of solid muscle on a six-foot, one-inch frame, thanks to hours spent each week pumping iron, supplemented by heavy doses of anabolic steroids. He was dressed in shorts, flip-flops, and a tank top stretched tight across his chest. His right arm was a full sleeve of tattoos that included skulls, eagles, snakes, and a naked female performing fellatio on a figure closely resembling himself.

"I said let her go!" Ty repeated, approaching Connor and the woman.

Connor sneered as he recognized the detective. "Well, if it isn't Tiberius Honchen. Looks like they'll make anybody a sergeant nowadays," he said sarcastically. "And who's the pretty boy behind you? Could that be Jeh-ruh-mee Rivers?" he asked in a mocking tone. "Hey, Rivers, I always wondered, is that dumbass nickname code for the length of your little prick?" he snickered.

Stepping up beside Ty, Three replied calmly, "No, actually my nickname stands for the number of women that dumped you to be with me. But thanks for asking."

"You fuckin' wiseass!" Connor roared. "You don't wanta be talkin' shit to me!"

Before Three could react, Ty said, "Back off, Connor, unless you want a battery on a law enforcement officer charge put on you."

"This has nothing to do with you or your sissy friend, Honchen. Me and my girl here were just having a little disagreement. Isn't that right, Andi," he demanded.

"That's right, officer. We were just arguing," she said, smiling.

Connor gave the woman a look, "Go ahead. I'll catch up."

Anxious, she asked, "Are you sure? You need me to call anybody?"

"Naw, it's cool. These guys don't have a damn thing on me. You go on."

Heading toward her car, Three Rivers stopped her. "Ma'am," he said, "come with me, please. I need some information from you."

As Three walked her to the police car, Ty said, "I haven't seen you since you got out of jail, Connor. You got a job?"

"I don't have to tell you anything, Honchen. I have rights." He paused and then laughed. "Ain't that a bitch? I didn't have any when I was a cop. Now that I'm just a citizen, I've got all sorts of rights! That means I can tell you to piss off since I haven't done anything. You heard her. She said she was okay. So, no laws violated? No reason to tell you shit. Isn't that right, *Sergeant*?"

Before Ty could respond, a voice behind him spoke up, "I can't believe it! Roy freakin' Connor! I ain't seen you since, uh, since, lemme see here, was that when you got arrested, or was it when the chief fired you?"

Ty turned to see Bobby, leaning against the hood of the car to keep from falling down. "Get back in the car, Hawkins," he said, his voice tight.

Bobby looked bleary eyed at Ty. "What for? You got a dangerous crinimal . . . uh, criminal here. And I'm your backup."

"I see the ole JBPD is still full of winners. Damn, Hawkins! You're tore up from the floor up, looks like. And just so you know, I met better people than you in jail, asshole."

"Hey! You can't talk to me that way!" Bobby yelled, bringing his hand from behind his back to reveal a container of pepper spray. Pointing the can at Connor, his index finger on the trigger, Bobby said, "I'm arrestin' you for aggervatin' the poh-lice. Turn around and put your back behind your hands . . . uh, your hands behind your back so Sarge can cuff you."

Looking at Ty, he mumbled, "Hey, Sarge, you got some cuffs? I think I left mine at home."

Connor burst out laughing. "You silly bastard! You haven't changed a bit. Still get knee-walking drunk and act a fool just like you always did."

Bobby yelled, "You prick!" Raising the can of pepper spray, he pressed the trigger. Screaming loudly, Bobby dropped the container, falling down and rolling back and forth as he clawed his eyes, trying to wipe away the burning chemical.

Connor and Honchen stood transfixed by the sight of a police officer stupid enough, or drunk enough, to shoot himself with the pepper spray. As Bobby's screams slowly faded to whimpers, Connor glanced at Ty with a big smile, "And that, ladies and gentlemen, was a demonstration of proper police tactics by one of Jax Beach's finest."

Ignoring Bobby, Ty picked up the can of pepper spray and looked at Connor, who was still smirking. "Roy, what happened to you? You held a position of trust, and you pissed it all away."

"I don't give a shit about your opinion, Honchen," Connor said. "But since you're so curious about what I think, I'll tell you. Nobody gives a shit about cops. People are always bitching at you. Everybody you deal with is pissed off or whining about something. You wanta know what finally pushed me over? It was at some rich bitch's beach party where I was working off duty. Everybody was eating steak and lobster and drinking top shelf stuff. I'd been working the damn thing for like six hours straight, and nobody ever asked me if I wanted something to eat.

"Then, get this. I'm standing beside where the waiters stacked the plates and shit from their dinner. Up comes the broad hostin' the party, half in the bag, looking all fine with her tits hangin' outta her bikini top. She comes up and asks me if I've eaten. 'Course I said no. Then she points at the stack of dirty plates and says, 'You know, officer, you can make yourself a nice plate from the food my guests didn't eat.'

"I came about half an inch from rippin' her head off right in front of her pissant guests. But I didn't. I just smiled and said I'd rather eat the ass end of a dog with diarrhea than the garbage her guests had dumped. Then I walked out. And that's when I knew that you don't get anywhere in this world unless you have money and power."

"And how's that money and power thing working out for you, Roy?"

Connor sneered, "Let's just say I'm doin' okay and leave it at that, Tiberius."

"Wow," Ty said softly, "I'm damn glad I don't live in your head, Connor. With an attitude like yours, I have a feeling our next meeting may involve handcuffs, mug shots, the works. And if you think I'm right about that, maybe you should consider doing your business somewhere besides Jacksonville Beach."

Without waiting for a reply, Ty walked over to Bobby, who by this time had made it to his hands and knees, mucous pouring from his nose, strings of saliva drooling from his mouth, his eyes the color of overripe tomatoes.

"C'mon, Hawkins. Get your ass up," Ty snapped.

"I, I'm sick," Bobby moaned. "I can't."

"You're a moron, Hawkins. Where did you get off thinking you could pepper spray Connor just because you didn't like the way he talked to you? You deserve this, pulling such a stupid stunt. Now get up, or I'll drag your sorry ass to the car feet first," Ty demanded.

Bobby staggered to his feet. Leaning heavily on the hood of the car, he made it to the passenger door and reached for the handle.

"Oh, no you don't," Ty objected. "You're not riding in my car with pepper spray and snot all over you. You're getting in *your* car. And I'm not making Rivers suffer for your stupidity. You're riding in the trunk."

Bobby looked heavy lidded at Ty. "Wh, What? Where?"

"Are you deaf? In your trunk," Ty said, signaling to Three Rivers to pop the trunk of Bobby's Lexus.

"Oh, man, I can't ride back there. I'll get carsick," Bobby wailed.

"I don't care if you puke all over your own car. That's your problem. Get in the damn trunk now, or I'll call Clay and tell him what you did. And I'll bet by tomorrow you'll be maximizing your opportunities outside the Jax Beach P. D.!"

Blinking tears from his eyes, wiping snot with the sleeve of his shirt, Bobby shuffled to the back of his car, head down. He glanced over his shoulder at Ty, a pleading look on his face.

"Inside," Ty commanded without a trace of sympathy.

Bobby climbed in slowly, curling immediately into a fetal position as Ty slammed the lid and walked back to where Connor still stood.

"Don't give me any shit, Connor," he said gruffly. "He may be a sorry excuse for a human being, but he's still a cop, and I'll take him over you any day of the week. So haul your ass outta here before I figure out a charge to put on you."

Connor opened his mouth but quickly shut it. Scowling, he spun on his heel, and walked quickly to his truck.

As he drove off following his girlfriend, Ty looked at Three Rivers and asked, "What's her story?"

"Name's Andi LaBelle. She's a barmaid at the Pier Club. She said they had a disagreement about where to go for dinner," Three said, rolling his eyes.

"Yeah, right. My wife and I have disagreements all the time about where to go for dinner, and I guarantee you it doesn't end up with me dragging her across a parking lot."

"I hear you. If there was any dragging to be done, Anne would be the one doing it, anyway! Your wife is one tough little lady."

Laughing, Ty said, "Did you catch Connor's rant?"

"Man, did I! That guy's a head case. And you're right. We'll see him again. He's got a vicious temper he obviously can't control. And how about his size? Even his eyebrows are pumped! I guarantee he didn't get that bulked up just from pounding the weights. The sucker's on steroids, I bet, and it's making that temper of his about three times as bad. At least when he was a cop, he had some incentive to hold it in. Now there's no telling what he might do."

"You're right," Ty agreed as he went to check on Bobby. Hearing loud snores coming from the trunk, he said, "Come on. Let's get our resident jackass home and head back to the party before the beer and food's all gone."

Chapter 5

As Bobby Hawkins headed for his pepper spray rendezvous with Roy Connor, the party resumed its previous, earsplitting volume. Clay went back to the grill, where he discovered Danny Malone flipping the meat like a pro. "Hey, man. I didn't expect to see you here. How you doing?" he asked, putting his arm around the shoulder of his best friend.

"I'm okay, thanks," Danny answered, glancing at Clay with a brief smile. Nodding at Fontana Jones, Danny observed, "No doubt in my mind she would have kicked Bobby's ass if you hadn't stepped in."

"You're right," Clay said. "The guy's gonna keep on screwing up until the chief fires him. Next stop, door greeter at the local shopping mall."

Danny laughed softly. Clay looked closely at his friend, trying to gauge his mental and emotional state barely a week after the deadly shooting on the beach. "How did it go with the department psychologist?" he asked.

"Fine. She said I'm crazy and should be committed immediately."

Taken aback, Clay said, "What? You're kidding, right?"

Danny grinned, "Well, she may not have said it exactly that way, but she made it clear that she thinks all cops, especially undercover dope cops, have to be a little off to do this job."

"I can't argue with that. After years of dealing with the quote, unquote, dregs of society, any sane person can get a little crazy if he doesn't do normal stuff on a regular basis. Like fishing, hunting, chasing women."

Danny looked sharply at Clay. "Do what? My straight-shooter buddy chases women? Come on!"

"Hey, I'm not talking about me. Or you for that matter. We both got lucky and married up, big time. There's no women around who could take the place of Dana or Rachel."

At the mention of his wife, a sad look passed over Danny's face, and he suddenly focused on basting the chicken breasts.

Seeing the change, Clay asked, "So how's Rachel taking it?"

"What? The shooting?"

Clay nodded.

"She doesn't know," Danny responded.

"You're kidding. How could she not know with the news coverage and all?"

"She's not feeling well. Been sleeping a lot, and you know . . . ," he paused, his voice trailing away.

"Is it the Lyme disease?" Clay asked.

Until she had contracted the debilitating disease, Rachel Malone had been a highly successful financial consultant, but a camping trip to the Osceola National Forest with Clay and Dana had changed everything. Days after returning home, Rachel developed what seemed to be nothing worse than a bad cold, followed by flu-like symptoms. She also noticed a minor bug bite and a rash on the back of her left arm that faded after a few days.

All of the symptoms eventually disappeared, so she never bothered to see a doctor. Over the next year, she began to suffer from various ailments. Her back would ache at times, accompanied by stiffness in her knees and ankles. Occasionally, she ran a low-grade fever. For almost two years, various doctors diagnosed Rachel's symptoms as the flu, a viral infection, fibromyalgia, multiple sclerosis, and even Lupus. One doctor suggested her symptoms were psychosomatic and recommended she see a psychiatrist.

Danny was not convinced his wife suffered from any of the disorders or diseases her doctors had surmised. In utter frustration, he began searching the Internet. Scanning websites listing every exotic disease known to medicine, he ran across one that referred to a tick-borne disease first identified in Lyme, Connecticut. There, he found what he had been searching for, reams of information that fit Rachel's varied and disabling symptoms.

Armed with the printouts, Danny took Rachel to her primary care physician, who refused to look at the data, rejecting it as unproven medical theory. Undeterred, Danny began searching for a doctor who specialized in treating Lyme disease, finally locating one in Daytona Beach. After a comprehensive examination, the doctor confirmed Rachel was in late-stage Lyme disease and needed immediate treatment.

"Yeah," Danny responded to Clay's question, frowning. "Lyme disease is weird. The symptoms are not too bad some days. But others? Man, I gotta tell you, they're horrible. And right now, they're bad. Worse than they've ever been."

"Are you making it okay with her not being able to work?" Clay asked.

"Aw, you know. Our insurance is balking right now at paying for the Lyme disease doctor, but I'm taking her to him anyway and covering the whole tab myself. I've taken on some extra jobs, so we'll be okay."

"You sure? Because Dana and I will be glad to help out until she gets over this."

Tapping Clay on the arm, Danny said, "I know that, buddy. I can't tell you how much I appreciate it, but we're cool. Now how about I get you another drink?"

As Danny headed to the bar, Ty and Three came through the patio doors. "After that experience, we need beer!" Ty bellowed over the music.

Reaching into the cooler, Danny grabbed four cans of ice-cold brew and began lobbing them rapid-fire at the two detectives. Dancing to the beat of the music, Ty effortlessly snagged each can out of the air as if he were a professional juggler. Flipping the first can to Three, Ty shoved the second one in his pocket, passed the third to Three with a behind-the-back toss, and caught the final beer just before it hit the ground.

To the cheers of the crowd, Ty popped the tab and chugged the beer in one long gulp. Then he crushed the can flat and spun it like a Frisbee back at Danny, who promptly dropped it, leading to raucous jeers from his fellow cops.

Ty laughed at Danny. "Son, did you really think you could get one of those beers past ole Honch?"

Bowing deeply in mock submission, Danny said, "Sergeant Honchen, you are the *man*!"

Chapter 6

Clay Randall and Danny Malone first met at Fletcher Middle School when they competed for quarterback of the football team. Both boys tended to be hotheaded and quick to respond to any challenge with their fists. The coaches loved seeing their players mix it up, and Clay and Danny gave them plenty to admire. But after they threw punches at each other for the third time in the first two days of practice, the head coach sat them both down for a talk.

He made Clay his quarterback on the strength of his passing arm. Danny would be the running back due to his speed and his absolute refusal to go down short of being gang tackled. Danny was so disappointed over not getting the quarterback position that he threatened to quit the team. The coach was not the sort of man to tolerate a threat from a thirteen-year-old kid. He was about to tell him to take a hike when Clay asked to talk to Danny alone. The coach nodded curtly and headed for the locker room, leaving the boys sitting on the stadium bleachers.

Clay looked at Danny, who turned his back to stare at two girls riding their bikes on the street beside the stadium.

"Hey, Malone, we need to talk."

Danny kept his back turned, ignoring him.

"Look, I know you wanted the quarterback position as bad as I did, but I can't help it if Coach picked me instead of you. Can we at least get along on the field so we can win some games?"

Danny glanced over his shoulder, a frown on his face. "I'm a better quarterback than you. I can't believe he picked you."

"It's probably because you're an even better running back than you are a quarterback. I've never seen anyone as hard to tackle as you. You're like a maniac when you get the ball in your hands. Maybe he figured putting me at quarterback and you at running back will win us the championship. I just hand off to you and stay out of your way."

Danny turned fully around and stared at Clay. "You mean that?"

"Sure," Clay said.

Danny grinned, "I've got two older brothers, and they were always beating up on me. I had to learn how to run or fight to keep from getting my butt kicked. Sometimes I'd be running and fighting at the same time."

Clay laughed, thinking the guy wasn't so bad after all. He stuck out his hand. "Friends?"

Danny shook his hand. "Friends," he said. "But I still think I'm a better quarterback."

None of their buddies expected Clay and Danny to become best friends considering their personalities and upbringing. Clay's formative years were spent with two parents that were loving but strict. When his dad died of a heart attack when Clay was only twelve, his mom worried he would grow wild without a strong male influence. Instead, he developed a maturity beyond his years.

Meanwhile, Danny was growing up largely unsupervised. His father was an alcoholic prone to extended absences when he went on binges. His mom suffered from severe depression, sometimes staying in bed for weeks, getting up only to go to the bathroom and raid the freezer for ice cream, her food of choice. Danny had to get himself ready for school most mornings, including making his own breakfast. He often entered the kitchen to find a half gallon of ice cream melting on the counter, a spoon still in the container as if his mom would be right back for one more scoop.

A week after he turned thirteen, his dad left, never to return, sending his mother into an increasingly downward spiral of depression. By that time, his two brothers had left home, leaving Danny to cope with his mother alone. Many kids his age would have been resentful at what life had thrown at them. But not Danny. Instead, he learned to compartmentalize his feelings, showing everyone a fun-loving, joking demeanor that masked the hurt and pain he felt. His friendship with Clay became Danny's lifeboat in an ocean swirling with emotional storms.

At Fletcher High, they played football together, with Clay once again the quarterback handing the football to Danny. Their common interests included pretty girls, even dating twins at one point. Their contrasting personalities sometimes led to conflicts, one of which resulted in a trip to the emergency room. It happened in their senior year. The boys were at a party thrown by the parents of one of their football teammates. With the adults upstairs watching TV, several bottles of liquor materialized, livening the party dramatically.

Around eleven o'clock, as the alcohol began to loosen inhibitions, one of the football players came up with the idea of car surfing on the roof of Danny's old van. Danny said he was in as long as he could go first.

Clay argued, "You're drunk out of your mind, Danny. You're looking at a full ride at UNF in football. If you fall and break something, and you probably will, you can kiss your scholarship goodbye. That is if you don't kill yourself in the process."

"Screw you, Clay," Danny said, "I'm not drunk, and besides, I got great reflexes. Better than yours, even. Piece of cake."

Danny turned and trotted to his van, tossing the keys to Joe DeLattre, the center on the football team. "Crank 'er up, Big D," he yelled as he clambered to the roof of the van. "Let's show these pussies what car surfing's all about!"

Clay grabbed DeLattre's arm as he started to climb behind the wheel. "Joe, don't move this van. Danny's wasted. He's gonna fall and bust himself up, and it'll be your fault!"

"Whata you mean, my fault?" he snarled, jerking his arm away.

"That's just what I mean. You're driving, so when he falls off, the cops will hold you responsible!"

Danny leaned over the side of the van, obviously angry at Clay's interference just as he was ready to show off for everyone. "Back off, Randall! You're always too scared to do anything fun. You never take chances. You gotta learn to roll the dice. Do something to make you feel alive!" Looking over Clay's shoulder at DeLattre, he yelled, "Let's roll, Big D!"

The big center shoved Clay back and slammed the door, cranking the engine and revving it loudly. Danny stood up on the roof, holding his arms out as he whooped and hollered at the twenty or so kids still at the party who had lined up on both sides of the long driveway to watch the show. Clay headed across the lawn away from the van, refusing to watch what he knew was coming.

Instead of easing the accelerator down, DeLattre, highly intoxicated himself, jammed the pedal to the floor. The van leaped forward, instantly throwing Danny off his feet. Before he could react, his body slid across the roof, flying off the back and slamming hard onto the pavement.

The kids stared in horror at Danny, who was lying very still on the driveway. Clay came racing back, dropping to his knees beside his friend. "Danny! Are you okay?" When he didn't respond, Clay shouted, "Call 9-1-1!" A feeling of utter helplessness threatened to crush him.

I should have stopped him from pulling this crap, he thought. *Now, he might be dead.*

As he continued to stare in agony at his friend, afraid to touch him for fear of causing further injury, Danny's eyelids fluttered open. He looked around blankly. Finally, his eyes focused on Clay, who was leaning over him.

"Dude," he whispered.

"Yeah, Danny. I'm here. Talk to me," Clay said anxiously.

"Dude, you got a booger hangin' outta your left 'stril."

After the inevitable trip to the emergency room to treat a mild concussion, and after the cops arrested DeLattre for DUI and wrote Danny a ticket for riding on an unapproved portion of a vehicle, he promised his best friend he was officially retiring from car surfing.

Upon graduation, the boys headed up the road to the University of North Florida. While Danny's academic record in high school was barely adequate, his football skills earned him a scholarship. There, his coach's disciplined approach to the game and to life struck a chord in the young man, and he applied himself to his studies for the first time. Instead of partying, he kept his nose in the books, consistently making the Dean's list. Graduating with a degree in sports management, Danny was quickly hired as an assistant football coach at his old high school.

Meanwhile, Clay went the other direction. Tired of the hard work it took to maintain good grades in high school, and uncertain about what he wanted to do with his life, he neglected his studies, spending more time on scholastic probation than off. By the time he turned twenty-one, he had tried and abandoned majors in marine biology, psychology, and sociology and was nowhere near graduation. Frustrated with the direction his life was going, Clay impulsively joined the Jacksonville Beach Police Department after an exciting encounter with an officer and a violent shoplifter.

In spite of going in different directions professionally, the two friends stayed close, leasing a condo together and spending their off days surfing, fishing, and enjoying the nightlife offered in downtown Jacksonville Beach. One afternoon, beers in hand, Clay and Danny sat on their balcony, feet propped on the railing as they watched bikini-clad young women stroll by. Clay had just shared several stories of fights and car chases and women skinny-dipping in the ocean during a full moon.

"Man, I can't believe all the crazy stuff you get into," Danny marveled. "It sounds like Jax Beach is party central for the whole county."

Clay nodded, taking a swallow of beer. "Guaranteed, bro. There's rarely a night that goes by when I'm not cuffin' and stuffin' half a dozen or so. They get shit faced and then pile out into First Street at bar closing to prove who has the biggest set of balls."

Danny laughed, fascinated at Clay's stories. "I gotta tell you, man. A teaching job is boring in comparison to what you get to do. I want something more exciting than grading history exams and coaching little jerks who remind me of me when I was that age."

Clay responded with a grin. "Then I have the perfect solution for you, bud. Go through the police academy, and I'll do everything I can to help you get hired on the PD. Then we can crunch crime together. Whataya say?"

Clinking his beer bottle against Clay's in a toast, Danny made a life-changing decision. He would be a cop.

Upon completing the police academy, and with Clay's recommendation, the chief hired Danny Malone, and he embarked on his exciting new career. Assigned as his FTO, or field training officer, Clay's task was to teach Danny what police work was really like, rather than the sanitized version taught in the academy. It didn't take long for Danny to get his first taste of the crazy side of police work.

Chapter 7

Midway through Danny's second week on the job, he and Clay got involved in one of those situations that becomes part of the institutional history of a police department. The kind passed down to new officers for years afterward. What cops called a war story.

It was a hot August night, nearing two o'clock, and the moon was full. Although experts insisted there was no correlation between moon cycles and people acting nutty, cops and emergency services personnel knew better. Danny drove the patrol car slowly north on First Street with Clay riding shotgun. In spite of the hot, humid night, they kept their windows down so they could hear anything unusual. Even with the air conditioner set on maximum, the temperature inside in the car hovered near eighty degrees.

Wiping sweat from his brow with the back of his hand, Danny glanced over at Clay. "Dude, how do you ever get used to wearing a ballistic vest in this weather? It fits so snug it feels like my whole upper body is in a sauna."

Clay grinned, "You get used to it. And if you're ever in a shooting, you'll be glad you're wearing it."

"I guess," Danny said as he scanned the empty street. "Speaking of shooting, where's all the action? From all the stories you've told me, I thought we would be breaking up at least a dozen fights every night. But so far, the most excitement we've had was refereeing a couple of eighty-year-olds arguing over which TV channel to watch," Danny said.

"Just be patient, Danny," Clay responded. "It can happen at any moment. One second, you're tooling along trying to stay awake. The next, you're running code. You get there, and two drunks or maybe half a dozen are going at it, so you just wade in. Some of them will stop fighting as soon as they see the uniform, but others will see your badge as a challenge. That's when you find out what you're made of."

"Well, I can't wait for the chance to kick some guy's butt legally."

Clay looked sharply at his friend and partner. "Danny, you don't wanta be committing a six o'clock rule violation."

"Remind me what that is?" Danny asked with a puzzled look.

"Don't tell me you've already forgotten your talk with the chief when he hired you."

Grinning, Danny answered, "Oh, yeah, that rule. Don't do something that'll get you on TV unless you're proud, etcetera, etcetera. That the one you're talking about?"

Clay stared at his rookie partner with a frown. "Danny, don't be clowning around about ethical stuff. The chief takes it very serious, and I do, too."

"Hey, bro, I was just screwin' with you. I know I can't do that kinda stuff. 'Cause if I did, I'd have a helluva time giving a legal, reasonable explanation for it. And anyway, it would just be wrong."

Clay smiled, "Wow! My rookie is actually learning something. I'm impressed."

"Hey, I'm like a dog. With the right incentive, I'm trainable."

Suddenly, a woman shrieked, "DON'T . . . STOP! DON'T . . . STOP!"

"Where did that come from?" Clay yelled as Danny slammed on the brakes.

"It sounded like it came from there," Danny said, his foot still on the brake as he pointed down the narrow alley between two buildings.

"Go! Go! Go!" Clay shouted.

Danny jerked the wheel to the left and punched it, tires squealing as the police car accelerated west through the dark alley. Reaching the parking lot behind the building, Danny jammed on the brakes, bringing the car to a sliding stop. Both officers leaped out and began shining their flashlights around, trying to locate the source of the screams.

Danny was nervous. He hadn't handled this type of call before, and he wasn't sure what he should do. Glancing at Clay, he figured if he followed his partner's lead he would be okay. Clay stopped, sweeping his flashlight to the right toward a black, dual-wheel pickup parked across the lot. "Look, can you see somebody in the bed of that dualie?"

Danny, looking the other direction, said, "No, where?"

"Over there to your right. Look, the truck's bouncing up and down. Come on," he said, shining his flashlight toward the vehicle. Glancing at his partner, Clay whispered, "Put your light in your left hand so your gun hand is free."

Danny immediately switched hands, "Sorry, Clay. Forgot a basic officer safety rule."

Making their way across the parking lot, their eyes swept left and right searching for possible threats. The sound of a woman moaning grew louder as they approached. Suddenly, she erupted again, "Yes! Harder! Don't stop now!"

Reaching the truck, Danny and Clay stared in disbelief at the scene. At first glance, it looked like a bear engaging in wild, uninhibited sex with a human female. But they quickly realized the bear was actually a huge man. Coarse, dark hair covered his naked body with the exception of his bald head, bare butt, and the soles of his feet. Under him, they could see a woman passionately moving in rhythm with the giant.

People having noisy sex in the back of a pickup was not unheard of in downtown Jacksonville Beach. What was unusual was the sheer size of the two love combatants. The officers' flashlights bounced off acres of sweaty, writhing flesh that appeared to fill the bed of the truck, side-to-side and front to back.

The enormous man was oblivious to the interruption, never altering his rhythm. The woman, almost as large as her partner, turned her head toward the bright lights, squinting in the glare. "Turn those damn lights off and get outta here! Can't you boys see we're busy?" she exclaimed.

Clay said firmly, "Police. Stop what you're doing."

Neither reacted to his command. The man kept stroking, and the woman, her legs wrapped around his buttocks, began moaning loudly again. "Drive it home Lester!" she screamed.

Clay yelled at the man. "Break it up! Get off her right now!"

Lester the giant continued without pause, rumbling in a deep bass voice, "Not now, man. Hold on, just hold on."

Danny looked at Clay, eyes wide. "It's like two elephants breeding, and one of them is a wooly mammoth!"

Clay bit his lip to keep from laughing out loud. As the two cops stood, enthralled by the spectacle, Lester growled, "I'm a'comin', Wanda. Get ready for the big bang!"

Suddenly, they bellowed in unison loud enough to shatter windows. Lester collapsed on top of Wanda, breathing like a wounded rhino. It was over. The woman kept her legs wrapped around the man as she turned to look at Clay and Danny. "Enjoy the show, boys?" she asked, showing no embarrassment.

"Would you please get up and put your clothes on now?" Clay said, exasperated. "And show me some ID while you're at it."

The couple untangled their enormous limbs and sat up, making no effort to hide their nakedness.

"Ma'am, please cover yourself," Clay pleaded.

"Listen to him, Lester. Ain't he polite?" she asked, leaning back against the side of the truck bed, a pair of 48HHs staring at the two officers.

Danny leaned over to Clay, "Damn, dude. Her nipples are bigger than my head."

Lester apparently didn't find Danny's comment humorous. Standing up in the bed of the truck, he roared, "Don't talk about my woman like that!"

Both officers stepped back, startled by the size and ferocity of the man. Clay debated drawing his weapon, deciding instead to try to calm Lester down by talking quietly to him. No one else had seen the wild exhibition, so he could let them both go with a warning. That is, as long as Lester didn't decide to defend Wanda's honor.

"Lester," Clay said, "I apologize for my partner's crude comment. He's a rookie, so he's not used to seeing people having sex in the middle of downtown Jax Beach. Now, you and your lady get dressed, and I'll let you go with a warning citation."

Lester shook his head violently. "Nope. That ain't good enough. He didn't show no damn respect for Wanda, and I'm gonna whip his ass unless he says he's sorry."

"Lester, it's okay," Wanda said, pulling a tee shirt the size of a small tent over her head to cover the objects of Danny's remark. "I guess he ain't never seen a full grown woman before. Prob'ly likes his women skinny with little titties like doorknobs."

"I do not," Danny objected, indignantly. "My girlfriend's got big–"

"Back off, Danny!" Clay interrupted, glaring at his partner. "Give Wanda an apology for talking about her that way."

Danny stared in disbelief at Clay. "Apology?"

"That's right," Clay said, hoping Danny would realize he could defuse the situation before they found themselves in the fight of their life with the naked giant.

Danny shook his head. "Officer Randall, could I talk to you a second over here?" he asked, gesturing over his shoulder.

Clay hesitated, not sure what Danny wanted. Finally, nodding his head, he said to Lester and Wanda, "Y'all hang on. We'll be right back. In the meantime, *please* get dressed."

Walking away a few steps, keeping the two lovers in sight, Clay whispered, "What is it, Danny?"

"Clay, why the hell do I have to apologize when she dissed my girlfriend? After all, what I said was true. Her nipples *are* huge."

Clay frowned, "You've got to be kidding me. You really think talking about some woman's breasts is okay? Try explaining a comment like that to the chief. Actually, you won't have to. Since you're a rookie, it'll be me trying to explain why I allowed you to say something so stupid. Now, get your ass back over there and apologize," he said tersely.

Danny glanced toward Lester and Wanda and then back to Clay. "You're right, partner. I screwed up. I'll fix it."

With a curt nod, Clay stepped over to the truck with Danny following. "Wanda," he said, "my partner has something he wants to say to you." Turning toward Danny, he said, "Go ahead."

Danny glanced down a moment before squaring his shoulders and looking directly into the woman's eyes, "Wanda, uh, I'm sorry if I offended you by comparing your nipples to the size of my head. It's obvious they're not quite that big."

"You little pissant!" Lester roared, launching himself from the bed of the truck and slamming into the rookie cop with almost four hundred pounds of redneck wrath. Danny flew off his feet, skidding on his butt across the asphalt parking lot and tearing the seat out of his uniform pants and underwear. Before he could react, Lester was on him, wrapping his paws around Danny's neck and yanking him off the ground as if he weighed nothing, his feet dangling in the air.

Clay hit the emergency 34 button on his radio and screamed for help. Then he raced across the lot, drawing his TASER and firing at the hairy back of the man who appeared ready to kill Danny. Both barbs struck Lester in the upper back, sending fifty thousand volts of energy into his body. But Lester gave no indication he felt anything. He continued to hold Danny off the ground by his neck, squeezing so tight his face was turning purple.

Seeing the TASER was having no effect, Clay drew his pistol, screaming, "LET HIM GO OR I'LL SHOOT!"

Before he could squeeze the trigger, Wanda came roaring by, knocking him down. She howled, "Lester, stop it!" Barreling forward, Wanda's three hundred pounds of female fury smashed into her lover. Lester didn't go down, but the impact staggered him. He dropped Danny, who fell to the pavement coughing and gagging.

With fists almost as big as his, Wanda pounded Lester in the face, head, and chest. He kept backing away, making no effort to defend himself from the crazy woman who had recently been the willing recipient of his amorous attentions. Finally, out of breath and exhausted, Wanda stopped her attack, although she continued to glare at Lester. "Are you crazy?" she demanded. "Do you want to go back to prison?"

Lester's face scrunched up in confusion. "What are you talkin' about, woman? 'Course I don't wanta go back."

"Then why did you jump on the little cop? He weren't hurtin' me none."

Lester dropped his head, his hands opening and closing reflexively. "I, I got mad when he talked bad about you. You know I don't like no man lookin' at you. Much less talkin' dirty to you."

"Well, Lester," she said, turning to Clay, who had regained his feet and was still pointing his gun at the giant, "you're just damn lucky this cop didn't kill you. Now don't give him no more trouble. You hear me?"

Lester nodded, turning to Clay, "Officer, I'm real sorry I lost my temper and hurt your friend. I know I gotta go to jail. But, 'fore I do, can I put on my clothes?" Still amped up from his first close encounter with deadly force, Clay could only nod.

Within seconds, cops began arriving from every direction. Lester, now docile, allowed himself to be handcuffed and carted off to the Duval County Jail where his cellmates welcomed him as a conquering hero for beating up a cop.

At the emergency room, Danny lay face down on the treatment table, pants down to his knees. His fellow cops teased him mercilessly as the ER nurse scrubbed and scraped asphalt from his backside. In spite of the pain and embarrassment, it was obvious he enjoyed the ribbing.

As they left the emergency room well after daylight, Clay said he hoped Danny understood how important good verbal communications could be, in most cases more critical than the ability to fight. He then asked his rookie partner and best friend what he had learned from the encounter with Lester and Wanda.

Danny thought about it a moment and then, cutting his eyes over at Clay, responded with a sly grin, "I've learned that if I ever run across another grizzly bear screwing a woman with nipples as big as my head, I'll shoot first and ask questions later."

Chapter 8

The warm spring air attracted thousands of sun worshippers to Jacksonville Beach, and this day was no exception. Up and down the beach, young women, pale from the winter, rubbed sunscreen on their exposed skin before lying on beach towels, their common goal to create just the right glow they hoped would attract the opposite sex. Young men walked, ran, played beach volleyball, and generally did everything in their power to catch the eye of the nubile beauties decorating the sand.

It had been a week since Roy Connor's parking lot encounter with the three Jax Beach detectives. He and his boss, Tony Savoy, sat in comfortable beach chairs beside Tony's penthouse pool, both drinking Scotch whiskey in cut crystal tumblers. As their eyes roamed over the young women in tiny bikinis down below, Connor told Tony about Bobby Hawkins' drunken attempt to use the pepper spray on him. Savoy laughed heartily as he visualized how stupid Bobby must have looked.

A criminal defense attorney in his mid-fifties, Anthony Joseph Savoy cut an imposing figure in the courtroom. Wearing his jet-black hair parted in the middle and falling over his ears, he carried two hundred and forty pounds on a six foot, three inch frame. Twenty years spent in the sun playing golf with his rich buddies had left heavy crow's feet around his dark brown eyes.

Tony was on marriage number three and trophy wife number two. Jessica, a willowy blond, part natural and part silicone, was a striking woman in her late thirties. In spite of her good looks and great flexibility in bed, Tony Savoy was constantly on the prowl, a man with an almost pathological need for new sexual conquests.

One of his pussy malls, as he called places where he attempted to score with beautiful women, was the beach in front of his condo. Several afternoons each week, Tony sat in the same chair as he admired the vast array of bare female skin, plotting ways to entice one or more of them into bed. A man with big appetites in all things in addition to sex, Savoy loved rich foods, Cuban cigars, alcohol of all types, and the occasional snort of coke.

He had made his money defending the rich who ran afoul of the law in Houston, Texas, a city known for its oil money, cattle, big-haired women, and dope. During a drug trafficking trial in Beaumont, an oil refinery town located seventy miles east of Houston, Tony had visited a strip joint to unwind.

There, he fell hard for a pole dancer named Kayla Forrester. Only twenty-two at the time, Kayla was gorgeous, with blond hair, blue eyes, and big breasts concealing not a trace of silicone. She was looking for a sugar daddy, and Tony was looking for fresh pussy. They were made for each other.

When the trial ended, he took her back to Houston and set her up in a condo a few blocks from his downtown office. Supplied with plenty of coke, her drug of choice at the time, Kayla repaid Tony with more sex than even he could handle. But it wasn't long before Jessica Savoy found out about Kayla and demanded a divorce. Having failed to get his wife locked into a pre-nup, and looking at losing millions, Tony begged and groveled, finally convincing her to give him another chance. When she insisted he move her back to her hometown of Jacksonville as the price for staying with him, Tony reluctantly agreed. What choice did he have?

Packing up his law practice, he relocated to Jacksonville Beach, careful to keep his wife from discovering that Kayla came along, too. Tony put her up in the Atlantic View Condominiums, which he leased through a dummy corporation to protect himself. Kayla made the lease payments with cash he deposited into her checking account. She could come and go as she pleased as long as she was available when Tony wanted sex, which was often.

Meanwhile, he bought a penthouse condo at the south end of First Street and opened his criminal defense practice in Jacksonville, specializing in defending dope dealers and white-collar criminals who could afford to pay his exorbitant fees.

One of Tony's first priorities was to hire an investigator to do the legwork for trial. Someone to hunt for dirt on potential witnesses to bring their credibility into question. He needed an investigator with intimate knowledge of the criminal justice system in Duval County.

A cop, preferably a former cop who might have left police work under a cloud. Tony wanted someone who wasn't afraid to bend the rules or even break them when the situation warranted it.

He discussed his needs with a fellow defense attorney one evening over drinks. The lawyer complained bitterly about a Jacksonville Beach cop named Roy Connor that arrested him for DUI years before. With obvious satisfaction, he described how Connor did something illegal involving another cop and got fired, eventually serving several months in the county jail. After doing his own background investigation into Connor's tarnished police career, Savoy was intrigued and set out to find him.

He found him working at a big box store unloading trucks. After a brief conversation, it was clear that Connor's prior law enforcement experience, native intelligence, and street smarts made him the perfect choice. It also didn't hurt that his massive physique, coupled with major ink on his arms, would be an intimidating sight when dealing with less-than-cooperative clients and witnesses. He offered Connor a job, and the man accepted on the spot.

Roy Connor quickly demonstrated his value when Jacksonville Beach cops arrested a rich kid from Ponte Vedra for selling a half-pound of cocaine to an undercover officer. The nineteen-year-old was looking at heavyweight prison time, so his father hired the hotshot new defense lawyer from Texas to defend his son.

Connor knew the undercover officer from his time on the department. He also knew the man harbored a secret; he was a drug addict, hooked on prescription painkillers. He burglarized the cop's apartment while he was at work, looking for anything that could be used against him. Connor hit the jackpot, finding multiple blank prescriptions the detective had stolen from his doctor's office during a routine physical. On several of the scripts, the undercover cop had entered bogus prescription information, apparently planning to use them later.

While Savoy couldn't formally introduce the illegally-obtained evidence, he knew how to use it another way. At the deposition, Tony destroyed the detective, asking him questions about drug usage and implying he had evidence of his criminal acts. By the end of the depo, Savoy had him crying and admitting his addiction.

Realizing Savoy would destroy his prime witness in trial, the state attorney agreed to a plea deal giving the kid probation and a stern lecture from the judge. Word of Tony's skill at getting his clients off spread quickly throughout the drug culture, cementing his reputation as the ultimate fixer.

"I've heard of that cop, Hawkins," Tony said. "And what I've heard isn't particularly impressive. There are some competent police officers on his department. I've had a couple that challenged my exceptional skills in court," he said with a satisfied smirk. "But he's not one of them."

"No, he's not," Connor replied. "Bobby Hawkins is ten pounds of shit in a five pound bag, that's for sure."

Savoy burst out laughing. "Damn, Roy! You come up with the most outrageous expressions. You'd fit right in with some of those guys I knew in Houston."

As the afternoon wore on, the discussion turned to Tony's expanding list of drug dealer clients and their various legal woes. During pre-trial interviews, he questioned them extensively to learn what they had done to attract the attention of the cops in the first place. Did a disgruntled ex-employee of the organization turn snitch? Or was it a rival dealer looking to expand his territory? Their responses led Tony to conclude that most of them were personally responsible for their legal problems by being stupid or careless, or both. In every case, he saw how his clients could have avoided detection and arrest if only they had been more careful.

"You know, the typical drug dealer has an IQ equal to an armadillo," Tony said. "Actually, now that I think about it, an armadillo's probably smarter," he grinned, his eyes constantly roaming the beach.

"Whataya mean, Tony?" Connor asked, feeling a pleasant buzz from the alcohol.

"What I mean is, those brainless assholes I'm defending don't have a lick of common sense. They start out playing it safe. They pay attention to their surroundings when they do a deal, and they stay in the background so they don't draw attention to themselves. They don't discuss their business on traceable cell phones. But as soon as they start making piles of money, they go brain dead. They buy the biggest damn SUV they can find, put twenty-inch rims on it, and add a ten thousand dollar stereo system.

"Then, they really get stupid. They eat out every night at high-dollar places and tip the valet twenty bucks to park their car. They go inside and order the biggest steak in the house, and leave a hundred dollar tip for a forty-dollar chunk of beef. Then what happens, Roy? Tell me."

Connor had been half listening to Tony, preoccupied as he squinted at a voluptuous young woman in a pink string bikini strolling on the beach below. Turning back to Tony, he said, "Huh? What did you say?"

"I said, 'Tell me what happens next, Roy.' Haven't you been listening?"

"Well, I was until I saw that fine piece of pussy. Then my pecker took charge, and, well, you know how that can happen," he said with a grin.

Tony smiled, "Yeah, okay. Now, pay attention here. I'm trying to tell you something important."

"Right. You were saying dope dealers are dumbasses."

"Yeah, I was. After all that cash starts rolling in, they lose their mind and start throwing it around like they're just begging to get busted. You were a cop. Didn't you notice when some guy, a car wash attendant or a grocery store bagger, for example, suddenly started throwing money around like he just won the lottery?"

"Sure, I did," Connor nodded. "I didn't work dope, but I could spot somebody who was dirty a mile away."

"That's what I'm talking about. These guys are so dimwitted they deserve what they get. Most of the time, they get caught because they're dealing to an undercover police officer. I mean, come on. How hard is it to spot a cop posing as a druggie, anyway?"

Connor raised his eyebrows, "Hey, trust me, Tony. It's not that easy if the cop is a good actor. But there aren't many of those around. Especially at the old Jax Beach PD," he said, his mouth turned down in obvious distaste at the mention of his old department.

Tony nodded, "You know, if I was running a drug organization, nobody would ever find out."

Connor looked quizzically at Savoy. "What are you talking about, Tony? You? A drug dealer?"

Savoy replied, "Yeah, so? You think I can't?"

Connor leaned forward in the deck chair, rubbing his coarse chin whiskers as he shook his head. "I don't know. Never thought about it, I guess. Drug dealing isn't the same as . . . I don't know, running a lawn cutting business or a restaurant, something like that. I just can't see you doing that."

"Why not?" Savoy asked.

"You're a successful lawyer, Tony. You've obviously got plenty of money," Roy said, waving at the opulent surroundings. "It doesn't make sense why you'd want to get into such a dangerous business. People get killed all the time in the drug trade, you know?"

"Yeah, I know," he said with a dismissive wave. "Here's the deal. I'm bored out of my skull. The typical prosecutors I face in court are all fresh out of law school with no experience in a courtroom. Hell, they're so pathetic they can't even beat me on a day when I've got a world-class hangover.

"Roy, there's something you obviously don't understand about me. I have to win at whatever I do. And I *do* win most of the time, but it's to the point that winning cases isn't enough of a challenge to me anymore. I want something that'll cause my pulse to race. Something that has an element of danger to it."

"Hell, Tony, if you want danger, take up skydiving or swimming with sharks! But drug dealing? I don't know, man. Giving up your law practice for something like that sounds whack to me," Connor said, frowning.

"Oh, I'll keep my practice. It pays the bills. My, what should I call it . . . hobby? Yeah, my hobby will satisfy my craving for excitement. So, what do you say? Want to join me in my little adventure?"

Before Connor could answer, the terrace doors slid open, and Jessica Savoy came gliding out. Wearing a white terrycloth robe that barely covered the essential parts, she said in a silky voice, "Hello, boys. Don't mind me. It's time for my daily soak in the hot tub."

As she strolled past Connor, her hip brushed against his arm. He caught the scent of her perfume and marveled once again at the woman's stunning body.

Tony took a swallow of his drink. "Hey, babe, Roy and I are discussing business here. Give us a few minutes, will you?"

Jessica looked at her husband with a smile that didn't reach her eyes. "Tony, there shouldn't be any secrets between a husband and wife. Remember?"

Without waiting for a response, she turned her back on them and bent over to turn on the jets. Connor's eyes lit up as her naked buttocks came into view. Slipping off the robe, Jessica stepped nude into the hot tub. Winking at Connor, she settled into the swirling water, leaned back, and closed her eyes.

Connor struggled to keep from ogling her body, clearly visible through the foaming water. Glancing at Tony, he saw the man staring at his wife with . . . what? Hatred? Contempt? He didn't know, but it damn sure wasn't love.

Heaving himself to his feet without a backward glance at Jessica, Savoy growled, "Come on inside," and headed into the penthouse.

As Connor got slowly to his feet, he stared at the beautiful woman in the hot tub. Suddenly, Jessica opened her eyes and blew Roy a kiss. Resisting the urge to tear off his clothes and leap into the hot tub on top of her, he walked stiffly to the door. Something told him to stop and look again. She was waiting.

Arching her back, Jessica raised her hips. The water sparkled like diamonds in the afternoon sunlight as it rolled off her shaved groin. Connor stared at the erotic sight a moment before shifting his eyes to meet hers. The look she gave him was one of appraisal, of challenge. Like she was making him an offer and asking if he thought he was man enough to accept. He was amazed at the woman's audacity, coming on to him with her husband only feet away. Reluctantly, he stepped into the penthouse, hearing her hearty laugh as the door closed.

"What the hell was that all about, Tony?" Connor asked as he entered the living room, finding Tony sprawled on the couch.

"The bitch is still paying me back for Kayla. That was over a year ago, but she won't let it go."

Looking over his shoulder to ensure Jessica was still outside, Connor asked quietly, "You think she knows Kayla's here?"

"No way. She's just a vindictive bitch. I closed a very lucrative practice and brought her back to her hometown. All to try to make it up to her, but she won't let it go. She hasn't let me touch her once in the past six months. Parades around here naked all the time. Gets my blood pumping and then cuts me off cold if I even try to cop a feel."

Connor thought it ironic that Tony was pissed at his wife for snubbing him when he was the one who was chasing after every piece of ass he could get his hands on.

"Can't you dump her? Get a divorce?"

Shaking his head, Tony replied, "No pre-nup. She'd take everything I've got. It looks like I'm stuck until she gets over being pissed at me, finds another sucker to marry, or accidentally falls over the railing drunk one night. I can only hope."

"Damn, that sucks, Tony," Connor said sympathetically. He thought some women, no matter how beautiful and sexy, were not worth the pain and suffering they inflicted on a man. However, with her hot tub exhibition fresh in his mind, he thought she might be a woman worth a little pain for the pleasure of her company.

If she comes on to me again when Tony's not around, he thought, *I might just have to grab a taste of that.*

Face impassive, revealing none of his lascivious thoughts about his boss's wife, Connor said, "So Tony, just outta curiosity, what would I be doing in this sideline business you're proposing?"

"I've already established contacts through some of my wealthier clients. Now I need a front man. Somebody to run the day-to-day operations while I'm in court. Make trips to close deals, pass the cash, and ensure the dope gets back here safely. And I need somebody to recruit and oversee the street-level dealers. Somebody I can trust not to rip me off. You know, I need somebody, preferably you, to run things while I take care of the money end, negotiate the deals and so forth."

Connor stared at the ocean as he wrestled with the idea of getting mixed up in a potentially lucrative venture that could also land him in jail for a long time. "I just don't know if I want to do something that could put me away until I'm too old to care about getting it up anymore."

"What are you talking about? Worst case scenario, you got me to defend you. And, not to brag, but I'm the best there is," Tony said with a smirk.

"Yeah, Tony, you're all that and probably more. But if I get busted, that means you're busted, too. Kinda hard to defend me when you're sitting at the defense table as a co-defendant, don't you think?"

Tony grinned, "Roy, my man, you're worrying too much. I've already told you I know how to run an organization that will be invisible."

Connor looked down at his hands as he continued to think it over. Sensing he was weakening, Tony said, "You're making fifteen hundred a week now. With your extra duties, I'll bump it to twenty-five hundred. How's that sound?"

Connor did the math in his head and realized he would be knocking down a hundred and thirty thousand a year starting out. "That sounds pretty good, Tony, but I'm sticking my neck way out here. I'm an ex-cop with a conviction on my record. I'm looking at a lot of time if things go wrong. I think that calls for a bigger pot to match the risk. Like, I don't know, like thirty-five hundred a week."

Tony smiled, "Come on, Roy. You're not going to get caught unless *you* do something stupid, and you won't do that, I know. Tell you what, three to start. Then after three months, assuming everything is going well, I'll pay you thirty-five hundred. How's that?"

Connor stared hard at his boss. The man had to be insane to be thinking about doing something like this. But it was a lot of money, more than he had ever made as a cop. He shrugged, thinking, *I'll take the crazy bastard's money if he wants to throw it my way.*

Leaning forward, he shook Tony's hand. "What the hell. Why not?"

And with that handshake, a new drug organization was born.

Chapter 9

His beach shootout with Dante Brown still years in the future, Danny Malone was excited to be starting his new assignment as a drug detective on the Community Response Team. Excited, that is, until Commander Mike Wilson greeted him unceremoniously. "Malone, what the hell are you doing?" he demanded.

Danny stuttered, "Si, Sir? Doing about what?"

"The way you're dressed, that's what."

Even more confused, Danny asked, "What way, Commander?"

Rolling his eyes, Wilson said, "Your assignment is undercover. Do you really think some pothead or speed freak is not instantly going to make you as a police officer?" he asked, eyeing Danny's short hair and neat clothing. "You look exactly like what you are. A cop. Face slick as a baby's butt. Creases in your jeans. And to top it off, you're wearing a damn golf shirt! How do you expect to convince a dope dealer you're strung out when you look like that?"

Danny looked down nervously, certain he was about to be bumped back to patrol before he even started as a detective. "Well, Commander, I, I wasn't sure what my first assignment would be, so I, uh . . . ," his voice trailed off.

Wilson said, "Tell you what. I'll give you one, no, make that two hours since you're obviously a little slow. Two hours to change your appearance to fit the job assignment you begged and pleaded to get. Now, go!"

Danny didn't hesitate, dashing out of the building in a panic as he tried to imagine what Mike Wilson would find acceptable for an undercover detective. With one minute remaining in the two hours, he came bursting through the door of the Detective Division.

Wilson was in the conference room talking to Clay, by now a detective sergeant. They heard a voice ask breathlessly, "Where is he?"

Startled, the secretary, Linda Greene, said, "Excuse me? How did you get back here? This is a restricted area."

"Mrs. Greene, don't you recognize me? I'm Danny Malone."

Linda was speechless, unable to do more than point wide-eyed at the conference room.

"Thanks," he said, hurrying toward the room as other detectives gawked at him. Standing to the side of the open door, Danny knocked three times.

"Come in," Wilson commanded gruffly.

Sidling into the room, Danny grinned at Clay before turning to Wilson. "Is this better, Commander?"

Wilson stared at Danny, no expression on his face. Clay, on the other hand, burst out laughing. Danny had concealed his short blond hair under a greasy, shoulder-length set of black dreadlocks. He sported a scraggly goatee that hung down to a faded yellow tank top paired with green plaid skateboard shorts and black hi-top sneakers. The look was completed with tattoos of daggers and barbed wire on both arms and a snarling jaguar on the right side of his neck.

"What the hell did you do to yourself, Danny?" Clay asked, continuing to laugh.

"The commander told me I had to change my appearance, so I did."

"But you've never had any tattoos," Clay protested. "How did you get those so fast?"

Danny grinned, "They're temporaries. They last a few days and then wash right off. At least, that's what the directions said."

Clay shook his head in amazement. "Okay, so how did you grow a goatee in two hours?"

"Pretty cool, huh? I got it at a costume shop in Jacksonville."

Remembering he was trying to impress his new boss, Danny asked nervously, "What do you think, Commander? Is this a good undercover disguise?"

With a deadpan look, Mike Wilson said, "It's not bad if you're planning on hustling a bunch of wannabe gangster skateboarders."

A stricken look on his face, Danny said, "I, I was just trying to create a character so I'd blend in on the street. Do you want me to change?" Glancing at his arms, he grimaced, "The, uh, ink won't come off right away, but I can wear long sleeves if you want."

A tiny smile twitched the corner of Wilson's mouth. "Naw. Keep the damn outfit. One thing's for sure. Looking like that, you're not gonna have to worry about some cop groupie sniffing around and distracting you from your job." Sliding a folder across the table, he continued, "Here, read this intelligence report. Then go check it out."

Danny opened the folder and scanned the documents quickly. An elderly woman was complaining about two men possibly dealing drugs out of a house across the street from her. The file contained numerous dates, vehicle descriptions, and license tags the lady had recorded. According to her notes, each vehicle only stayed a few minutes while one person went inside the house. Most of the visitors exited with a small bag they would lock in the trunk before driving quickly away.

In spite of his limited knowledge of the drug culture, Danny knew the information was consistent with the way dealers operated. Closing the folder, he stood up, nodding to Wilson, "I'll get right on it, Commander."

"Good. Now get out of here before I change my mind about you working in my division."

Grinning at Clay, Danny nodded to Commander Wilson and headed out to work on his first case as a narcotics detective. He jogged through a misting rain to his assigned car, parked a block away at the city's golf course. As an undercover detective, he would have to get used to hiding his ride well away from the police lot. He knew smart criminals made a habit of driving by looking for undercover cars.

His assigned car was a hand-me-down. To save money, the department transferred patrol cars to detectives when the vehicles got too old and beat up for everyday use. Take off the emergency lights and siren, slap on a two hundred dollar paint job, and, *voilá*, a new unmarked was ready to go.

Cranking the engine, Danny hit the wipers to clear the windshield, at the same time turning on the AC. Nothing happened. No wipers. No air conditioner. Within seconds, the windows began fogging up. He tried the defroster. Again, no luck.

Danny drummed his fingers on the steering wheel. If he went back to the station and asked Wilson for another car, the old bastard might change his mind and boot him out of the division after all. On the other hand, the car wasn't drivable, so he couldn't follow up on the drug complaint. Then Wilson would boot him for not completing the assignment.

I'm screwed either way I go, he thought. *Unless I take my truck. We're not supposed to use our own cars in case we have to make a traffic stop, but what the hell else can I do?*

Figuring he was making the right decision, Danny climbed out, slamming the door with a satisfying bang as he headed back to retrieve his truck.

Chapter 10

By ten that night, Danny had been watching the possible drug house for five hours. Three hours into the surveillance, sweating as if he were in a sauna, he yanked off the wig and tossed it to the floor. It was driving him crazy, so hot it made his scalp feel like it would spontaneously combust. To make matters worse, Danny discovered he was apparently allergic to the dye in the temporary tattoos, causing him to scratch his arms and neck until they were raw. He was quickly learning that undercover work involved long periods of boring surveillance often resulting in nothing more tangible than a sore butt and a constant need to pee.

Nell McCoy, the elderly complainant, lived in a small cinderblock house directly across the street. Widowed for many years, she sat in a straight-backed chair, notepad on her lap, pen at the ready, keeping a sharp eye on that sliver of the world she could see through the tiny living room window.

Until the week before, Mrs. McCoy had been content to watch and record the comings and goings of the two men, Jason Benson and Greg Harper, according to the intelligence report Danny reviewed. She was curious, but not enough, in her words, to bother the police. That all changed the day they backed out of their driveway so fast the car jumped the curb and mowed down her neatly trimmed hedge. To make matters worse, they raced away without stopping, leaving ruts in the lawn and a six-foot gap in her prized shrubbery.

After two days, neither man had attempted to contact her with an offer to repair the damage or even to apologize. Mrs. McCoy was very upset, so she finally called the police to complain about what she called the callous murder of her beloved hedge. When told an officer would come to her home to make a report, she refused, saying she feared retaliation if they found out she had called the police. Still determined to see the two men receive punishment for their crimes, Mrs. McCoy drove to the police department and personally delivered her detailed notes on dates, times, and descriptions of cars and people, the same notes now resting on the seat beside Danny.

Her story had some validity, as Danny discovered during his surveillance. Thirteen cars had visited the house so far, each following the five-minute pattern Mrs. McCoy had reported. Meanwhile, the car apparently belonging to the occupants had not moved from the driveway. Danny wondered why they backed in. Were they just being good neighbors, wanting to avoid another trip through Mrs. McCoy's hedge? Probably not. Or did they park the car so it would block the view of nosy neighbors who liked to watch from their front window? A more likely scenario, he figured.

Danny watched Jason Benson come out twice within fifteen minutes, each time taking something from the trunk and quickly carrying it into the house. As the door closed behind Benson after the second trip, Danny's cell phone vibrated.

"Malone," he answered.

"Danny, you still on that First Street stakeout?" Clay asked.

"Hey, Clay. Yeah, still here."

"Anything happening?"

"Maybe. Lots of cars with in and out traffic. Just in the past few minutes, one of my targets has made two trips to get stuff out of the trunk of his car. Only problem is, I couldn't see what he took out."

"I just finished the paperwork on one of my cases, and I don't have time to start anything new before the end of the shift. You want some company?" Clay asked.

Smiling, Danny said, "Sure, man. Come on by. I'm in a condo parking lot half a block south of the target's house. You got the address?"

"Got it. Be there in five. You need anything?"

"Yeah, if you got anything that'll stop itching, bring it. I must be allergic to the ink in these tattoos. I'm going crazy scratching."

Clay laughed, "That's what you get for going overboard with the disguise. You didn't need all that ink and that ridiculous-looking wig."

"Yeah, lotta good that does me now, bro. Just get over here with the medicine."

Clay pulled into the parking lot ten minutes later and climbed quickly into Danny's pickup, handing him a sleeve of antihistamine tablets.

Danny hurriedly ripped open the package and chewed two of the tablets. "Thanks, man. My skin feels like raw meat from all the scratching."

Looking around the cab, Clay asked, "Where's your city car? You're not supposed to be driving your own vehicle."

"Man, that piece of crap didn't have wipers or AC. The windows got so fogged up I thought for a second I was back in high school," he said, his eyes suddenly glazing over as the mention of fogged windows and high school brought back vivid memories of sex with the head cheerleader in the back seat of his car.

Blinking, Danny grinned, "Wow. I flashed back on Laney Edwards and the fun we used to have in my car. Remember her?"

"Uh, *yeah*," Clay said, rolling his eyes. "It would be kinda hard to forget her since I was dating her twin sister, Raney. However, we're getting off topic. Your city car, remember? Why didn't you check out another one?"

"Come on, Clay. I had just gotten my ass reamed by Wilson for the way I was dressed. I wasn't about to go back in there to whine about my car. I was afraid he'd boot me out of the division for being a pain in the ass."

Clay laughed, "Nah. Knowing Mike, he probably would have put you on a rusty beach cruiser from the property room." Peering at the tattoos, he asked, "Are you going to show off your ink to your new girlfriend?"

"Hell, no. Rachel wouldn't understand. She's never been around cops. She's still trying to get used to the idea that her boyfriend packs a gun."

Danny pointed at the house. "Hey, check it out. There's one of the guys. His name's Jason Benson. The other one is Greg Harper."

"Either one got a rap sheet?" Clay asked.

"Two misdemeanor arrests for possession, less than twenty grams, on Benson. Nothing on Harper."

As they watched, Benson went to the car, opened the trunk, paused as he looked both ways, then reached in and pulled something out. Slamming the lid, he quickly went back inside.

"Okay, that's three trips in the past half hour," Danny said. "I smell dope big time."

"It looks suspicious, I'll give you that. But hold up. We don't know that it's drugs. Maybe he forgot to get some groceries out of the trunk."

Danny frowned at Clay. "Groceries? C'mon, man. Give me a break!"

"I'm just sayin'. Working dope, you have to be careful that you don't jump too soon and screw up a good case. All you've got right now are suspicious acts that may or may not indicate illegal drug activity. You're gonna need more if you want to make a good case on these guys."

"Okay, my brilliant detective sergeant friend," Danny said with mock sarcasm. "Tell me how I can get more."

"You work at it, Danny," Clay said. "This job's not easy. You're going to spend a helluva lot of time bored out of your skull, spotting on a house or a car for hours with nothing happening. Occasionally, though, you get lucky. You see a deal go down right in front of you, and that's when all the boredom pays off."

"Like now, you mean?" Danny said, excitement rising.

"What? I don't see anything."

"Benson just stuck his head out the door, looked both ways, then ducked back inside real quick. Something's about to happen. I can feel it," Danny said, grabbing the wig and jamming it on his head.

"Wait," Clay cautioned. "Chill a second until we see if he comes back out."

"But we need to get in closer before they go mobile. I bet they're gonna come out with the bag like the old lady said and take off in that piece of shit car. If they do, we're screwed since I don't have any lights or siren on my truck."

"I didn't walk here, Danny," Clay said calmly. "My car's right over there," he said, pointing toward the other side of the lot. "If we need to go mobile, we can."

Within five minutes, both men came out the front door, Harper carrying the black gym bag. Slinging it over his shoulder, he led the way around the side of the house.

"They're heading to the beach," Danny said excitedly. "I bet a deal's going down!"

Clay put a hand on Danny's shoulder. "One thing before we go. Be cool."

"What do you mean?" Danny asked.

"It's just that you sometimes jump before you consider all the alternatives. I don't want you to get hurt. Or me, for that matter. That's all."

"Yes, Mother," he grinned. "And I'll be sure to wear my raincoat and not step in any puddles on my way home from school. Now, can we go?"

Chapter 11

Clay adjusted his ankle holster before climbing out. As Danny came around the front of the truck, he noticed for the first time how his sergeant was dressed.

"Damn! I can't believe I missed the clothes! Wilson ripped me for wearing the same kinda stuff. What's the deal?"

As they continued across First Street, Clay said, "Mike was laughing his ass off after you left. Couldn't you tell he was just messing with you?"

"Hell, no! I haven't been working for him for years like you. Are you telling me I was dressed okay?"

Clay grinned, "Well, let's just say that I can pull off the preppy look better than you, so no, you weren't dressed okay. The rebel skateboard persona is definitely more your style."

Danny gave him the finger, mad at himself for falling for Wilson's practical joke and at the same time irritated at the commander for screwing with him.

Clay said, "Hurry up, let's cut through the parking lot so we can get to the beach ahead of them." They took off running, slowing when they came to the beach walkover. Clay held up his hand, stopping so fast that Danny bumped into him. "Look. They're just now hitting the walkover behind their house," Clay said. "Let's see where they go."

"How the hell are we going to see them after they get on the beach?" Danny asked. "There's no moon tonight," he said, scanning the dark sky.

"There'll be enough light from the parking lot to see what they're doing," Clay answered. "Come on. Let's get off this walkover before they see us."

When they reached the sand, Clay and Danny scanned the area where they had last seen their targets. "There they are," Danny said, pointing toward the base of the stairs. "Wait, I'm not sure. Is that them?"

"You need to invest in one of these," Clay said, pulling a small but powerful monocular out of his pocket.

Danny gaped at the device. "You carry a scope in your pocket?"

"Yeah, don't you?" Clay asked.

"Well, duh," he said, taking the device and trying to focus on the two men. "Nobody told me I needed a spotting scope to work undercover."

"Now you know. Wait. Can you see the big guy, Benson? He's opening the bag," Clay said, watching the man take out what appeared to be a small hand shovel. "Duck," he said urgently, pulling Danny down behind the stair steps. "They're looking around. Oh, man! I got a feeling I know what's happening," Clay said as he watched Benson slip under the walkover and start shoveling sand.

"What's going on? Tell me. I'm dyin' here," Danny said, squinting as he furiously twisted the focus dial on the scope.

"Turn it slowly clockwise until the view sharpens," Clay said.

"Finally," Danny said, relieved. "Okay, I see them. What's he doing, digging a hole?"

"Ten bucks says he's not hunting for shark's teeth. He's digging up their stash of dope," Clay said.

As they watched, Benson dropped the shovel and began pulling small, blocky packages out of the sand, handing each one to Harper, who stuffed them into the bag. Two, five, ten in all. From their position, the packages had the distinct look of blocks of marijuana. When Benson finished, he pushed the sand back into the hole with the side of the shovel blade. Finished, he smoothed the area with his shoe before coming out from under the walkover.

Harper reached into a side pocket of the bag, taking out rolling papers, a lighter, and a baggie of what was obviously marijuana. Rolling two joints, he handed one to Benson, fired it up, and then lit his own. Side by side, they kicked back on the bottom rung of the stairs, taking deep drags and holding the smoke in their lungs for several seconds before exhaling.

"Wow, that was obviously hard work digging up all that dope," Danny said sarcastically. "So I guess sampling the product must be their reward. Well, let's go ruin their day," he said, straightening up, anxious to make a big bust on his first day as a narcotics detective.

"Hang on, let's think about how we want to do this," Clay cautioned. "Assuming those packages are dope, which I'm almost certain they are, they're obviously not small time dealers. That means there's a very good possibility they're packing guns. If we charge up there without a plan, we may have a shootout on our hands."

Danny frowned as he pondered the options. Glancing at his tattooed arms, a thought came to him. "I look like a doper, right?"

Eyeing his friend closely, Clay said, "Yeah, so?"

"How about I stroll in their direction, maybe stagger a little like I'm stoned. Then, when I get close, I ask them if they've got any stuff. Tell them I smelled it, you know? Then try to buy some."

Clay started to object. "Hold up," Danny said, raising his hand. "Let me finish. While I'm doing my stoner bit, you slip around through the sea oats and come up from behind and we take them down. They won't have time to react."

Clay thought about it a moment and said, "There's a bunch of holes in your plan, but it's probably the best we can do right now. Okay, I'll call Dispatch and have a couple of patrol officers set up down the street and wait for our call. Give me two minutes to work my way back to the sea oats and down to their location, and then go into your act."

"Wait, Clay. I just thought of something. If I can convince them to sell one of those bricks to me, that'll give us an even stronger case, won't it?"

"You're starting to think like an undercover narcotics officer. But they're gonna expect you to flash some serious cash. You carrying a wad of Benjamins in your shorts?"

Danny pulled out five one-hundred-dollar bills. "I sold a couple of my guns yesterday. I can use this as flash money, can't I?"

"Long as you don't hand it over. If you do, we'll have to book it as evidence when we bust them. I can't guarantee Mike will be able to reimburse you right away. That okay?"

"Sure," he said with a shrug. "It's just money."

"Okay," Clay said. "We need a signal so I'll know when to swoop in just in case I can't hear the deal being made." He stared at the sand a moment before looking up. "I know. When you're ready to bust them, yank off the wig. That should throw them off long enough for me to get there."

"Cool. Sounds like a plan," Danny said.

Clay reached down to his ankle, pulling his pistol. Looking at his friend, he asked, "You remember to bring your gun?"

Danny strained to see Clay's face in the dim light, trying to figure out if this was another joke like Commander Wilson had pulled on him. "Yes, I've got my damn gun," he said indignantly, drawing it from its concealment holster in the small of his back. "My eyes may not be good enough to spot a gnat on your ass at a hundred yards, but there's nothing wrong with my memory."

Clay grinned, "Just checking."

Danny laughed quietly. "Always screwing with your best bud. Okay, let's synchronize our watches."

Clay looked at him, one eyebrow raised. "We're not in the movies. I think an estimate will be sufficient."

Danny smiled, "Gotcha, dude."

Clay gave Danny's shoulder a squeeze, suddenly serious. "Just be careful. This is no game we're about to play."

Chapter 12

As Clay made his way cautiously over the dunes, he called the dispatcher on his cell and requested patrol officers for backup. Danny watched as he headed toward the next walkover, concealed from view of the drug dealers. In spite of Clay's ribbing about synchronizing watches, he waited exactly two minutes. Taking a deep breath, he started walking with an exaggerated stagger, doing what his fellow cops called a stoner stroll.

Danny could see Benson and Harper lounging on the walkover steps, the pungent odor of burning marijuana drifting his way. Suddenly noticing Danny, Benson casually dropped the joint, kicking sand over it as he signaled to Harper to do the same.

As Danny drew close, he pretended to see them for the first time. "Yo, dudes, what's happnin'?"

Both men stared suspiciously at Danny. "Ain't nothin' happening here, man," Harper said.

"Say, uh, you guys know where I might find some smoke? I been up and down this damn beach, and there ain't nobody holdin'. They're all sayin' the cops are like everywhere. Hell, it ain't that way in Miami. I can score stuff anywhere down there."

"So why didn't you stay in Miami?" Benson asked.

"Good question, man. See, I got this little problem down there with a deal that went sour. I decided a change of zip code would be, like, a good idea."

Harper said, "What makes you think we have any dope?"

"Well, 'cause I caught a whiff of burnin' hemp," Danny said, using what he hoped was realistic doper slang. "And I thought y'all might have some extra I could buy from you."

Benson and Harper stared at Danny, giving nothing away.

"If it's about money, well, that ain't no problem. I got the cash if you got the stash. But hey, if it don't work for you, that's cool. I'll just keep lookin' for some weight."

The two dopers looked at each other, a silent signal passing between them. "You don't look like the type to have the cash to deal in weight," Harper said, taking in Danny's skateboard ensemble.

"I do alright, man. I made a sweet deal before I left Miami. I got enough back in my truck to swing a couple of pounds if you know where I can find some," he said. "And I got a hundred or so on me now, just in case I run across somebody that might have some product I can, you know, like, sample?"

"Wait here," Harper said, grabbing the black bag and climbing the stairs to the top with Benson behind him. Halfway across the walkover, they stopped. Clay crouched almost directly beneath them, listening to every word they said.

"What do you think? Do we really wanta deal with this fool?" Benson asked. "He doesn't seem like the type in spite of what he claims. That bit about a deal gone bad in Miami sounds like bullshit, too. I'm just not sure we can trust him, you know what I'm saying?"

"Yeah, you're right," Harper said. "But remember we're three weeks late on paying our man in Boca, and he's getting antsy for his money. We need to move the rest of the stuff quick, or we're gonna be in deep shit. So how about we sound this guy out a little more? See if he's all talk or really a player. If he's serious about wanting two bricks, you go with him to get his money. Cool?"

"Yeah, I'm cool with it," Benson said. "Let's go see if this freak is for real."

As they headed back across the walkover, Clay silently paced them underneath, stopping when he reached the stairs. He was now in perfect position to leap out at Danny's signal.

"What's your name, man?" Benson asked.

Without hesitation, Danny said the first name that came to mind, a kid from elementary school he used to fight with regularly. "Billy. Billy Duncan. And you?"

"I'm Jason, and this is Greg. So let's see some money," Benson said.

Danny reached into the pocket of his shorts and pulled out the wad of bills. Fanning them, he said, "I was wrong. Looks like I got five hundred. How about I get a look at the stuff?"

Harper kneeled on the sand and opened a side pouch of the bag. He pulled out a baggie containing a half ounce of weed. Handing it to Danny, he said, "One half ounce of prime stuff."

Unzipping the baggie, Danny sniffed the contents, the sharp odor filling his nose. Although he had no idea what top-grade marijuana smelled like, he smiled as if he approved.

"This is some good shit," he said, smiling at Benson and Harper. "But like I said, I'm lookin' for a couple of pounds. Think you can help me out?"

"Depends," Benson said. "You said you had more cash, but you didn't say how much. The price is three large. Can you handle that?"

"No problem," Danny said. "When can you deliver?"

Harper said, "Jason will go with you to get your money. When you get back, the stuff will be here waiting for you."

"That's cool. Let's go," Danny said.

Before they could leave, Clay jumped out of his hiding place, leveling his gun at them as he yelled, "Police! Get down!" Even in the dim light, the shock on their faces was evident, including Danny's.

"I SAID GET DOWN! NOW!" Clay shouted when they didn't react. This time, all three men complied. He said sternly, "If any of you so much as twitches, I'll assume you're attacking me, and I'll put a bullet in your head. Do I make myself clear?"

A chorus of 'Yes, sirs' was the immediate response, including from Danny. Clay grabbed his cell and called the street supervisor, who arrived within minutes followed by two patrol officers. Clay pulled the sergeant to the side, whispering, "The one with the dreadlocks is Danny Malone. Don't let your guys blow his cover. And have them cuff him like the others. Then I'll take it from there."

"You got it, Clay," he said.

Turning to Danny, Clay said, "I heard you say you're Billy Duncan."

He responded in a cocky voice, "Yeah, what about it?"

"We've been looking for you. Miami sent us your mug shot last week. Said they got word you booked up here to shake the heat from Metro narcotics. You and I need to have a talk about why you're here in our town."

"Screw you, asshole! I ain't sayin' nothin' without my lawyer," Danny snarled, getting into his role.

Turning to the patrol sergeant, Clay said, "I'll transport this guy myself. He and I need to have a little discussion about the right way to talk to the police."

"He's all yours, Sergeant," he responded. "What charges you got on these other two?"

Benson and Harper stared at Clay, anxious looks on their faces. "I'll tell you in a second. Shine your light in the bag," Clay said. The patrol sergeant lit up the interior of the bag, revealing the wrapped packages of marijuana. "Looks like about ten bricks of weed. Charge them with possession and delivery of a controlled substance. I'll be in to talk to them in a little while, right after I take care of motor mouth here."

Clay held Danny's arm as the officers took Benson and Harper away. As soon as they were out of earshot, Danny said, "Wow, quick thinking, bro. You gave me street cred with those dirtbags. Now, pop these cuffs off. The sergeant got a little enthusiastic when he locked them down. I can't feel my right hand."

Clay glared at him. "You're a dumbass, you know that?"

"What the hell are you talking about?" he said, jerking out of Clay's grasp.

"I'm talking about you agreeing to go to your truck with that doper. You never, and I mean *ever* split up from your partner when you're doing a deal like this. That's almost guaranteed to get you hurt or killed. Or worse, get me hurt or killed."

"I was just gonna do it to try to pump the dude for information on his supplier. You know, try to move up the chain and get the bigger fish."

"You know nothing about drug undercover work, Danny, but this is so typical of you. You're always too quick to jump without thinking it through. Your first day on the job, and you think you're an experienced narcotics officer. Well, listen up, partner. You're not, and if you ever pull a stunt like that again I'll bust you straight back to patrol."

"You wouldn't do that to me, would you?" Danny asked, suddenly concerned.

"You're damn right I would. Look, you're my best friend, Danny, but, like I've told you before, police work is not a game. It's serious stuff, and it's even more critical when you're working undercover. Some of these people won't hesitate to kill you if they think you're a cop. Danny, listen close now. You've got to make some serious changes in the way you do things, or you're not going to make it as a cop. You have to think about the consequences of your actions first instead of just doing the first damn thing that pops into your head. You're way too impulsive, and that's a deadly trait for a cop."

"Come on, Clay. This is Danny you're talking to."

"I know who I'm talking to. If you were anybody else, I would have already called Mike and told him I was booting you out of CRT."

"Okay, okay, I'll work on it," Danny said with a shrug. "Now, can you take these cuffs off before my hands turn black and fall off?"

"You're just agreeing to shut me up," Clay said in disgust. Releasing the cuffs, he grabbed the bag containing the dope and walked off.

"Clay," Danny pleaded. "Hey, bro, don't be mad at me. I told you I'd work on it."

Clay kept walking. Danny stood watching until he was out of sight. Jerking the wig off and dropping it on the sand, he slowly trudged after his friend.

Chapter 13

Dressed in shorts and a tank top that displayed his heavily muscled body, Roy Connor flopped down in a deck chair beside Tony Savoy at his beachside condo pool. He popped open a cold beer and drank half the can in one swallow, wiping his mouth with the back of his hand as he let out a satisfied belch.

The previous ten months had been very profitable for their venture into the world of illicit drugs. They started small, building the organization from the ground up. Roy had recruited his street-level operatives from a dealer that left for a twenty-year prison hitch. Tony was right. Most drug dealers were stupid or careless, and they subsequently paid the price. The way he saw it, their loss was his and Tony's gain.

They were grossing thirty thousand a month, and each month was better than the one before. During his law enforcement career, he never realized how many people actually used cocaine. But he was happy they did, especially since the clamoring for their product was putting almost five thousand a week in his pocket.

"Any luck with the beach pussy today?" he asked as a well-built young woman walked by wearing just enough fabric to avoid arrest for indecent exposure.

"If I had gotten lucky, you wouldn't have found me sitting here," Tony said. "Speaking of pussy, what have you found out about Kayla?"

Connor hesitated, knowing what he was about to tell Savoy would make the man go ballistic. "I found out some stuff. But are you sure you wanta know?"

"I asked, didn't I?"

Connor took a deep breath as he leaned forward, staring at his feet. "Okay, here's the deal. She's got some tall, skinny kid staying with her. A heroin addict named Trey Jessup. He's got her shootin' up with him. You probably noticed she's been losing weight over the past couple of months. But there's more than just her shacking up with the guy. Jax Beach cops busted him for heroin possession a month ago, and word on the street is he turned. He's apparently giving them information about drugs at the beach."

"What?" Savoy exclaimed, lunging to his feet. "You're shitting me!"

"Tony, chill!" Connor said.

Looking around, Savoy saw people staring at them. He slumped heavily into his chair, waving at Connor to continue.

"And no, Tony, I'm not shittin' you. How do I know? Several things point to it. Wait, hear me out," he said, holding up a hand before Savoy erupted again.

"You're an attorney. You defend dopers. What does it mean when a guy gets busted for heroin possession, taken to the police department for booking, and then gets released without going downtown to the county jail?"

"Son of a bitch! The cops got him to agree to work off his charges in return for information on where he gets his drugs. That's what it means."

"Exactly. Of course, the big question is whether he knows your name. My informant tells me Jessup's been screwing Kayla, and, during a little pillow talk, she apparently told him she had a rich guy paying the lease on her condo. My source said he gets his money dealing coke. So you need to consider the possibility that Kayla dropped your name, even by accident. If she did, the next question is whether this guy gave up your name to his handler. And—"

"Who's he snitching to?" Savoy interrupted.

"A drug cop named Lonnie Washington."

"I know him. I defended a couple of crap-for-brains dopers he arrested and won both cases. He's pretty good at what he does, but I'm better," Tony said with a smirk. Then he frowned, "If the guy knows about me, Washington will probably get it out of him. This is potentially very bad."

"Hold on, Tony. You didn't let me finish. He doesn't know. At least he didn't as of two days ago."

"How do you know?"

"I have somebody who works with Jessup at the Pier Club. She said he's a part-time bartender. She dated him for a while before he started shacking with Kayla. She told me Jessup rattled off his life history after a blowjob one night, including all the details of his arrest and his conversation with Washington. She hates drugs, so she dumped him when she found out he was a doper. Kind of ironic isn't it, considering she's with me now," Connor said, grinning.

"How did she get all that information from him with just a blowjob?" Tony asked, curiously.

"Simple. When Andi LaBelle goes down on you, she's the best there is, ever was, and ever will be."

"Sounds like my kinda woman," Savoy leered.

"Uh-uh, no way, Tony. She's all mine. You got more women than any normal man can handle."

"Okay," Tony laughed. "But, if you get tired of her . . ."

"Right. You'll be the first to know."

Savoy said, "Alright, let's get back to business. So you feel confident that Jessup didn't tell the cop about me as of two days ago. Do you know what he did say?"

"Yeah. Andi said he told her Washington was really pressing him to give up his source for heroin or something of equal value. Jessup said he was afraid to give up his supplier, so he told him he knew about a major coke dealer on the beach pushing large volume. Jessup told her he knew he'd fucked up, that the cops would pull Kayla in, so he played him off by saying the guy would kill him if he gave up his name.

"Washington got pissed when he wouldn't cooperate and was gonna book him, so Jessup gave him a small-time PCP dealer that he knew. That got him off the hook for the moment, but Washington told him he would tell the state attorney he still needed prison time for refusing to give up the coke dealer. I'd say he's definitely a weak link that can bring the whole operation down if he rolls over."

For several long moments, Savoy said nothing as he stared at the waves rolling onto the beach. Abruptly, he asked, "You ever kill anybody?"

The ex-cop stared at Savoy for a long moment, curious where this was going. "Yeah, once, about a year after I got on the PD. Why?"

Tony said, "Tell me about it."

Connor shrugged. "Not much to tell. I rolled up on a robbery in progress. Guy came running out of a stop and rob carrying–"

"Whoa," Savoy interrupted. "What the hell is a stop and rob?"

"That's what cops call a drive-in grocery. You know, a carryout. They're on just about every damn corner in this country, and they're always getting robbed, so . . . stop and rob."

Savoy grunted, gesturing for him to continue his story.

"Anyway, the guy came running out with a gun in his hand just as I pulled on the lot. I jumped out, and he took a shot at me. He missed. I didn't. I filled him up with six rounds. He didn't even have time to bend over and kiss his ass goodbye."

As Connor told the story, he grew animated, re-living the intensity of the shooting and its immediate aftermath. He had never suffered through any of the mental or emotional trauma that many cops endured after taking a human life. Remorse over killing a scumbag robber was not an emotion he had felt then or since.

"Okay, Roy, I guess you're wondering why I asked if you had ever killed someone."

Connor looked shrewdly at Savoy. "I didn't think we were taking some bullshit trip down memory lane. What you got in mind, Tony?"

"You realize we have a thriving business going here, much more lucrative than my law practice."

"Yeah, so?"

"And from what you're telling me, we may have a problem with this Jessup asshole, as well as Kayla. Now, if they go away somewhere, our problems disappear. Would you agree?"

Connor thought about what Savoy had said, weighing it from a cop's viewpoint. "It's not as easy as you make it sound, Tony."

"Why not?"

"Well, for starters, you've already said Washington is a good detective. If Jessup and Kayla suddenly end up dead–"

"Wait! Hold on!" Savoy exclaimed. He took a deep breath, "I didn't say I wanted you to kill them."

"The hell you didn't," Connor objected. "You asked me if I ever killed anyone. Then you told me how they were a problem that needed to go away. What was I *supposed* to think?"

"Alright, Roy," he said, frowning. "I'm going to make it very clear, so listen closely. When I asked if you had ever killed anyone, I was simply curious. Okay? I'm not telling you to kill anybody. In fact, I'm telling you specifically *not* to kill anyone."

"Then what do you want me to do? Wave a magic wand and make them disappear?"

Tony bellowed, "Use your damn brain! You have one, don't you?"

Roy stood up abruptly. No one talked to him that way without getting an ass whipping. He glared at Savoy and started to let loose a string of curses, but he held back. The man had rescued him from the loading dock and put him in charge of a major drug operation. And paid him very well, too.

Swallowing his pride with great difficulty, he choked back the words he wanted to say and slowly sat down. When he felt he could respond calmly, he said, "Yeah, Tony. I have brains. I'm just not clear on what you want me to do to Jessup and Kayla. Okay, you don't want me to pop them. I got that. But you want them gone. So I assume you want me to scare them so bad they'll haul ass outta here. Is that it?"

Smiling again, Tony said, "That's the idea, Roy. Scare them into thinking they're going to die. Just don't actually do it."

Connor sat back in the beach chair, staring at a woman in a thong bikini a short distance away. Bending over to pick up a shell, he got a clear view of her well-toned buttocks. *Damn, why does every fine woman on this beach have to wiggle her naked ass in front of me when I can't do anything about it?* Tearing his eyes away from the woman, he thought about his career as a cop. He had never bought in to the idea of being a public servant, of treating citizens like customers. He believed most people were dirtbags who deserved whatever bad things happened to them.

Connor had been especially hard on homeless people and prostitutes, beating some with his fists, spraying others with heavy doses of pepper foam. You took the fight to them, you attacked first, and you cut no one any slack. That was Roy Connor's policing style.

He said, "You're probably right, Tony. If I did them, Washington would assume either their supplier killed them or hired someone to do it. Cops get seriously pissed when someone takes out their CI. They would put pressure all over the beach to find out who did it."

"Yeah, I can see that," Tony nodded. "But we have to do something to get them out of here. If we do nothing, and he knows my name, there's a good chance this Jessup character will give me up. I can't have that, Roy. And neither can you."

Connor continued to stare at the woman, now standing in shallow water at the ocean's edge as tiny waves broke over her ankles. He wondered what he could do or say that would frighten them into silence as well as leaving town. He had stepped over the line many times in his police career, legally, morally, and ethically. Intimidation was his specialty.

Maybe threats would be enough, he thought. *But what if they're not? If things get dicey, and one of them tries to escape, what would I do? It was no big deal to pop that guy during the robbery. That was self-defense. But this is different. Suppose it's Kayla that's getting away and not that pissant needle freak. What a waste of a sweet piece of meat, even if she has turned into a doper. I don't know. Jessup? Yeah, I could do him if it came down to it. But Kayla?*

Concealing those thoughts, Connor turned to Savoy, "What's the deal with Kayla? If she said anything to Jessup, you know it was probably while she was stoned on the shit. Man, she just doesn't seem like someone who would deliberately burn you. I mean, look, you set her up in a fancy penthouse. Give her plenty of money so she doesn't have to do shit except party and keep you happy. There's no way she would deliberately hurt you. She has to know that she'd be back pole dancing in some two-bit strip joint in Texas if it weren't for you. And so what if she's doin' Jessup? She's still available whenever you want her, isn't she?"

"Roy, you're letting your cock do your thinking for you. You–"

"I haven't ever touched her, Tony!" Connor protested.

"I know you haven't, but I've seen you looking at her. The heat rising off you is enough to power a small city. I won't argue that she's hot. But, Roy, she's obviously a junkie. This asshole she's letting stay in my penthouse has ruined her. For the past couple of weeks, I haven't seen her sober once, and her ability to satisfy my needs has deteriorated because of it. Even if she didn't tell Jessup about me, it's just a matter of time with the junk she's sticking in her arms before she slips up and runs her mouth. She's a liability to me, and that makes her a liability to you."

Connor had worked for the man long enough to know he took care of people loyal to him. He didn't particularly like Tony Savoy, but he respected him for possessing many of the same traits he prized in himself. "So if I take this on, what's in it for me?" he asked.

Savoy smiled, "Make them believe they will die slowly and painfully unless they leave and never come back, and your bank account will grow by twenty grand. That work for you?"

"I just wanta make sure you're talking about Kayla, too." Connor said.

"Yeah, her, too. That'll save me four thousand a month in lease fees."

Connor gazed out at the ocean, weighing the risks versus the obvious financial benefits. "Okay, suppose I agree. To convince them I'm serious, I'll have to come across like a stone cold killer. You know?"

"Yeah, so?"

"Well, I was just thinking. To pull that off, I can't very well ring the doorbell and politely ask them to invite me in, can I?"

Tony paused, then said, "No, I guess that would look pretty stupid considering the message you're trying to get across."

"My thoughts exactly. So here's what I'm thinking. I need to be hiding in the condo when they show up. Then I ambush 'em, tie 'em up, maybe stuff a gag in their mouth. That should freak them out enough that by the time I get around to laying death threats on them, they'll be ready to book for parts unknown."

Tony's eyes lit up. "I like it, Roy! I like it a lot. Damn, you're good!"

Connor took the compliment with a nod, focused on the plan that was still forming in his head. He asked, "So how do I get in the place?"

Tony grinned, "That's easy. With a key." Reaching into the back pocket of his shorts, he pulled out a thick wallet. Thumbing through numerous credit and business cards and a wad of fifties and twenties, he pulled out what at first glance appeared to be another credit card.

Eyeing the piece of plastic, Connor asked, "What? I'm supposed to get in the penthouse by slipping the door lock with a credit card? I never learned that trick, Tony."

Savoy laughed heartily, "No, no, my friend. This isn't a credit card. It's a keycard for a keyless door lock. They use these instead of regular keys in the place. This will open Kayla's door. But it'll do more than just that, too. It's a master keycard that I got my hands on when I leased the place. It'll open every door in the whole building, including every condo."

Connor reached over and took the card, holding it up to his eyes. "Damn, this is a handy device. Good thing I'm not into high-end burglaries. This little baby could make somebody a fortune."

Pocketing the card, Connor stood up. "Okay, consider it done."

Leaning forward, Savoy put his hand on Connor's arm, staring intensely at him. "Good. Just remember, while you've got them scared shitless, find out whether they dropped a dime on me. I need to know."

Chapter 14

Over the next week, Connor obtained the equipment he would need. He talked to Andi at the Pier Club and got Jessup's work schedule. He would be working Friday night from nine until bar closing at two. Kayla club hopped every night, so he was confident the condo would be empty.

On Friday night shortly after one o'clock, Connor drove to the Atlantic View Condominiums, parking across the street in the public lot. It was a clear night, the temperature a comfortable sixty degrees. Dressed in his usual attire of shorts, tank top, and flip-flops, Connor looked like most of the people who called the beach home. He carried a black canvas bag on his shoulder containing his equipment.

Approaching the entrance doors, he stopped, slipping behind a line of shrubs. Peering through the bushes, he spotted a uniformed security guard. The rent-a-cop came out the door, turning and pulling on the handle to ensure it locked behind him. Walking quickly to the opposite end of the parking lot, he climbed into a rusty, older model pickup.

Connor watched the man, barely visible through the windshield, as he lit what at first glance appeared to be a cigarette. The driver's window was open, allowing the sound of country music to follow the sharp smell of burning marijuana across to where Connor stood. Over the next fifteen minutes, the guard continued to sit in his truck as he smoked two joints.

What's going on? Connor wondered. *The security company is supposed to shut down at midnight. So what the hell is he still doing here?* He thought about casually strolling through the front entrance as if he lived there but quickly dismissed that idea. He figured the guard probably knew most of the tenants on sight. If so, the man might be suspicious of someone he didn't recognize going in with a bag that looked like it contained burglar tools. He also didn't want the guard to see his face and be able to describe him to the cops.

Connor stood watching the security guard, debating his options. The asshole was seriously screwing up his plans. The longer he stood hunched over in the bushes, the greater the chances someone would see him and notify either the guard or the Jax Beach cops. His initial plan to go through the front door using Tony's electronic keycard was rapidly falling apart. Unless the guard smoked enough dope to pass out within the next few minutes, Connor knew he would have to find another way to get inside.

Five minutes later, when the guard still had not moved, Connor had to act. Keeping the bushes between himself and the guard, he went around the end of the building to the exit door leading to the main hallway. Inset four feet, the door gave him a measure of concealment. Sliding the keycard into the electronic lockset, he watched the tiny red light change to green. Easing open the door, he gave a sigh of relief to see an empty hallway. *I should have gone in this way from the get-go*, he thought.

Once inside, he allowed the door to close with a soft click before hitting the stairwell. Climbing rapidly to the tenth floor, he paused to catch his breath. Peering through the small observation window in the door, he could see the entire length of the hallway. From Savoy, he had learned the other penthouse on the floor was vacant, so there was no need for stealth.

Connor went down the hallway to 10B and slid the plastic card into the electronic slot above the door handle. Nothing happened. The light stayed red. He pulled it out and reinserted it. Again, nothing. Cursing, he yanked the card out and wiped it on his tank top. A third try yielded the same results.

"What's the deal? Tony said this was a master keycard. The bitch must have changed the code," he grumbled. Standing in front of the door, his hand poised with the card inches from the slot, he tried to decide what to do. Suddenly, the elevator dinged as it arrived, sounding unnaturally loud in the empty hallway.

"Shit!" he muttered, sprinting to the stairwell. Just as the exit door closed behind him, the security guard came out of the elevator, turned to his left, and walked unsteadily the opposite direction.

Damn! Stoned out of his gourd and still making his rounds, Connor thought. The security company had apparently begun providing guard service later than midnight. That complication, coupled with his inability to get into the penthouse with the keycard, was going to require a new plan.

Within minutes, he was back in his car, heading south on First Street. Pulling into the parking lot of the Pier Club, Connor killed the engine as he pondered his problem. The front door opened, and Andi LaBelle walked out, dressed in a tight, black mini-skirt that barely covered her cheeks, coupled with a red tube top at least one size too small. Connor waved at Andi, who responded with a grin and a quick flash of her breasts. As she got into his truck, he smiled, seeing the perfect remedy for the stress brought on by the temporary failure of his mission. Anticipating the pleasure her lips and body would provide, Connor pulled her close. Andi came willingly.

Chapter 15

Shortly after eight the following Monday morning, Connor arrived back at the condominium complex, this time neatly dressed in a navy blue suit, white shirt, and patterned red tie. He wore black-rimmed glasses and a brown hairpiece. After shaving off his goatee and trimming his scraggly mustache, Connor no longer looked anything like the man who had slipped into the building the previous Friday night.

He parked his rental car, a plain, four-door sedan that shouted government issue, near the front entrance. A young security guard was standing a few feet away eyeing him curiously. The kid was skinny, dressed in a grey uniform that hung loosely on his body.

Piece of cake, Connor thought. He stepped out of the car unhurriedly, allowing his coat to flare open. The guard's eyes widened at the sight of the gun and badge riding on Connor's hip. Striding purposefully to the door, he said in an official tone, "Good morning. I'm Special Agent Jerome Travers, FBI. What is your name, young man?"

The security guard stared nervously, clearly intimidated. "Uh, my, my name is Mickey Feldman."

"Mr. Feldman," Connor said crisply. "I'm here to conduct an interview with a tenant in this building. I would appreciate your cooperation by opening the door and then going about your business."

Feldman swallowed hard, his Adam's apple bobbing. "Uh, I'm supposed to ask for the name of the tenant you're visiting and then call to make sure they're expecting you, and, uh . . .," he said, his voice fading away.

The glare Connor gave the young man was intense. "You don't understand," he said sternly, eyes locked on Feldman's. "I don't need the tenant's permission. *Or* yours for that matter. I want to be clear as to your intentions before I take any action that you will regret. Now tell me, and think hard before you answer. Are you refusing to cooperate with the Federal Bureau of Investigation, Mr.

Feldman?" Connor demanded, putting his face within inches of the young man.

Mickey Feldman began shaking, "N, No, sir, I, I'm not refusing to cooperate, sir," he said, turning toward the entrance. "Let me get the door for you, sir."

Feldman scurried to the entrance, looking apprehensively over his shoulder at Connor. Fumbling his keycard out of his pocket, Feldman dropped it. Cursing under his breath, he quickly scooped up the card, his hands continuing to shake. Connor stood watching behind the young man with an amused smile on his face.

In his haste to get the keycard into the lockset, Feldman inserted it backward. Yanking it out, he turned the card over and slammed it back in, breathing an audible sigh of relief as the red light turned green. Jerking open the door, Feldman stepped to the side like a hotel doorman welcoming a guest. The only thing missing to complete the hilarity of the scene, Connor imagined, would be for the kid to remove a plumed hat and bow low as his lord and master swept by.

"Go right ahead, sir. And be sure and let me know if I can do anything else for you," Feldman said, avoiding looking at Connor.

"Thank you, Mr. Feldman," Connor said, striding into the building. "Go about your rounds. I can find my way to the correct residence."

"Yes, sir. I'll just take a walk around," he said, heading out the door without a backward glance.

Connor watched until Feldman walked around the south corner of the building. He then went into the ground floor hallway, looking left and then right at the fire exits located at opposite ends of the building. Seeing no one, he entered the waiting elevator and ascended to the ninth floor. Stepping off, he went directly to 9B, which was situated directly below Kayla's penthouse condo.

Tony had said most of the condos were vacant, and he hoped 9B would be one of those. He rang the doorbell and waited. After three tries with no response, Connor pulled the master keycard from his pocket and inserted it, smiling when he heard the lock release. He opened the door and stepped inside, quickly confirming the condo was vacant.

Marveling at his good luck, he left, riding the elevator back to the lobby and exiting the building past the empty security desk. Just as he wondered where the kid had gone, Mickey Feldman approached from the north end of the parking lot.

"Are you finished, sir?" he asked, respectfully.

"Yes, I am, Mr. Feldman, and the FBI thanks you for your cooperation."

Feldman flushed at the compliment. "Thank you, sir. Uh, may I ask you a question, sir?"

Pausing, pretending to consider the request, Connor said, "You just did, Mr. Feldman. Is there a second question you wish to ask?"

"Oh, I, I didn't mean, I, uh . . . ," he stuttered, thoroughly flustered.

Smiling, Connor responded, "It's okay, Mr. Feldman. What's your question?"

"I was just wondering what it takes to be an FBI agent," Feldman said. "You know, do I have to have a college degree or anything like that?"

Connor thought, *Is this kid for real?* Hiding his amusement, he answered, "Young man, you must possess a college degree with a grade point average approaching 4.0, have a spotless record going back to the day you were born, and, most of all, demonstrate fidelity, bravery, and integrity, character traits the F., B., and I. stand for. Now, do you have what it takes to be one of us?"

During Connor's detailing of the requirements to join the prestigious organization, Mickey Feldman's shoulders had begun to droop. When he finished, Feldman, said, "I, I only got a GED. And I got arrested a couple of times. Nothing major, of course," he added hastily. "It was just a DUI and like a little bit of pot in the car. And, and . . . ," Feldman said, his voice fading away.

Seeing Connor's flat stare, he said, "Well, anyway, thank you for letting me know. Maybe I'll check into it."

"You take care, son," Connor said, nodding curtly as he headed to his car, already making plans for his return that night.

Chapter 16

Shortly after midnight, Connor drove past the condo building looking for Kayla's car. It was gone, as he expected. Much to his dismay, however, Jessup's old pickup was in its usual spot.

The son of a bitch didn't go to work after all. Screw it. I can't wait any longer. I gotta get this done. Driving two blocks north, Connor parked, retrieved the backpack containing the tools he would need, and hiked quickly over to the beach. As he walked south on the hard-packed sand, he strapped on the backpack, which blended with his dark clothing and black boots.

Approaching the building, Connor's eyes drifted to the Kayla's tenth floor condo. Lights shone from several windows, a good indication Jessup was there. His suspicions were confirmed when he observed a very tall man step through the double glass doors onto the balcony. He pulled a compact set of binoculars from his backpack and focused on the balcony. Trey Jessup was leaning on the railing facing the ocean as he talked on a cell phone. Standing at the edge of the sea oats to break up his outline, Connor knew he was invisible to the man.

Several minutes passed before Jessup ended the conversation and went back inside. Connor waited to see if he would come back to the balcony. When Jessup didn't return, he headed to the north side of the building. Looking through the small window set in the door, he confirmed the hallway was empty. Before entering, however, he went searching for the security guard. He wasn't hard to find, once again sitting in his car, and once again smoking a joint.

Retracing his steps, Connor entered using the keycard. Taking the stairs to the ninth floor, he entered 9B and made his way onto the balcony. He took several deep breaths of the salty ocean air to calm himself. Pulling off the backpack, he removed a thirty-foot length of black rappelling rope designed to hold several hundred pounds. On either end, he had previously tied a knot to make it easier to throw with accuracy. Looking up, he gauged the distance to the top of the balcony rail of 10B to be about fifteen feet.

Connor listened carefully for sounds from the condo above. Hearing nothing, he coiled half the length of rope in his left hand and the other half in his right. Then he leaned out, tossing the rope toward the balcony railing above. His first effort was unsuccessful, the knot bouncing off his head as it fell back down.

Cursing, he tried again. This time, the knot flew over the railing and landed with a soft plop on the balcony. Connor waited for a reaction from 10B. When none came, he began flipping his end of the rope. After multiple attempts, the knot bounced off one of the steel bars of the balcony railing and hung straight down. From there, it was a simple matter of playing out additional rope until he could grab the knot.

He shouldered his backpack and, grasping both lengths of the rope, stepped onto the top of the railing. He effortlessly pulled himself up until he could see into the condo. Hanging ten floors above the ground, Connor scanned the kitchen and a small portion of the adjoining dining room that was visible to him, barely straining as he held his weight with only the strength in his arms.

Seeing no movement, he hoisted himself onto the balcony, landing lightly on the balls of his feet. He pulled up the rope and shoved it into the backpack. From another pocket, Connor removed a .45 caliber pistol. He was ready. Slipping through the door, he stood in the darkened kitchen trying to pinpoint Jessup's location. The place was silent, the only sound a single chime of a grandfather clock.

Connor went as far as the archway leading to the formal dining area. The centerpiece of the room was an immense oak table surrounded by ten high-backed, cowhide-covered chairs. Seated at the head of the table, Jessup faced away from Connor. In spite of the man's six foot, nine inch frame, the chair back was high enough that only the top of his head was visible. As he watched, Jessup's head sagged slowly to the side, coming to rest on his shoulder.

Looks like he's asleep, Connor thought. But just in case, he waited and watched for a full minute. When there was no further movement, he approached from the rear, gun ready. What he saw made him smile. The man was completely out. He observed a length of flexible rubber tubing wrapped around Jessup's puny bicep. An empty syringe lay by his foot.

Removing his backpack, Connor retrieved the rope, a roll of black duct tape, and a stun gun. Glancing at Jessup, he realized there was no need for silence; the man was so stoned he wouldn't have heard a bomb go off beside his chair.

He put the stun gun on the table in case Jessup awakened before he got him restrained. Connor peeled off five equal lengths of duct tape, enough to pin Jessup's arms, legs, and head to the chair. The rope around his upper body would complete the job of fully immobilizing the doper. Connor looped several coils of rope loosely around Jessup's chest and the chair. Leaving it untied for the moment, he grabbed the first strip of duct tape and wrapped it around Jessup's wrist and the arm of the chair. As he continued to snooze, Connor taped his other wrist, followed quickly by wraps around both legs, pinning them to the chair legs.

This left only his head free, which continued to loll on his shoulder. Connor tightened the coils of rope around Jessup's chest and knotted the ends together. Pulling the man's head upright, he wrapped the last length of tape around his forehead and the narrow, rounded peak of the chair.

Connor glanced at his watch, pleased to see it had taken only seven minutes to secure Jessup. Figuring Kayla would be partying at the bars until closing, he felt no need to rush.

Chapter 17

Connor leaned back against the table, his arms folded. As he watched, Jessup stirred. Blinking slowly, he licked his lips once, twice. When he discovered he couldn't turn his head, a confused look crossed his face. Then he saw Connor. "Wha's goin' on?" he slurred.

Connor didn't speak, staring coldly at his captive.

"Who are you, man?" Jessup asked, trying to raise his hand to his face. Lowering his eyes, he saw the duct tape pinning his wrists to the arms of the chair. Connor saw no sign of fear, just continuing bewilderment.

"Talk to me, man. You want some dope? I got some weed in the other room," he said, wiggling the fingers of his left hand as he tried to gesture toward the master bedroom. "I got some smack, too, if that's what you need. In fact, I just been doin' a little pop myself. You want some? Huh? Talk to me, man!" Jessup said growing agitated at Connor's silence.

Connor leaned forward, speaking softly, "I'm going to ask you a few questions, and I expect straight answers. If you lie, I'll know it, and that'll piss me off. And if I get pissed, I'm gonna give your balls a tune up with this little device," he said, holding up the stun gun so Jessup could see it. "Ever take a ride on one of these babies?" he asked, pointing the electric weapon at the man's groin.

Jessup stared at the weapon. "No, and I'd rather not start now. Ask your questions, and I'll answer them or tell you to take a flyin' leap up my ass," he responded contemptuously.

Connor's anger flared at the man's disrespect and apparent lack of fear at having his balls turned into electrified jelly. *Trussed up like a pig waiting for the butcher knife, and the bastard has the audacity to talk shit to me*, he thought. Without warning, he drove the stun gun into Jessup's testicles and squeezed the trigger. Jessup screamed, his body jerking uncontrollably as the current slammed into his groin. Connor stopped after a couple of seconds, and Jessup collapsed back into the chair, breathing harshly. "You . . . sorry . . . motherfucker," he wheezed, eyes full of pain.

Connor hit him a second time, holding the device in place for a full five seconds. Jessup screamed even louder this time, jerking his hips left and right as he tried to get the device away from his groin. By the time the current stopped, he was crying.

"Please, please stop! I'll tell you whatever you want to know! Just . . . please don't. No more," he begged, tears streaming down his cheeks.

Connor watched impassively for a few moments, then said, "Okay. First question. Did you get popped for possession recently?"

Unable to take his eyes off the stun gun, Jessup croaked, "Yeah, man. I got busted about a month ago."

"Second question. Did you talk to a detective named Lonnie Washington after you got arrested?"

Jessup hesitated this time, glancing up into Connor's eyes and then immediately back down to the device.

"I'm not hearing any words coming outta your mouth. That makes me think you might be planning to lie to me. Is that what you're doing, Trey?"

"No, that's not it at all," he protested, trying to shake his head to emphasize the point. "I was just tryin' to remember if I heard that name before. What name did you say again?"

"You heard the name just fine. I'm starting to get irritated, Trey. You need a little encouragement?"

"NO! NO! I remember now! Washington. Black guy."

"Okay, good. Now, let's move on to the bonus round. Did you agree to work off your drug charges by giving Washington information on drug dealers in the beach? Think carefully before you answer because my hand is getting tired of holding this thing on your balls, and my finger might just slip on the trigger. You don't want that, do you?"

Trying again to shake his head, Jessup said, "No, I don't want that. I'll tell you everything."

"Okay. I'm listening," Connor said, pointing the stun gun at the floor.

"The cop wanted information on whoever's dealing all the coke here in the beach. I told him I didn't know nothing about no coke, that I'm strictly a junk man. But he didn't buy it. Said he knew I was snortin' shit up until about three months ago, before I switched to smack. I'm like, 'Where'd you hear that shit, man?' And he's like, 'I heard it on the street.' He said the word was some businessman or something was over all the cocaine distribution on the beach, and he wanted the name in exchange for dropping my possession charge."

"What did you tell him?"

"Shit, man, I was scared. Last thing I wanted was a trip to jail. I hear they like tall, white boys in there, you know what I'm sayin'?"

"I'll ask you once more only," Connor said, menacingly. "What did you tell him?"

"If I tell you, will you let me go?"

Connor leaned forward, his eyes narrowed, "You're not in a position to bargain, asshole!"

Jessup's eyes darted between the device and Connor's face. "I told him I didn't know the guy's name, but he was supposedly a lawyer."

"What else?"

"I told him there's some muscled-up guy handling the distribution and collection and stuff, you know, while he like stays in the background and counts his money."

"And where did you hear that, Trey?" Connor asked as he watched a flood of emotions cross Jessup's pasty-white face. When half a minute had passed with no response, Connor said, "You keep stalling, and I'm gonna zap your balls until they explode. For the last time, who told you all that shit?"

"Okay, okay," he said, warily eyeing the stun gun. "It was, it was a while back. I heard Kayla talking to the guy on the phone. She was asking him stuff about some drug dealer he was defending in court. I could tell from the conversation that he's the one covering the rent for this place. She doesn't work. She's like his on-call pussy."

"You ever hear a name?"

"No, never," Trey said.

Connor saw his eyes shift when he denied knowing the name. "You're lyin', you piece of shit!" he yelled, triggering the stun gun again.

When he released the trigger, Jessup sobbed, "Please, please, I'll do anything. I'll tell you anything. I beg you. Just please stop."

"I'll ask you again, Trey," Connor said, calmly. "Did you ever hear a name?"

"Tony. She said Tony one day when she was high. She doesn't even remember doing it, and I never brought it up. And I swear I never told the cops."

"Why should I believe you?"

"It's the truth, I swear. I didn't tell Washington the name because I was afraid he would figure out who he was and arrest him. Then Kayla would lose this place, and I'd be out on the street."

Connor laughed softly, "You kept your mouth shut just to keep living in this fancy place, huh? That's cool. Take care of yourself first. That's something I can understand. Now tell me about the other guy. She mention his name?"

Sweat pouring down his face, mingling with tears from the latest assault, Jessup said, "No. She just said he was like a giant, all muscled up, with a shaved head. She said he got a charge out of hurting people, and . . . ," Jessup stopped, the light of recognition dawning in his eyes.

"What is it, Trey?" Connor asked in a silky voice. "And what?"

"You're him, aren't you? You work for the lawyer. Aw, man. Look, I don't know shit. I just wanta get out of here. Let me go, and I swear I'll never say a word to nobody. In fact, I'll be out of the whole damn state in thirty minutes. I won't even stop to pack, and I'll give you all my dope, too. Whataya say, man?"

Connor stood up, a cold look on his face. Kayla had shot off her mouth to this doper, and he passed the information to Washington, all to keep himself out of jail. He stared at Jessup, thinking hard. If he let him go, Connor had no doubt that Jessup would take off as he promised. He was probably even telling the truth when he claimed he wouldn't snitch. At least, that is, until the cops caught him.

Problem was, the guy had an outstanding possession charge. If he took off, cops could pick him up on an arrest warrant anywhere in the country. Then he would come back to Jacksonville to stand trial. When that happened, there was nothing to stop him from trading what he knew about Connor in return for a reduced sentence. Although Jessup didn't know his name, a smart cop like Washington would easily identify him.

As he continued to study the frightened eyes of his captive, Connor realized he had no choice. He couldn't let Jessup just walk away. He picked up the gun from the table.

Trey's eyes widened at the sight of the weapon. "Hey wait, man! Listen, there's cash in the bedroom closet. It's on the top shelf inside a computer box. Seventy-five hundred bucks. It's all yours. If you or your boss got a beef with Kayla, that's cool. She don't mean shit to me."

"You know, all those promises sound okay on the surface, but I'm not sure I can trust you. See, my boss doesn't like loose ends and I don't either. You're a loose end, Trey. If I let you go, it may come back one day to bite us in the ass."

Picking up the duct tape, Connor pulled off a strip. "I'm gonna tape up your mouth. Your screams a little while ago sounded like a girl, I have to tell you. Act like a man instead of a whining pussy."

As Connor approached, Jessup exploded, bucking and straining against the tape as he spewed curses at his executioner. After watching him struggle in vain a few seconds, Connor leaned forward to tape his mouth. At that moment, Jessup spit in his face.

Connor roared, grabbing his captive by the throat and choking him viciously. Jessup let fly with another load of spit, driving Connor completely over the edge. Grabbing the strip of tape off the floor, he slapped it on Jessup's mouth. Breathing hard now, in a full-on frenzy, Connor looked around wildly, first at the stun gun, then at the pistol.

He was reaching for the firearm when his eyes fell on the mounted head of a Texas longhorn steer on the wall in the living room. The horns were each almost three feet long, curving up to sharp points. With a wild gleam in his eyes, he ran over and jerked the head off the wall. Lugging the trophy back, he savored the look of pure terror on Jessup's face. Using his powerful shoulder and arm muscles, he drove the horn into Jessup's chest, ripping through the sternum, puncturing the heart, and breaking two ribs. The sharp point came to rest only after punching through the back of the cowhide chair.

Jessup twitched once, twice. Then, with one last, ragged breath, nothing. For several seconds, bright blood continued to flow from his mouth down the front of his shirt as he gazed unseeing at the monstrosity embedded in his chest.

Connor stared as he wiped Jessup's spit off his face with the sleeve of his shirt. Suddenly, he heard a sound at the front door. *Oh, shit, Kayla's back*, he thought. Turning off the dining room lights, he rushed into the kitchen just as the front door opened.

Chapter 18

Connor knelt on the far side of the kitchen's marble-topped island, waiting to spring if Kayla came into the dining room. Instead, she went straight into the master bedroom suite, never looking that way. He could hear noises as she started undressing, dropping her shoes on the hardwood floor with a flat clunk, first one, then the other. Seconds later, he heard the shower.

He slipped into the bedroom, stun gun in hand, positioning himself beside the door to the bathroom just as the shower stopped. Within seconds, Kayla walked into the bedroom naked, toweling her hair dry.

As she passed Connor, he jammed the device against the sensitive skin of her lower back and pulled the trigger, at the same time wrapping his arm around her neck in a chokehold. Kayla's back arched as the device sent waves of pain crashing though her body. Stopping the device after a few seconds, Connor continued applying pressure to her neck until he felt her body sag. She was out cold.

Lifting Kayla's limp form, Connor dropped her unceremoniously on the bed. For a moment, he admired her firm breasts and flat stomach. As his eyes roamed over her lower abdomen, he noticed a small heart-shaped tattoo with the initials T. S. inside the heart. *Tony Savoy. The son of a bitch has his women branded like cattle.*

Before she could regain consciousness, he flipped her onto her stomach and taped her hands behind her back. Turning her over, he sat down on the bed to wait. Within a minute, Kayla's eyelids fluttered several times and then opened.

When she saw Connor, she drew in a sharp breath, "What are you doing here? What did you do to me?" Seeing him leering at her naked body, Kayla tried to turn away, but Connor brutally jerked her around to face him.

"You son of a bitch! You're not supposed to be here without Tony. When I tell him what you've done to me, he'll kill you with his bare hands!" she spat.

Connor grinned. "You stupid whore. Who do you think sent me here?"

Glaring at her captor, she said, "You're lying! Tony would never do that! Untie me!"

"That's not gonna happen. At least not until you answer my questions. Then maybe I'll consider your request."

"I'm not requesting anything!" she screamed. "I'm *telling* you to untie me and get the hell out of my house right now!"

"Shut up, bitch!" Connor snarled, slapping her face hard. "You're not in a position to tell me anything! If you keep running your mouth, I'll tape it shut. Got it?"

Lips pressed together tightly, blood trickling from the corner of her mouth, her eyes showed fear for the first time.

Connor nodded, "That's better. Are you going to answer my questions, or do I *really* have to hurt you?"

"What do you want to know?" Kayla asked, her apprehension visibly growing.

"Did you tell Jessup about Tony? And just so you know, I've already heard from him. So don't try to lie."

Kayla stalled, "What did Trey tell you?"

"I'm asking the damn questions. Answer me!"

Taking a deep breath, she said, "I may have mentioned something about Tony helping me out with the rent and stuff. But I never used his name."

"Then how did Jessup know it?"

Kayla said, "I don't know, Roy. I swear I never told him! I'm not stupid. I know what Tony's into. I mean, come on! I'd have to be the dumbest bitch in the world to snitch off the guy who's keeping me in a million dollar condo and a new car every year and clothes and plenty of money. All I have to do in return is screw him whenever he wants. I would never mess up a deal like that."

Connor's eyes roamed over her body as he considered her words. *Okay, maybe she didn't deliberately drop Tony's name to Jessup. If she didn't, there's no reason to kill her. Except that Tony's also crazy over her letting Jessup crash in his condo and tap his personal stock. But maybe there's a way outta this for her. And if I pull it off, she should be grateful.*

"Kayla, what you're saying makes sense," he said in a friendly tone. "But Tony's a hard man. You know that."

"You don't have to tell me that. When we were back in Texas, he got away with beating a guy almost to death just for grabbing my tits. I guess with him being a big time lawyer and all, he must have had friends in high places. I know all about Tony's dark side. That's why I would never think of crossing him."

"Well, you see Kayla, we got ourselves a real problem here."

"What kind of problem?" she asked warily.

"I was sent here to kill you and Jessup."

She gasped, "You, You're kidding!"

"I wouldn't kid about shit like that," he said earnestly.

"There's gotta be some kind of mistake or something! Tony loves me!"

"C'mon, Kayla," he said. "The man doesn't love you. He loves what you do for him and to him. That's all."

She started to cry. "Roy, please don't kill me. I never told Trey or anybody about Tony. Yeah okay, I was giving Trey some on the side. Tony's getting old, you know? He doesn't come around as much as he used to. Then when he does, he's only interested in me getting him off. I was lonesome in this big place. Trey was just somebody to be with. That's all."

"Bullshit. You've been hanging with Jessup for the heroin. It wasn't about sex or being lonesome. Look at you. You've lost weight. Your skin color is getting pasty. That stuff is eating you up inside. You've still got a fine body, but it's going downhill fast."

"Roy," she murmured, a sudden, calculating look in her eyes as she stared at his crotch, flicking her tongue over her full lips, "I'll do anything, and I mean anything, if you'll let me go."

Connor felt the heat rise in his groin. He wanted to take her right then, right there, tied up and all, the gory scene in the dining room gone from his mind. Standing abruptly, hands shaking, he loosened his belt and dropped his pants. Spinning Kayla onto her stomach, he prepared to mount her from the rear.

She flailed against his lower abdomen with her bound hands, yelling, "Wait, Roy, I don't like it like this! Untie my hands!"

But Connor was too far gone to hear her. The lust he had harbored toward her raged out of control, and nothing she said or did was going to stop him from finishing.

She let out a piercing scream, startling Connor and causing him to pull away. Taking advantage of the opportunity, Kayla flipped over and kicked him in the groin as hard as she could.

Now it was his turn to scream as blinding pain shot through his body. Connor fell backward, banging his head on the hardwood floor. Kayla didn't hesitate, lunging off the bed and running, her hands still taped behind her back. Heading at a dead run for the front door, she stopped suddenly when she saw Trey Jessup's lifeless body pinned to the chair. She was still frozen when Connor's fist crashed into her temple, knocking her down.

Ignoring the mind-numbing pain in his groin, he quickly taped her ankles together and then her mouth. Picking her up, he raged, "If you screwed up my pecker, I'll figure out a way to bring you back to life and kill you again!"

Pain beating in rhythm with each rapid heartbeat, Connor was almost beyond rational thought. Reaching the patio, he heaved Kayla over the railing, pausing only until he heard the distant thump of her body striking the concrete pool apron ten stories below.

Limping to the bedroom, he passed Jessup's body without a glance. He grabbed Kayla's large shoulder bag and upended it on the bed, pawing through the usual items all women seem to keep close at hand. As he picked up her wallet, a packet of heroin fell out. "Bitch was gonna kill herself sooner or later with this shit, anyway," he said, tossing it on top of the dresser.

He continued to sift through the contents until he found her cell phone. Scrolling through the address book, he located Tony's name and number. Though the pain was driving him mad, he recognized the importance of removing anything linking Kayla to his boss. The phone went into his pocket.

Checking each room once more, Connor went out the front door, leaving it slightly ajar. He took a couple of halting steps toward the stairs before turning and hobbling slowly to the elevator. Walking ten flights to the bottom with the screaming pain in his groin was not going to happen. Wrapping his hand around the pistol in his pocket, he thought, *Anybody gets in my way is dead.*

Connor encountered no one as he reached the lobby and hobbled out of the building. As he headed for the beach, he passed Kayla Forester's final resting place without a backward glance.

Chapter 19

"Are you ready, babe?" Clay asked Dana, standing at the open terrace door as he watched the sun climb out of its watery bed. The soft ocean breeze felt cool on his face, just right for a run on the beach.

"Just about," she answered.

Cat leaned back in her stroller as Taz, the family Rottweiler, nuzzled her hand wanting his ears scratched. The large dog was her personal, four-legged bodyguard. Wherever she went, Taz was always nearby, a level of devotion Clay and Dana deeply appreciated.

"Let's get going. We're burning daylight here," he urged.

"Clay," she replied, exasperation in her voice, "you throw on shoes and running shorts, and you're ready to head out the door. Meanwhile, I've got to get Cat *and* me ready. How about helping out a little? Put her shoes on while I stretch."

"I can do that," he said with a disarming smile as he slipped on his daughter's pink sandals.

As he pushed Cat's stroller onto the terrace, she looked back with a frown. "Daddy, where is Taz?"

"Oh, was he going with us?" he teased.

"Yes, Daddy," she said.

"OH-kay," he said in mock disgust. Stepping inside, Clay retrieved the dog's lead from the utility closet. When Taz heard the chain rattle, he came lumbering up to Clay in anticipation. "Come on, Taz. Your biggest fan requests your presence on the terrace," he said, patting the dog's head affectionately.

Clay pushed Cat in the running stroller over the hard-packed sand as Dana and Taz matched his pace. To pass the time, they talked about her upcoming gallery show in St. Augustine and the investigations he and his teams were conducting. At the four-mile mark, they stopped to rest before the return trip on First Street. Clay handed his daughter a sippy cup filled with apple juice and a bottle of water to Dana.

"Have you talked to Rachel recently?" he asked.

She shook her head, frowning, "Not since last week. She's been down with the flu symptoms again."

"Maybe it's really the flu this time," Clay said hopefully.

"I doubt it. It's the same pattern the Lyme disease takes every time. She's been going through these ups and downs for quite a while now. I feel so sorry for her," Dana replied sadly.

"Yeah, me too. And for Danny, also. You know, it seems like he's destined to be the caregiver to the women in his life. First, it was his mom. After she died, he broke down and told me he felt guilty about not being able to help her get over her depression. I tried to tell him it wasn't his fault. I said if anyone should have stepped up to help, it was his older brothers. But he was absolutely convinced it was his fault. And now with Rachel, it seems like he's doing the same thing. I think it's a control thing with Danny. Rachel's Lyme disease, like his mom's depression, are things he can't control, and that makes him nuts. But at the same time, he won't ask anyone for help."

"Like refusing a loan from us?" Dana asked.

"Exactly. Danny will never admit he needs anything, no matter how bad things get," Clay said.

"Daddy," Cat interrupted, crossing her little arms. "It's time for my ride."

Clay smiled at his daughter's impatient look. "Okay. I guess mommy and I have talked enough." Lifting her out of the stroller, he put her on his shoulders and began dancing and jumping around as Taz ran in circles barking at them. Cat giggled and clapped her hands at the familiar ritual.

After a few minutes, they headed through the soft sand to the parking lot to begin their return trip. As Clay reached the pavement, he was about to lift Cat off his shoulders when she said, "Daddy, why is that lady outside with no clothes on?"

"What lady, Cat?"

"Over there," she said, pointing toward the condo pool area to his right.

Clay and Dana looked in that direction, but they couldn't see over the fence bordering the property. Thinking she was probably seeing a nude sunbather, Clay said to Dana, "Can you check it out? I don't want to be accused of peeping at a naked woman."

Going to the fence, Dana stretched to see over the top. Gasping in shock, she cried out, "Clay, come here! Quick!"

Clay ran to her and peered over the top. Kayla Forester's lifeless body lay sprawled beside the pool, both arms oddly positioned beneath her. Blood stained the concrete apron in a rough circle around her body. Running to the stroller, he grabbed his cell and dialed 9-1-1.

"Jax Beach 9-1-1," the dispatcher answered.

"This is Commander Randall. I've got what appears to be a homicide at the Atlantic View Condominiums, 900 First Street, North. White female by the pool on the beach side. Have the on-call detectives respond right away. Also, I need an evidence technician, wait, make that two ETs. And send a couple of patrol officers for crowd control."

"You got it, Commander. Are you there with the body?" the dispatcher asked.

"Not yet. My wife and I were coming off the beach and saw her over the fence. I'm going to check it out," Clay said, breaking the connection.

"Wait here. I'll be back," he told Dana, grabbing his gun and ID from the running stroller. Vaulting the fence, he went swiftly across the grass to the pool. Drawing near, his mouth tightened at the sight of the terrible injuries to the body of the young woman. Staring intently, the heart tattoo on Kayla Forester's lower abdomen caught his eye. *A boyfriend? Or maybe the guy who pitched her off the balcony.*

Returning to the fence where Dana waited, Clay spoke softly, "I'll be here awhile."

"Is it a suicide?" she asked.

Clay shook his head. "Not hardly. People planning to kill themselves don't usually tape their hands and feet together before they take a dive off a balcony. And they don't tape up their mouth, either. It's a murder, straight up."

Dana's nodded, knowing her husband was anxious to get back to the crime scene. "Cat and I are heading home. Just call when you can."

"Do you want me to get an officer to take you?"

"No, don't worry about us. Taz is a great protector," she said, standing on tiptoe to give him a kiss.

Focusing on the crime scene as Dana and Cat left, Clay gazed up at the tall building, eyeing each balcony carefully. The woman would more than likely have come from one of the higher floors, considering the extent of the injuries. He was searching for something, anything, to indicate which railing she had gone over. He was still scanning when the first officers arrived.

Chapter 20

The area around the pool filled rapidly with police officers, detectives, and evidence technicians. The ETs erected a frame with plastic sheeting to screen Kayla's body from view.

"Have you got all your shots? I want to see what the backside looks like," Clay said to one of the ETs.

"Got 'em, Commander, both stills and video. You want to flip the body over?"

"No. Let's just raise it up far enough to check for bullet holes or anything like that."

Clay donned a pair of latex gloves as he positioned himself at Kayla's head. As they rolled the body, bones ground and popped.

"Damn, it feels like she's broken in half," the ET said. "And look, Commander, her hands are bound with what looks like the same kind of duct tape."

"I see that," Clay grimaced, imagining the terror the woman must have felt as the hard pavement rushed up to meet her. "Be sure every piece of tape is preserved for prints."

"Will do, Commander," the ET responded.

Detective Rafe Santos came up behind Clay. "What the hell happened to her?"

"Someone helped her take a dive off one of the balconies, it appears. Probably one of the higher ones, considering the damage," Clay responded.

Santos stared at the body for a long moment before stepping away, a sick look on his face. The grisly scene could depress even the strongest person. The ability to compartmentalize emotions was a necessary defense against the more stressful aspects of the job. Clay maintained by ensuring he didn't close himself off from the world outside of police work, a world that revolved around his family and close friends.

"Okay, Rafe, pull it together. We've got work to do. Get the rest of the guys and start canvassing the building," he directed. "I want every tenant interviewed. We need to find the balcony she launched from."

"I'm on it, boss," he said, leaving to round up the other detectives.

An hour later as technicians from the medical examiner's office bagged Kayla's body, Clay's phone chirped.

"Clay, are you on?" Danny Malone asked.

"Yeah, Danny. What's up?"

"You need to come up to 10B right away."

"What do you have?"

"Uh, you gotta see this for yourself."

"On my way," Clay said, heading for the building entrance.

As the elevator doors opened on the tenth floor, Danny stood waiting. "It's this way," he said, gesturing to the right.

"Okay, so why so mysterious?" Clay asked.

"First, let me give you some background. The building has two condos per floor. Normal occupancy rates in these buildings are around seventy-five to eighty percent, but the slowdown in the housing market has hit this place hard. Right now, there are only six occupied units out of twenty in the building. The condo we're going to, actually you'd probably call it a penthouse, is 10B, and it's leased. The other one on this floor, 10A, is vacant."

Consulting his notebook, Danny said, "There are occupied units on the second, fifth, sixth, and eighth floors. One, three, four, seven, and nine are empty, although the units are completed."

Pausing a moment, he checked his notes again. "That's it. Come on in and take a look."

"Wait, Danny," Clay said, putting a hand on his arm.

He turned back with a questioning look, "Yeah?"

"How did you get into 10B?" Clay asked, concerned about entering a private residence without a search warrant.

"The door was standing open when we got here. The building security guy, Mickey something . . . hang on, I've got his name written down here somewhere. Let's see, Mickey Feldman. He was inside, and, let me tell you, the kid was freaked."

"How did he get inside?"

"The first thing he does every day when he comes on duty is check each floor to make sure everything's secure. When—"

"Wait a second," Clay interrupted. "This is a limited access building. You can't get in the front door if you don't live here unless the security guy buzzes you in. So why does he have to check all the floors?"

"Feldman said they've had some problems with people climbing the beach side of the building, going from balcony to balcony with ropes or something like that. Then they pry open the patio doors of vacant condos and go in and have parties. I've read a couple of reports on that over the past few months."

"I remember now. Go ahead."

"Feldman said he checked the first nine floors, and everything was fine. When he got to 10B, though, it was standing open an inch or so. He knew it was a leased unit, so he figured someone must be in there. He knocked several times but got no response, so he decided to check it out to make sure there hadn't been a burglary," Danny said, heading down the hall toward the condo.

Walking beside him, Clay asked, "Where's the rest of the team?"

"Interviewing the other tenants in the building," Danny said as they arrived at the door.

Three Rivers stood at the entrance to the condo, a strange look on his face.

"Hey, Commander," he said. "Imagine the hundred craziest things one person could do to another. I bet what you're about to see won't be on that list."

"Okay, you've piqued my curiosity," Clay said, stepping around Rivers into a large foyer. Paintings of oil wells, cowboys, and longhorn cattle decorated the entry, reflecting a love for all things Texas. Seated just inside the door, the security guard, Mickey Feldman, jumped to his feet. Clay introduced himself, shaking the kid's clammy hand.

Directing Feldman to wait by the front door, he continued into the living room. The sparkling waters of the Atlantic Ocean dominated the view from the floor to ceiling windows. Clay imagined the furnishings would look more at home in a rustic cabin along the Rio Grande River than in a Florida beachfront penthouse.

Matching eight-foot couches made of cypress and covered in tanned cowhide were set on opposite sides of the living room. A natural limestone fireplace covered most of the south wall. As he reached the arched doorway to the dining area, Clay came to an abrupt stop, staring in disbelief at the Longhorn steer head protruding from Trey Jessup's chest, its glass eyes seeming to gaze back at him.

"One thing I believe we can all agree on," Three said, standing directly behind Clay. "The man definitely got the point."

Totally focused on the scene, Clay didn't react. However, Danny burst out laughing. "Three, you're the most irreverent son of a bitch I've ever known!"

Looking at Danny solemnly, Three retorted, "I'm disappointed in you, Detective Malone. Show a little respect for the recently departed. I mean, really. Laughing like that in the presence of death. Look at the guy's tee shirt. He's obviously a Gator fan, and now he has to spend eternity with a Texas Longhorn stuck in his chest. It's a dark day for the Gator Nation."

Clay glanced at the security guard sitting in the foyer, wide-eyed at Rivers' flippant attitude toward a murder victim. "Cut it out, Rivers," he said softly. "We have company. Use your head."

"You're right, boss. Sorry about that," he said under his breath.

Clay turned back to the body, mentally cataloging every detail of the crime scene. A flexible strip of rubber hose wrapped tightly around the man's left bicep. An empty syringe on the floor at his feet. Puncture wounds in both arms, some fresh, more old and scarred. A tiny drop of blood had clotted at the site of what was apparently his last drug trip. Clay thought it likely the ME would find additional injection sites in numerous hidden locations, essentially any place the addict could find a vein.

Looking around the room, Clay saw drug paraphernalia on a marble-topped bar to the right of the table. He kept his hands in his pockets to avoid disturbing any evidence as he stepped over to the bar. A lighter lay beside a large metal spoon bent in the classic position to heat heroin, thereby turning it into a liquid suitable for injection.

Clay asked his detectives, "Can I assume the rest of the place is secure?"

"Yeah," Danny responded, "it's clear. We think the woman must have jumped or was pushed from the balcony over there," pointing at the sliding glass doors.

Speaking quietly so Feldman couldn't hear, Clay said, "Trust me, the woman didn't jump. Not with her feet taped together and her hands bound behind her back." Looking back at the body, he continued, "The guy's so skinny he looks like a concentration camp survivor. Did you find any more dope or paraphernalia?"

Three answered, "A tiny bit of powder, maybe half a gram, in a glassine envelope on the dresser by the wallet."

"Do we know who he is?" Clay asked.

"I found his wallet and driver's license in the master bedroom," Three said, handing the items to Clay.

"William Lamar Jessup, III," Clay read off the driver's license. "Twenty-eight years old, Gainesville address."

"Wait, Clay," Danny interrupted. "That name sounds familiar. If he goes by Trey, then I believe he's a snitch for Lonnie Washington."

"Okay, Three, call Washington to confirm whether the guy's his snitch. If he is, tell Washington I said to get over here fast. I want to know what intel he has on this guy and also the woman. Call Ty while you're at it and tell him I said to call out the rest of CRT. Also, get someone rolling on a probable cause affidavit for a search warrant."

"On the way," Rivers said, heading for the door.

Clay turned to Danny. "Tell me about the woman."

"Her purse is on the bed. Everything's been dumped out of it," he said, leading the way into the master suite. "The name on her DL is Kayla Ann Forrester, age twenty-five."

"Any record through NCIC or FCIC?"

"She had a DUI arrest in Jacksonville six months ago. She also had a hooker arrest three years ago in Beaumont, Texas, and one speeding ticket in Atlantic Beach about a year ago. No active warrants. That's it."

"Any idea where she got her money to pay for this place?"

"No," Danny responded. "We may find something when we do a full search, but, so far, there's nothing to indicate how a current or former prostitute could afford a multimillion dollar condo, or why she's living with a heroin addict who just happened to get himself skewered with a Longhorn steer."

"Okay, when we get back to the office, get on the horn, uh, no pun intended," Clay said with a smile. "Call that police department in Texas and dig up what you can on her. Find out who she associated with besides this guy. Oh, and by the way, she had a small heart tattoo on her lower abdomen with the initials T. S. inside the heart. I know it's a long shot, but see if you can find the person that goes with those initials."

"Okay. We probably should press that goofy security guard, too," Danny said.

"You think he knows something about it?" Clay asked.

"Not sure. But his hand was so wet when I shook it that I wanted to boil mine as soon as I let go."

"Yeah, I was wishing for a towel myself," Clay said. "I'm not sure about Feldman. His nervousness seems more like a scared kid than a killer worried that we're on to him. Besides, look at him. What does he weigh, maybe one-twenty? I'm not convinced he's strong enough to drive that horn all the way though the guy's body and the chair. Then there's the dead woman. She probably weighs as much as him. It just doesn't feel right to me."

"I accept that, but we still need to question him about how he found the body."

"Okay, you're right," Clay said.

"What was that?" Danny asked, holding up a hand to stop Clay. "I thought I heard something, but I'm sure it wasn't what I thought."

"What are you talking about?"

Grinning, Danny said, "I thought I heard the great, the omnipotent Detective Commander, Clayton Allen Randall, say to his minion that he, the humble detective, was right about something."

Clay stared at Danny a moment, unsure if he should laugh or explode. He knew his friend was just trying to keep him loose. If another detective had said it, Clay would have responded in anger. But it was Danny. "Screw you, minion!" he laughed, heading out of the bedroom.

Chapter 21

The chair where Mickey Feldman had been sitting was empty. Detective Santos was in the dining room taking measurements of the horns for his report.

"Rafe, where the hell is the security guard?" Clay demanded.

"Isn't he in the chair, Commander?"

Trying to remain calm, Clay said, "No, he's not. That should be obvious from my question."

Santos stepped into the hallway, looking both directions. "He's, uh, he's not here, Commander. I've only been in the dining room a few minutes. He couldn't have gotten far."

Danny chirped Rivers. When he responded, Clay asked, "Do you have an eyeball on the security guard, Mickey Feldman?"

"Sure do. He's sitting in a red pickup on the parking lot. You need him?"

"Yes, bring him back up to 10B, please."

"Okay. Uh, wait. You're not gonna believe this. The guy's tokin' on a joint. Right in broad daylight. Stand by while I snatch his ass through the window!"

"He's kidding, right?" Clay asked.

"Commander Randall wants to be reassured that you were kidding about that last transmission," Danny said.

After a few moments of silence, Three responded, "Sorry, boss. I got a little carried away. I saw it done one time in a cop movie, and I always thought that would be a cool way to remove a perp from a car."

Clay looked at Danny and Rafe in disbelief. "Did Rivers leave his brain at home? Never mind. Give me your phone." Hitting the transmit button, he said tersely, "Detective Rivers, if you enjoy your current assignment and wish to continue in that position beyond the next five minutes, then listen up. Remove Mr. Feldman from his vehicle in a professional manner, which involves opening the door and inviting him to step out. Preserve any evidence of a criminal offense that might be present, and take him straight to HQ. Now, is that sufficiently clear to you?"

"Yes, sir," Three said. "On my way. Sorry, boss."

Five minutes later, Rivers radioed that he would be 10-15 with one white male to HQ. Calling Danny on his cell, he told him Feldman had been halfway through a joint when he surprised him. He said to tell the commander that he acted very professional when he arrested the kid. "Tell him I also advised him of his rights already," Three said. "Is he still pissed at me, Danny?"

"Not all that much. At least I think I've talked him out of assigning you to a traffic post at the next bicycle rodeo at Seabreeze Elementary," he laughed as he hung up.

Within minutes, Ty Honchen arrived and took charge of both crime scenes. After briefing the sergeant on the status of the investigation, Clay and Danny headed to police headquarters.

Walking down the hall toward the booking area, Clay said, "You handle the interview with this Feldman kid. Three's BS is getting to me this morning."

"Clay, he thinks it's his mission in life to keep everybody laughing. He has trouble sometimes turning off the joke machine, but he's a good guy. He'd never do anything illegal or unethical. That counts for a lot, don't you think?"

"Yeah, it does. I like Rivers. I just wish he would learn when to be serious and when he can act like an idiot." Arriving at the interview room, Clay said, "You go on in. I'll watch from the viewing room."

Danny stepped in and closed the door, while Rivers took a chair behind Feldman. Sitting down across from the terrified security guard, he said, "Detective Rivers tells me he advised you of your rights."

Feldman nodded his head, a panic-stricken look on his face.

"Do you understand your rights as they were explained to you, Mr. Feldman?" Danny asked gently.

The kid, stammered, "Ye, Yes, sir."

"Understanding those rights, do you wish to speak to us now?"

"I, I guess so."

"Mickey. Can I call you Mickey?"

"Yes, sir," he answered timidly.

"Do you understand why you're here?"

"Yes, sir."

"Okay, tell us why."

"Uh, because I, uh, because I was smokin' dope, and the detective caught me," he said, peering over his shoulder at Rivers.

"That's right, Mickey. He caught you smoking marijuana. You know, that can be a serious offense."

"Yes, sir. I don't hardly have any more. About enough for one or two more joints, I think." Eyes filling with tears, he asked, "Am I gonna go to jail again?"

"We haven't decided yet, Mickey. It all depends on you. Let's talk about what happened in 10B this morning. Okay?"

Wiping his eyes with the sleeve of his shirt, he said, "Okay. Yes, sir. What do you want to know?"

"Let's go through your story from front to back. Start with what you did when you got to the tenth floor. Tell us everything."

Over the next hour, Danny took him through the events of the morning several times, listening for discrepancies from one telling to the next. He was consistent in his story, as consistent as anyone could expect from a twenty-one year old with a marijuana habit.

Convinced that Feldman was a witness and not a suspect, Danny asked a closing question. "Mickey, did anything out of the ordinary happen today, anything unusual at all? I mean besides the homicides."

Feldman frowned in concentration. Finally, he said, "No, not today. Not that I can think of."

"Okay, Mickey, I think–"

"Of course, there was the thing yesterday, but . . . ," he said, pausing.

"What thing yesterday?"

"I, I don't know if I'm allowed to tell," he stammered.

"Tell me what? If it involves the deaths of those two people in any way, you have an obligation to tell me. It's your honor-bound duty as a security guard," he said, playing on his ego.

"Well, if you're sure."

"Trust me on this, Mickey. I'm positive," Danny said firmly.

Twisting his head back and forth to relieve the stress, Feldman said, "Well, there was this guy from the FBI that came by yesterday.

He said he had to interview somebody in one of the condos. I told him I couldn't let him in without an invitation from a resident, and he got all up in my face. Asked me was I refusing to help the FBI and made like I would be in trouble if I didn't do what he said. So I let him in, and he told me to go on and do my rounds. He said he could find the right condo. So that's what I did. Then a little while later, he came back out and thanked me for my help. And, I guess that's about it," he said.

"Did the agent give you a name and show you a badge?" Danny asked.

"He sure did. Well, he didn't actually show me a badge, but I saw one on his belt right beside a big gun in a holster. He said his name was Agent Jerome Travers," Mickey said.

"Did he show you official identification from the FBI?"

Frowning, Mickey shook his head. "Well, no. I mean he had a gun and a badge and said he was a FBI agent. He was one, wasn't he?"

"I'm sure he was, Mickey. Don't worry about it. Tell me what he looked like."

"He was big. Over six feet, I know. I'm five-eight, and he was way taller than me. And he was like a weight lifter or something."

"What makes you say that?"

"It was his clothes. His arms were so big the coat looked glued on. It didn't hardly move when his arms moved, you know? And his shirt. He had trouble turning his head because the collar was so tight. He was huge is what I'm sayin'."

"Anything else you remember?"

"Let's see. He had on black glasses, and he had a mustache, and there was somethin' about his hair. It looked kinda like a wig. It just didn't look real. That's about all I can remember."

"Okay, Mickey. You've been very helpful. Wait here with Detective Rivers for a minute," Danny said, stepping out of the room.

"What do you think?" he asked Clay.

"He doesn't strike me as someone who could plan and carry out what appears to be a professional hit. The kid's very immature and seems totally intimidated by authority. He's a simpleminded pothead who probably thought he'd just smoked some bad dope when he saw

Jessup. But I'm very interested in this alleged FBI agent, Jerome Travers. I know a lot of the guys at the local office, and I've never heard that name. The physical description is weird, too. An FBI agent wearing a wig? Come on! I'm not buying that."

"Same here. You think it was the killer casing the place?" Danny wondered.

"Could be. I'll call one of my buddies in the Jacksonville office and run the name by him. It'll be a simple matter to clear up if there is such a person. But if there's not . . . "

"What about the kid's marijuana possession?" Danny asked.

"It's a minor issue. Tell him we're letting him go for now, but we may have to charge him later. Keep him on the hook in case something else breaks. And tell Rivers I said to write up a Code One on the dope possession and hold it in case we need to file a case later."

"Done," Danny said, heading back into the interview room to give Mickey Feldman the good news.

Chapter 22

"Mr. Savoy?" Tony's secretary breathed over the intercom in her sultry voice. Andora Sanderson stood almost six feet tall without heels, with a body and face Greek sculptors would have loved to immortalize in marble. And she could type over one hundred words a minute.

Tony had managed to keep his wife from visiting the office since hiring Andora two months before. Jessica thought a sixty-year-old widow with five children and eight grandchildren was still his secretary. Tony knew there would be hell to pay when Jessica found out about Andora. No amount of talking would convince her that he wasn't sleeping with the gorgeous Amazon. Of course, he was doing exactly that, and the sex was so good that he was already thinking of making her wife number four. With a pre-nup this time, he vowed.

"Yeah?" Tony responded, only half listening as he reviewed notes for an upcoming drug trafficking trial of a rich kid he was defending.

"Mr. Connor is here to see you."

Tony looked at the closed door and frowned. *Damn*, he thought. *I don't have time for this.* With a heavy sigh, he said, "Send him in."

Andora opened the door and stepped inside as Connor followed, giving her amazing body an appreciative look as he passed. Tony glanced up at Roy before focusing his full attention on Andora's taut rear end as she left his office. He sat there a moment, his mind relishing the memory of her extraordinary sexuality.

"Hey, Tony!" Connor said, snapping his fingers in front of Savoy's face. "You in there?"

Savoy blinked, shook his head, and scowled at the man standing in front of him. "What do you want, Roy? I'm up to my ass in trial prep. I've got so much legal crap going on I hardly have time to jump my secretary."

"Yeah, I hear you, man. She's one fine piece of ass."

"So, what do you need, Roy? Like I said, I'm busy," Tony said impatiently.

"Heard the news yet?"

"What news?"

"About certain events in Jacksonville Beach."

"Roy, cut it out! I told you I don't have time for your games! I've been holed up in this office for the past two days getting ready for a trial. I haven't had the TV on or seen a newspaper, so just tell me what the hell you're talking about so I can get back to work."

"The problem with Kayla and Jessup is taken care of. They won't be talking to the cops about our operations," Connor said, watching Savoy closely.

Tony leaned back, lacing his fingers behind his head as he propped his feet on the desk. "Okay, you've got my attention. Tell me everything. What happened? Where are they?"

Sitting on the edge of Savoy's desk, Connor grabbed a hand-rolled cigar out of the polished cherry humidor and lit it. "You were right about Kayla dropping your name to Jessup, at least your first name. But she also told him you were a lawyer. She told him about me, too. Not my name, just my physical description. Anyway, near as I can figure, he never gave us up to his handler at the police department."

"What do you mean? Either he did or he didn't."

"He never actually told me he talked to Washington about us before . . . well, before things got out of control."

Tony's eyes narrowed, his feet hitting the floor with a bang as he leaned forward. "Out of control?" he growled.

"Yeah, that's what I said. Outta control. The asshole went crazy on me. I had him taped to a chair so I could interrogate him, and he started screaming and cussing, and . . ."

"And what," Tony demanded.

"And, well, the bastard spit in my face."

"Damn, that would piss me off," Tony grimaced. "You kick his ass?"

"I took him out," Connor said calmly.

"You . . . what? You took him out? What the hell are you talking about, Connor?" he demanded, standing up abruptly.

Smiling, Connor said, "You know, I popped him."

"You mean you hit him with your fist, right?" Savoy asked, suddenly uneasy.

"Uh, no, Tony. I mean I killed his ass."

"You, you killed him?" Savoy stuttered, feeling the blood drain from his face.

"Damn right I did. He spit in my face, Tony. Twice. What did you expect me to do? Grin and say, 'Thank you, may I have another loogie?'"

Savoy stared at Connor, wild-eyed. "You killed him because he spit in your face?" he shouted, unable to believe what he was hearing.

"That's right. Nobody spits on me and walks away! Nobody!" he exclaimed.

Savoy sat down heavily, putting his head in his hands. "Okay, Roy, let's both chill out." Raising his head, he looked at Connor, "How did you do it?"

A sheepish look crossed Connor's face. "I, uh, I stabbed him with your steer head."

Savoy was confused. He had heard the words, but they made no sense to him. "What are you talking about? What steer head?"

"You know, the one you got hanging, or I should say, used to have hanging on the wall in the living room. *That* steer head."

In disbelief, Savoy railed, "Are you saying you took my Texas Longhorn off the wall, the longhorn I personally shot and spent three thousand bucks to get the head mounted, the one I had shipped here in a special box that cost me another grand to be sure it was protected. You're telling me you used my trophy to kill the son of a bitch?"

"Yep, that's what I'm saying," Connor responded defiantly.

Shaking his head, Tony slumped back in his chair, removed his glasses, and rubbed his eyes, visualizing his treasured longhorn as a deadly weapon. With a deep sigh, he said, "I don't understand. I specifically told you to scare them. That's all. And what about Kayla? Tell me you didn't hurt her, too, Roy."

Connor watched his boss closely as he explained, "She came in right after I finished Jessup and almost caught me. I barely had time to duck into the kitchen. Fortunately, she went straight to the bedroom and took a shower. When she got out, I grabbed her and tied her up, taped up her mouth so she couldn't scream, and tossed her over the balcony."

Savoy's mouth dropped open. "You threw her over the balcony?! But, but, why? Why did you have to kill her, too? I just wanted you to scare them so they would take off, not kill them!"

"She got away from me and saw Jessup. I couldn't very well let her go then, could I?"

"Why the hell not?" Savoy asked in a whisper, the enormity of what Connor had done flooding his brain.

"Come on, Tony, use your head. If I had let her go, how long you think it would have taken her to call the cops on me. On both of us?"

Savoy stared off into space as he tried to make sense of it. Two murders. What a fucking disaster. He wondered what Connor would do if the police named him as a person of interest, the buzz phrase cops used now instead of calling someone a suspect. But he knew the answer. *If they put pressure on Roy, he'll roll over on me in a heartbeat to save his own ass.* Nervous sweat trickled down the back of his neck at the thought of facing a double murder charge. *Think, Tony,* he told himself. *You're a damn lawyer. Use your brain to figure a way out of this shit.*

Getting unsteadily to his feet, he walked over to the built-in bar and poured a double shot of whiskey, downing it in one gulp. Filling the tumbler a second time, he stared at his law school diploma on the wall above the bar as if it would give him inspiration. *Let's see. There's no physical evidence tying me to the murders. Any prints or DNA will be Connor's. He can claim I hired him, but there's no evidence of that. If he tries to pull me into it, I can say he confessed to me that he was screwing Kayla and went crazy when he caught her in bed with this Jessup asshole. And he can't claim attorney-client privilege to keep me from talking because I'm not his attorney. Yeah, that might work.*

As he was about to congratulate himself on creating a plausible story, reality hit home. Connor killed them in the condo he had leased for Kayla. Would the cops find his connection, even though he had purchased it through a series of cutouts? *Maybe. Possibly. Probably, damn it,* he thought, taking a ragged breath.

The murders would generate huge publicity, the media salivating over the unusual way Jessup and Kayla were killed. And Jessup being a snitch would put additional pressure on the cops to solve the murders. They would pour all their resources into the investigation if they thought a high-profile dope attorney was involved, especially one that had kicked their asses in court so many times. Savoy also had no doubt that, if Connor truly believed he was going down, he would spill his guts about their drug business in an effort to make a better deal for himself.

As the shockwave of what Connor had done rolled over him, Tony's heart began racing. He imagined cops breaking down the door of his penthouse at three in the morning and dragging him off in handcuffs, his bitch wife cheering them on. No more romps on his office couch with Andora. No more Scotch and Cuban cigars. No more prime, twenty-ounce, medium-rare steaks chased with two hundred dollar bottles of Cabernet Sauvignon. No more of anything he valued.

Tony began to hyperventilate. Bending over, he grabbed the wastebasket beside the desk just in time to catch his lunch of blackened Ahi tuna and poached pear salad. Heaving for several seconds after his stomach emptied, he collapsed into his chair, face pasty white and dripping with sweat.

Through it all, Connor placidly smoked his cigar as he watched Savoy's meltdown. "You okay, man?" he asked, false concern in his voice.

"No, I'm not," he wheezed.

"Come on, Tony, you gotta pull yourself together. You can't be flipping out on me. We've got our business to run, and you've got a trial to get ready for. This little incident will blow over."

"Blow over?" he asked, incredulously.

"That's right, blow over!" Connor said, talking louder. "At least it will if you don't do something stupid. In a couple of weeks, the police will be off on some other case, and this'll be old news. You just take care of your end, and I'll take care of mine. And we'll be cool. Okay, partner?" he asked, leaning over the desk.

Tony shrank back in his chair, realizing for the first time that Roy Connor was crazy. He wondered what the man might do if he didn't go along, quickly deciding he didn't want to find out. "Okay, Roy. You're right," he said in a placating tone. "But we need to back off for a while. Stop everything until things quiet down."

"No. Uh-uh, Tony, that's not a good idea. If we shut down even for a couple of weeks, our customers will find another source. We have bills to pay up the line that call for a steady cash flow coming in. Tell you what. You worry about defending your rich drug pukes and let me worry about the commercial end of our business."

Tony started to object until he saw the flat, menacing look in Connor's eyes. He shivered inwardly, wondering if Kayla and Trey Jessup had seen that same frightening look just before he killed them. "Uh, yeah, okay. Whatever you say," Tony mumbled.

"That's great," Connor said cheerfully. "You know, I see this partnership getting bigger and bigger. Hell, maybe we'll take over cocaine distribution in the whole fuckin' country!" he laughed, heading out the door.

Tony walked on unsteady legs to the floor-to-ceiling windows overlooking downtown Jacksonville. Many times, he had stood in that same spot on the twentieth floor imagining he was king of all he surveyed. As hard as he tried, he couldn't dredge up any of those pleasant feelings now. Instead, thoughts of Kayla filled his mind. The sweet Texas girl with the fabulous body. The great sex. The way she could lift him out of a bad mood with her crude but hilarious jokes. He almost smiled.

Then she was gone, her memory pushed out by rising panic. He had always lived life on the edge. Taking risks in the courtroom. Constantly pursuing sexual conquests. Getting into the drug trade. But all those paled in comparison as he contemplated life in prison. Or a death sentence.

Rubbing his face, feeling the stubble from two days without shaving, Tony cursed Roy Connor. He had made a terrible mistake ever getting involved with him. Now he faced the ultimate challenge, assuredly dangerous, potentially deadly . . . how to get the crazy ex-cop to take the fall all by himself.

As Tony continued to stare at the city's skyline, as afternoon light faded into evening, no answer came to mind.

Chapter 23

For the next two weeks, Clay had his detectives chasing leads on the double homicide. A call to the Special Agent in Charge, or SAC, of the Jacksonville FBI office confirmed his suspicions. No Jerome Travers worked in that office. In fact, there was no agent by that name employed by the FBI, period.

Three Rivers worked with the security guard to create a computerized composite photograph of the fake agent. The guard was adamant about the man wearing a wig, so Three created two composites, one with a wig and one with short hair. The photos coupled with the vehicle description had generated no leads so far.

Lonnie Washington was especially angry over Jessup's murder. If he had convinced him to talk, Trey Jessup would probably still be alive. Washington haunted the areas where Jessup hung out trying to develop any scrap of information that would point toward his killer. He was striking out, also.

As Tony suspected, the media were in a frenzy over the killings, ticking off Trey Jessup's short life in a series of bullet points that included former high school basketball All American, scholarship to the University of Florida, busted for heroin possession, dropped out of school, troubled young life ended by a steer horn.

And then there was the young and beautiful Kayla Forrester. Bound, gagged, and tossed over the balcony of her multi-million dollar oceanfront condo. Reporters dug into her past, uncovering the details of her prostitution arrest in Texas. Speculation was rampant that she was either a high-class call girl or a plaything for some rich guy. How else could she have afforded such an opulent lifestyle, the media asked.

Clay insisted that one piece of evidence, possibly a critical piece, be held back. The heart tattoo with the initials was something he had his detectives digging hard to identify. Danny did Internet searches in the Jacksonville area as well as in Houston and Beaumont, compiling a list of men with those initials.

Entering Clay's office, Danny dropped a stack of papers on the desk. "Here's the printout of guys with the initials 'T. S.' from here and Texas," he said.

Staring at the large stack, Clay said, "Give me the short version."

"Okay, there are about five thousand men with those initials in the target areas."

Although he expected it, Clay was still disappointed. "Crap, I was hoping it would be a manageable number," he said, shaking his head.

Seeing Danny grinning, he asked, "What?"

From his notebook, Danny removed a witness statement and slid it across the desk.

"What's this?"

"Read it," Danny said, sitting back and crossing his legs, the grin still on his face.

Looking at him a moment longer, Clay dropped his eyes to the page and started reading. Within seconds, he sat up straight, his pulse quickening as he read the statement. Finished, he looked up. "Talk to me."

Leaning forward, Danny said, "Dispatch got a phone call from this guy this morning. Said he wanted to talk to a detective about Kayla Forrester, that he might know something about her. So I called the guy back. After we talked a minute, I asked him to come in for a witness statement. That's what you just read. The guy owns a tattoo parlor in Jacksonville. He said when he heard the name Kayla Forrester and saw her picture on TV, he remembered her. He said she came into his shop about a year ago and wanted some ink. I asked him what he gave her, and where, and he was right on the money.

"But here's the interesting part. When I asked him why he remembered her out of all his customers, he laughed. He said partly because she was a fox, his terminology, and partly because of where she wanted it. Mostly though because she got completely naked while he was doing it. He said she watched his eyes the whole time he was doing the tat. As you can imagine, considering what she looked like, he said he had a hard time focusing on his work."

"Yeah, I can see where that might have been a little distracting," Clay said dryly. "So, did she tell him what the initials stood for?"

Danny shook his head. "No, unfortunately. She just said it was for a special guy who would get a real charge out of seeing his own initials the next time he went down on her."

"Well, I'd say this narrows the list of possibilities to this general area."

"I agree," Danny said, "but that still leaves several hundred men with those initials. However, he did give me one additional piece of information that may be helpful. He said he remembered her getting into a pickup with some big guy when she left his place."

Clay's eyes narrowed at the information. "Big guy. Where have we heard that before?" he asked, derisively. "Could he give a description?"

"Pretty general, considering it's been a year. Maybe six feet or a little over, heavy, but not fat. More like a weightlifter or a bodybuilder."

"Does he remember enough about the guy to do a composite?"

"I asked him, but he said he couldn't recall anything about the guy's face, except maybe a goatee and mustache. Or maybe not. So, no help there."

"That it?" Clay asked.

"Yep."

"Okay, any ideas on where to go now?"

"Not at the moment, but I'll keep working on it," Danny said, getting to his feet.

"Hang on," Clay said, raising his hand.

Danny sat back down. "What's up?"

"Dana and I were talking the other day, wondering how Rachel is doing."

Danny's whole demeanor changed at the mention of his wife. His shoulders seemed to droop, and his voice grew faint. "She's, uh . . . you know, could be better, could be worse."

"Is the new doctor giving you any hope that she can beat the Lyme disease?"

"You know how noncommittal the medical profession is. They never guarantee anything. If they did, and it didn't work out, every lawyer in town would be lining up to sue."

Clay nodded in agreement. "I know you don't like to talk about money, but I'm your buddy. So, how's that going?"

"Aw, it's a little tight, but we're making it. I'm pulling in some extra jobs, and we've cashed in a couple of CDs. But on the bright side, the meds she's taking are starting to have a positive effect."

"Hey, that's great!" Clay said enthusiastically.

"Well, it's not time to start celebrating. According to the doctor, the improvement is there, but you'd play hell measuring it. He described it as Rachel taking a hundred mile trip, and so far she's gone about twelve inches."

Clay shook his head. "When you explain it that way, I can see how a person can get discouraged." Realizing how negative that sounded, he scrambled to recover. "But, of course, improvement is improvement, right?"

Danny smiled, "It's okay, bro, and you're right. Any improvement is good."

"Well, anyway, the offer still stands. Dana and I want to help," Clay said.

"Clay, you've made that offer so many times recently that I'm getting embarrassed to keep turning you down," Danny said. "So, we could use some help."

"Really? Good, how much you need?" Clay asked, reaching for his wallet.

With a straight face, Danny replied, "I got this e-mail yesterday from a dude named Jenmar Spluckles. He said he was the Prime Minister of Denmark. Or was it Norway? Anyway, he said he's got twenty-four million dollars, and he wants to give it to me. Can you believe it? And all I have to do is send him a million dollars to show my good faith. So whataya say, partner?" he finished, sticking out his hand with a big grin.

Clay tried to give Danny a stern look, but he couldn't maintain. Bursting out laughing, he said, "Danny, I don't know how you do it. You have this natural ability to say the most outrageous crap in the most sincere way. That's obviously what makes you the best undercover cop around. Now, get the hell out of here and go find our killer."

Leaping to his feet, Danny clicked his heels together and snapped off a salute. "Yes, sir!" he exclaimed, bolting for the door, laughing hysterically.

Chapter 24

In the weeks following the two homicides, detectives checked and rechecked the few leads they had. In the meantime, Connor was ramping up his drug operation. To solidify his grip on the growing organization, he began using some of his trustworthy street dealers for out-of-town trips to south Florida and Georgia, trips he had previously made himself. That left him free to oversee the entire process and ensure his share of the profits grew well beyond what Tony had paid him.

Emboldened by his newfound wealth and power, Roy decided it was time to find out if the offer Jessica Savoy made to him that day in the Jacuzzi was real. He rang the doorbell late one afternoon after confirming that Tony was in his office. Watching the peephole intently, Roy saw a shadow pass in front, causing the small amount of light that shone through to dim. He grinned, knowing she was on the other side of the door looking at him.

"Just a minute," she called.

Thirty seconds later, the door opened to reveal Jessica standing nude, smiling at him, left hand on her hip, right arm extended toward the top of the door.

"I was beginning to think you weren't going to accept my invitation," she said, reaching out and squeezing his groin.

For a moment, Connor was speechless, gaping at the beautiful, voluptuous woman. But only for a moment. Stepping inside, he closed the door and threw the deadbolt. Without a word, he turned and scooped her up in his arms, carrying her through the living room and out onto the terrace.

"Wait," she said breathlessly, "let me make a quick call while you turn on the Jacuzzi and get comfortable."

Connor put her down, and she grabbed the phone from the patio table. Hitting the speed dial, she called Tony's private number.

After half a dozen rings, he answered gruffly, "Yeah."

"Tony, some of my girlfriends are due here in a few minutes to talk about the sorry men we're married to. I'm sure you wouldn't want to be here."

"Whatever," he said, hanging up on her.

Jessica put the phone down and turned to see Roy in the Jacuzzi. He had taken her at her word, shedding his clothes and dropping them on the deck. As she stared at his chiseled upper body, Roy arched his back as she had done, raising his hips out of the water to reveal his erection.

Laughing in delight, Jessica stepped into the water and quickly mounted him, holding her arms over her head as he fondled her breasts. As the water swirled around them, their bodies moved in perfect time with each other.

Over the next two hours, they indulged their sexual fantasies throughout the penthouse. Leaving the Jacuzzi, they tried out the lounge chair until it began creaking as if it would break. Going inside, they used various other pieces of furniture before finally taking over the king-size bed in the master bedroom, the bed Tony had shared with Jessica until she banished him.

They continued their exploration of each other like two animals in heat until, finally exhausted, they fell apart. Lying on their backs, Jessica draped her leg over Connor's hips while he laced his fingers behind his head, marveling at the physical attributes and sexual prowess of this woman. He shook his head.

"What?" Jessica asked.

"I was thinking what a dumb shit Tony is. Having a hot piece like you at home and getting his rocks off with other women. I just don't get it."

"With Tony, it's not about having the best sex right here at home. Well . . . actually it is. Not the 'best sex' part, but the 'at home' part. That's what Tony has a problem with."

"What do you mean?"

"I'm wife number three, in case you didn't know. I was selling real estate back in Houston, and Tony came into our office one day looking to buy some investment property. He liked what he saw in me, and, quite honestly, I was looking for someone with money. So it worked out for both of us.

"Within a week, I blew him and screwed him until he could hardly stand up. Next thing I know, he's getting a divorce and asking me to marry him. Of course, he tried to get me to sign a pre-nup, but I told him I wasn't signing anything that left me with nothing if he decided some little bimbo could replace me. When he still balked, I pushed him down in his chair, unzipped his pants, and gave him a blowjob like he had never had before. Then when he was about to come, I stopped. He's like, 'What are you doing? Why did you stop?' I looked him straight in the eye and told him to think about the marriage he could have had, with sex as often as he could handle it. Then I left. Before I got to my car, he's running out the door, holding up his pants and yelling that he'd marry me without a pre-nup."

Connor burst out laughing. Jessica was one strong bitch in addition to being good looking and a great lay. Her toughness was especially attractive to him. She was like him in many respects, focused solely on her own wants, needs, and desires.

"So, you never said what you meant about the 'at home' part."

"It's simple. Tony gets bored easily. No matter how great the sex is with me, he's continually looking for new conquests. It's like he thinks every beautiful woman he sees must have a uniquely-shaped pussy that will feel different and better than mine," she said, laughing.

Connor laughed with her. "I like your style, Jessica. We think a lot alike. Both of us look out for number one. First, second, and last. That's the only way to be. Anything less, you're a wimp, and you deserve all the crap life throws at you."

"U-m-m-m, Roy," she murmured, rolling on top of him, straddling his hips as she ground her pelvis back and forth. "I love to talk, but I think it's time for a little more exercise. What do you think?"

He didn't need to speak to show his agreement.

Chapter 25

Connor was soon pulling in seventy-five hundred a week over and above expenses. Knowing he couldn't dump the cash into a savings or checking account, he purchased a safe. Within a month, it was full, so he rented the largest safety deposit box available at a local bank. Twice a month, he would fill a briefcase and visit the bank, transferring stacks of money to his box.

He was now in control of all the money, dispensing payments to his dealers, negotiating deals with his suppliers, and even paying Tony Savoy, all in keeping with their reversal of roles in the organization. Whenever Savoy asked for an accounting of the drug proceeds, Connor would underestimate the take by thousands of dollars, knowing Savoy wouldn't challenge him.

Tony no longer received any pleasure from the illicit organization he had conceived and put into place. Connor's killing of Trey Jessup and Kayla Forrester worried him so much that he would begin to hyperventilate if he thought about it very long. On the personal side, panic attacks were wreaking so much havoc with his libido that he had become impotent.

Staring at his secretary's body no longer evoked the animal lust that was once an integral part of Tony's personality. Desperate, he demanded that Andora do a striptease for him in his office to try to get him aroused. Unaware of his current erection problem, she had grown increasingly tired of his constant demands for sex, linked to his promise to divorce his wife and marry her. She refused him this time unless he agreed to pay her a bonus, say a thousand dollars. In desperation, Tony grabbed his wallet and threw ten one-hundred-dollar bills on the desk.

Smiling, she scooped up the bills and stuffed them into the pocket of her skirt. Tony settled into his high-backed chair, unzipped his pants, and got ready for his pride and joy to appear in response to the erotic show Andora was about to provide.

Swaying to a tune she heard in her head, she slowly removed her skirt and blouse, revealing a red thong and matching bra that barely contained her ample breasts. She glided around the office, shaking her hips provocatively as she looked over her shoulder at Tony, her tongue sliding over and around her full, red lips. Coming closer, Andora unhooked her bra and dropped it in Tony's lap. Then, leaning over him, she brushed his face lightly with her breasts. Tony smelled her perfume, a subtle scent that never failed to excite him. Andora turned around, wiggling her butt provocatively as she slipped out of her thong.

These were acts that normally caused a major spike in Tony's testosterone, leading to a wild romp on his desk or the floor. As he stared with longing at her assets, he looked down to check his status. Nothing was happening there.

Kneeling between his legs, she took his flaccid member and began stroking it. Still nothing. She grimaced, "Tony, I'm working my butt off here, and you're like a corpse. What's the deal?" she asked, flopping his penis back and forth between her thumb and forefinger.

He shoved her away, yelling, "I don't need this shit! Get the hell outta here!"

Snatching up her clothing, she left the room in a huff, her bare butt swaying as if to taunt him. Slamming the door, she left Tony staring at his shriveled penis, unable to believe it had failed him after so many years of faithful service.

For the next hour, he sat motionless in his chair, his mind a swirling mass of emotions. He was only vaguely aware of the phone ringing half a dozen times, but he made no attempt to answer it. His thoughts kept circling back to one simple fact. This shit was all Roy Connor's fault. Sure, he hired the asshole. He could even admit he had almost twisted Connor's arm to join him. However, that was all the blame he was willing to accept.

In Tony's mind, everything started going sideways when Connor killed Jessup and Kayla. That put him, the Honorable Anthony Joseph Savoy, Esquire, in extreme legal jeopardy. He imagined what it would be like to sit at the defendant's table facing a murder charge. The prosecutor would point an accusing finger at him as he denounced Tony Savoy, the evil mastermind behind the killings of two young and innocent people.

He could see Connor sitting on the witness stand all cleaned up, his tattoos concealed under a new suit. He would get emotional, telling the jury that Tony Savoy threatened to have him killed if he didn't follow orders. The hell of it was that Connor's gift of bullshit might convince them he was telling the truth. Of course, they couldn't let the bastard off completely. Connor would probably get a few years out of it, maybe even less than that. But odds were high they would hammer the flamboyant attorney on trial with him.

Then there was Jessica. Her arrogance and independence grated on him. Over the past month, he had begun to suspect she was fooling around on him, calling and telling him not to come home because she had a bunch of cackling bitches coming over. Yeah, right.

She had never shown any interest in developing friendships with other women. Nor in reading books, for that matter, a recent activity that supposedly involved joining a book club. It was strange now that he thought about it. The meetings took place on different nights each week, always lasting until midnight. He had been so absorbed in his own worries that he had missed the obvious signs.

Tony began to get angry. He had always been the one to call the shots. He controlled people and events, not the other way around. Connor was the reason his life was spiraling out of control. Maybe Connor was the one screwing Jessica. After all, she came out on the patio that day and stripped right in front of the big bastard. She didn't even care that her husband was watching. He was probably the one drilling her for everything she was worth.

As his fury grew, Tony's apprehension drained away, and with it his fear of Connor. It suddenly became clear that he had allowed Roy Connor to become the alpha dog. In contrast, he, larger-than-life Tony Savoy, had become just one of Connor's pack animals.

But no more. He leaned forward, yanking open the middle drawer on his desk and pulling out a .40 caliber semiautomatic. Hitting the magazine release, he checked to ensure it was loaded. It was. Tony shoved the weapon into his briefcase and stood up.

At that moment, his private line rang. Glancing at the screen, he saw his home number. He debated answering it. What else was there to say? Reluctantly picking up, he said, "What do you want?"

Not reacting to his sarcasm, Jessica said, "Tony, I just wanted to let you know that my lady friends are about to arrive. I'm hosting the wine club here this week, so don't come home until at least eleven or so."

"Where do you expect me to go in the meantime?" he asked angrily.

"I'm sure one of your bimbos will be happy to accommodate the great man."

"Screw you!" he shouted, his hand squeezing the phone so hard his knuckles turned white.

"Not likely. Not by you anyway," she said sweetly, hanging up.

Tony threw the phone against the wall where it shattered into pieces, scarring the dark oak paneling. Taking deep breaths, he struggled to get control. If he needed any last bit of incentive, the phone call had just provided it.

He took one final look at the striking view of the Jacksonville skyline, watching as the sun began to slide below the horizon. As the orange and yellow faded to blue and black, he headed for his car, a man on a mission.

Chapter 26

Tony drove like a madman all the way to the beach, running red lights and whipping through traffic like a racecar driver. The thought of a cop trying to pull him over flashed through his mind once, to be instantly banished. He no longer cared about anything except putting his hands on his lying, scheming bitch of a wife.

It was dark by the time he drove into the underground parking garage of his building, taking a vacant spot next to Jessica's car. He cut the engine, sitting motionless as his mind once again sifted through various scenarios, all of them involving his wife cheating on him. It made no difference that he had been a serial womanizer his entire adult life. In Tony's world, there were certain inviolate rules that applied only to women. At least those women married to him. Being unfaithful was the ultimate insult to his manhood.

Jerking his briefcase out of the back seat, Tony strode rapidly toward the building entrance. The security guard saw him coming and rushed to open the door. "Good evening, Mr. Savoy," he said.

"Any visitors to my condo today?" he asked, curtly, not acknowledging the greeting.

"One moment, sir. Let me check the logs."

Savoy waited impatiently, drumming his fingers on his briefcase as the guard clicked through several screens on the computer at his desk.

"Uh, yes, sir. Logs show a Mr. Roy Connor was cleared to your floor."

"When?"

The guard glanced at the screen again. "He arrived at 4:32 p.m., sir."

Tony frowned, "When did he leave?"

The guard said, "Mr. Savoy, there is no checkout time recorded for Mr. Connor."

"What the hell does that mean?"

"Well, sir. It could mean one of two things. Either Mr. Connor is still visiting, or he left without being checked out through security."

"And how could he have left without you knowing it?"

"Sir, sometimes we get called away by a property owner to deal with a problem. When that happens, a visitor could leave and not be logged out. It doesn't occur often, but, you know, sometimes . . .," he said, his voice trailing off.

Tony spun and walked quickly to the elevator. The penthouse occupied the entire ninth floor of the building, accessible only with an electronic keycard or by a security guard authorizing entry. As the elevator rose toward his floor, Tony opened the briefcase and retrieved his pistol, slipping it into the waistband of his pants and buttoning his suit coat over it. Reaching the ninth floor, he went hurriedly to his condo, unlocking the door and stepping inside.

He stood very still, listening. From the master bedroom came distinct moans of pleasure. *That bitch!* he seethed, recognizing the sounds she used to make when he was the man enjoying her favors. Now, she was making those sounds with his partner, his employee. It was too much. Anger pulsed through his head as he went through the living room and down the hall to the bedroom. He paused outside, listening as the sounds of passion grew louder. He could hear a man's voice, Connor, telling his wife what he was going to do to her.

She moaned in response, "Oh, yes! Yes!"

Tony's eyes narrowed, his heart racing. Yanking his coat open violently, a button popped off and hit the floor with a soft plink. He pulled the pistol and slowly turned the knob. Then, all caution gone, Tony shoved the door hard and charged into the room. It hit the wall with a loud bang, causing the two lovers to jump.

There on the bed was Jessica, his wife, her legs in the air, toes pointed at the ceiling, mouth open in shock. Roy Connor, naked, was on top of her. Tony locked eyes with him, expecting to see fear or at least apprehension at the gun pointed at him. He saw instead a look of satisfaction, of triumph, of power.

"Get off her!" Tony growled.

"Tony, put the gun down," Roy said calmly as he climbed off Jessica and edged toward the side of the bed.

"Stop right there or I'll shoot!" Tony commanded.

Connor stopped, muscles tensed for action. Tony maintained enough distance so he couldn't reach him. If Connor got his hands on him, he knew it would be all over. In spite of his bulk, he was soft; he would be no match for the big man.

"Okay, Tony, whatever you say," Connor said soothingly. "I'm cool. But, hey, can I at least put my pants on? This is kinda awkward, you know," he said, gesturing at his nakedness.

Tony glared. "Awkward? You're damn right it's awkward! But not because your dick's hanging out. It's awkward because it was jammed up my wife's pussy!"

"Tony," Jessica said in a trembling voice, "I, I'm sorry. I just, I don't know what to say."

"How about you don't say shit to me, bitch? How about I shoot you right in your cheatin' cunt if you open your mouth again? How about that?"

In abject fear, Jessica sagged against the headboard, pulling the sheet over her body and crossing her arms over her breasts.

Turning back to Connor, Tony spoke in a dead voice, "You know, it just came to me, Roy. You've solved my problem. I've been worried for weeks that the cops would figure out you killed Kayla and that guy. I'd wake up all hours of the night every time I heard a sound, just knowing the cops were breaking down my door to haul my ass to jail. But I don't have to worry about it anymore, and I have you to thank. Well, you and my whore wife," he said, glaring at Jessica, who appeared to be trying to sink into the wall.

"What are you talking about?" Connor asked.

"I'm glad you asked, Roy. See, it's like this. I come home after a hard day defending fine, upstanding citizens falsely accused of heinous crimes. Doing my honorable duty as an officer of the court. I get home, expecting a hug and a kiss from my beautiful wife. Instead, what do I find?" he asked, pausing. Hearing no response, Tony yelled, "I asked a damn question!" as he shook the gun menacingly.

"Please, Tony," Jessica begged, covering her head with her arms, as if by doing so she could ward off a bullet. "Don't hurt me. I'll do anything you want."

"I don't want anything you've got, Jessica," he said, shifting his attention back to Connor. "So, what's the answer, Roy?"

"Fuck you! I ain't playin' your game."

Tony smiled. "Okay, you don't want to play? That's fine. I'll answer for you. What do I find when I come home, expecting to get that hug and kiss? Well, I find my employee. The guy I took off a loading dock making minimum wage. And what's he doing to express his appreciation for all I've done for him?" Tony demanded, glaring with hatred as his voice got louder. "He's screwing my wife in my own bed! That's what he's doing!"

The gun shook violently as Tony struggled to get his emotions under control. He took several deep breaths, never taking his eyes off the naked man in his bed. Connor watched him closely, keeping his face expressionless.

In a harsh voice, Tony barked, "Roll over. Get face down on the bed and put your hands behind your back. And lace your fingers together real tight."

"Up yours, asshole!" Connor roared.

Tony fired, the bullet punching into the mattress inches from Connor's leg. Jessica screamed as Connor shouted, "You idiot! What the hell are you doing?"

Smoke from the round drifted toward the ceiling as Tony stared at Connor, his expression unchanged. "I know exactly what I'm doing. Now, turn over and put your hands behind your back, or so help me the next round will be between your eyes," he said, raising the gun to point directly at Connor's head. He watched as Connor hesitated, knowing he was trying to figure a way out. When he gave a tiny shrug, Tony knew he had him. Connor rolled over slowly, shooting a venomous look at Tony.

"Jessica," Tony said, "get the handcuffs out of the nightstand."

Connor raised his head, staring at Tony. "What are you planning to do? This shit ain't funny."

"Roy, this shit stopped being funny a long time ago. Put your head back down. If you raise up again, you're a dead man." Looking back at his terrified wife, he commanded, "Get your ass moving, bitch!"

Jessica retrieved the set of handcuffs that in better times they had used as a prop in their sex games. Her hands shook badly, the cuffs clinking together as she held them out to Tony.

"What do you want me to do with them?" she asked nervously.

"Sit on his back and straddle his arms so he can't move. Then put the cuffs on and squeeze them down tight."

His voice muffled as he spoke into the mattress, Connor said, "Tony, this is going too far. You told me she wouldn't give you any, so—"

"If you think that's justification for humping my wife, you're dumber than I thought!" Tony yelled. "Now, shut up. And you, bitch, do what I told you."

Tears flowing down her cheeks, Jessica trembled violently. She swung her leg over Connor's upper body, pinning his arms under her thighs. Leaning forward, she started to apply the cuffs as her tears dripped onto his back.

The instant the cold steel touched his wrist, Connor exploded straight up, causing Jessica to fly off the bed at Tony. Her flailing hands struck his right arm, causing his finger to jerk involuntarily on the trigger. The .40 caliber bullet blasted out of the barrel at almost a thousand feet a second, striking Jessica just above the right eye. The entrance hole was small, but the exit was large and messy, spraying blood, hair, and brain fragments across the room as she collapsed face down on the floor. Tony stared in horror as Jessica's body twitched involuntarily, blood pouring out of a two-inch hole in the back of her head. He couldn't move, his mind unable to comprehend the ghastly scene at his feet.

Connor didn't hesitate. He lunged off the bed, grabbing Tony's wrist and twisting, at the same time jerking the pistol from his limp hand. Pointing the gun at Tony, he snarled, "Now we'll see who's running this little game."

Tony gave no indication he heard him. Without hesitation, Connor jammed the gun against Tony's right temple and fired. Savoy collapsed on top of Jessica, his blood mingling with hers.

———————

Connor dressed quickly. Then, grasping a clean section of the bed sheet, he wiped the pistol thoroughly from barrel to grip. Kneeling beside Tony, being careful to avoid stepping in the gore, he put the pistol in Tony's right hand and curled his fingers around the grip. As soon as he released Tony's hand, it relaxed, and the gun slipped to the side. Connor was about to try again when he remembered his police training. A gun never stayed gripped tightly in a dead guy's hand. *This looks more realistic, and Tony's prints are the only ones they'll find on the gun.*

Stepping back slowly, he took a critical look at the staged crime scene. He thought they'd probably figure it for a simple murder-suicide. Especially if they assigned some dumbass detective like Jeremy Rivers to investigate it. Satisfied he had created a believable scenario, Connor grabbed a towel from the bathroom and scrubbed every surface in the bedroom he remembered touching. There were no glasses or dishes to worry about, since his standard practice was to walk in the door and jump Jessica as soon as they reached a relatively horizontal surface. Thinking of her gave Connor a momentary flash of regret. Then it was gone. There were plenty more women eager to give him what he wanted.

As for having to kill Tony, it was his own fault. The man had become a liability, constantly whining about going to jail. It would have been only a matter of time before he broke down and ran screaming to the police wanting to confess everything.

With a last look around, he went to the door. Hand wrapped in the towel as he gripped the knob, Connor stopped, suddenly recalling something he had learned in a homicide investigation school years before. He found the air conditioner control panel and dialed the thermostat down as low as it would go. The colder the surrounding air, the slower bodies decomposed, he knew, making it harder to establish the time of death. With the weekend starting, he doubted anyone would miss Tony before Monday when he didn't show up at his office. That meant he could now head down to the Keys to create an airtight alibi.

Connor knew the security guards had a record of him coming to the condo today, a potential problem. However, if they found his name in the visitor logs, he would say Tony had asked him to drop off some papers on his way out of town. He would claim he handed them to Mrs. Savoy at the door to their residence and then left town right after. If the cops asked why there was no record of him leaving the property, he would say the guard wasn't at his desk when he came back down, and he didn't have time to wait.

To make it work, he would have to slip out a side exit door. With a brief glance back at the bodies, he left. Within minutes, he was driving away, a big smile on his face as he marveled at the turn of events that had now put him in sole control of a growing drug empire.

Chapter 27

"Commander, you on?" Ty asked, hitting him on his cell.

Clay chirped back, "Yeah, Ty, can it wait? I'm in a meeting with the chief."

"Sorry, boss. It can't. We need you here at the Ocean Condos on South First Street. And the chief probably needs to come, too."

"Why? What do you have?" Clay asked, curious why Honchen was asking both of them to respond.

"Initial indications are a murder-suicide, husband on wife. The reason I need you both here is because of who it is. Tony Savoy and his wife, Jessica."

Clay cut his eyes over at Chief Wilson as he responded, "Are you talking about the attorney that defends all those drug dealers?"

"One and the same."

With a nod from Mike Wilson as he rose to his feet, Clay said, "We're on our way."

Within minutes, they pulled into the parking lot of the Ocean Condominiums and made their way to the ninth floor. Ty met them as the elevator door opened. "Hey, Chief, hey Commander. It's this way," he said, turning and heading through the open door into the penthouse.

They followed Ty down a hall to the master bedroom. One ET was bagging the hands of the bodies while the second tech shot digital photographs of blood spatters on the bed, floor, and walls.

Clay studied the two bodies, joined as one in death. A strange thing, though. Jessica Savoy was naked, while Tony Savoy was fully clothed in a suit and tie.

Ty said, "Near as we can tell, at least right now, Savoy came home, walked in the door, shot his wife, and then himself. Kinda like, 'Hey, babe, how was your day? Mine was shitty.' BOOM! Shoots her in the head. Watches her fall. Maybe looks at her a minute, decides he's got no reason to hang around. So, BOOM! One more time, he checks out with her. Weird, huh?"

"I see a more likely scenario," Clay said thoughtfully. "Savoy comes home and catches his wife screwing around. He threatens to shoot him. The guy manages to talk his way out. Then he kills her in a jealous rage. Suddenly, he realizes what he's done. He knows he's going to need the best defense attorney in the world just to avoid the needle, so he takes the easy way out."

The Chief frowned. "That sounds plausible, except for the part about letting the boyfriend leave. If he caught them in the act, why not shoot them both right then? What's the difference if he's going to kill himself anyway?"

Honchen raised a hand to get their attention. "I've got some information that puts a real twist on this case."

They both looked expectantly at Ty. "Okay, what gives?" Clay asked.

"First, there was a visitor last Friday at 4:32 p.m., according to the computer logs. And you're gonna say, 'You're shittin' me,' when I tell you who it was," he said, pausing.

Clay's eyes narrowed, "C'mon, Ty, no games. Who was it?"

"Ex-JBPD cop, criminal, and all-around asshole, Roy Connor," he said.

"You're shittin' me!" Clay exclaimed.

"See, Chief?" Ty grinned. "Do I know Clay or what?"

"Are you sure about this, Honchen?" Wilson asked.

"Yes, sir. He's a regular visitor to the Savoy penthouse according to the security logs."

"When did he leave?" Clay asked.

"That's the thing. There's no time noted in their logs. I asked their security supervisor, and he said it's not unusual for visitors to have no logout time because the guard has to leave his post to make rounds periodically. He claimed they've never had any problems since the building opened. Until now, that is," he finished with a shrug.

Wilson folded his arms as he leaned against the doorway. "What was Connor doing here?"

Ty responded, "Savoy hired Connor sometime back as an investigator for his defense practice. He could have had a legitimate reason for being here since he worked for the man."

"I have to tell you," Clay interjected, "this scene bothers me. She's naked, and he's fully clothed. Like this all happened right after he came home. It's like I speculated before. Savoy caught her in bed, possibly with Connor. The question in my mind is the same as the Chief's. Why would Savoy let Connor go if he was enraged enough to kill his wife? He was obviously out of his mind, so letting Connor or whoever it was go free doesn't square with that mental state. Put out a BOLO on Connor. I want him brought in for questioning. He was the last known visitor before two people ended up dead. That's worth a conversation with the man."

"You don't think this is a murder-suicide?" Ty asked.

"I don't know. That's why I want Connor questioned," he replied.

"Okay, boss. I'll put the word out. Do you want to sit in on the interview?"

"Absolutely," Clay said.

"Absolutely not," the chief said. "Commander Randall will not participate in the interview."

Clay cut his eyes over at the chief, starting to object, but Wilson stopped him. "I know how you feel about Connor. That's why you won't be in there. If you are, and he gets violent, anything you do will be viewed as payback for the crap he pulled on you in the past."

"Okay," Clay said, reluctantly. "But I want to be in the viewing room to watch the interview."

"That's fine," the Chief said. "As long as you stay out of the interview room."

"Alright. Ty, you said there were a couple of things. What's the other?"

"Remember the tattoo on Kayla Forrester's belly?"

Clay nodded, "Yeah, a small heart with the initials T. S. inside. What about it?"

Ty didn't answer, an expectant look on his face. Clay stared back, confused. Then it hit him. "T. S.! Tony Savoy! Damn!"

"I knew you'd get it," Ty said, grinning.

Clay turned to Wilson. "We've been trying for weeks to find out who those initials belonged to. We had information that someone rich was keeping her in that million plus condo, so Danny compiled a list of people with the same initials. But there were so many we were having trouble narrowing it down." Looking at Savoy's body,

Clay said, "I have a feeling the list has just been narrowed down to a very small number."

He continued, "Ty, start digging into Savoy's background, his associates, his friends, the works. See if you can find a link between the deaths of Kayla Forrester, Trey Jessup, and Tony Savoy. And be sure you include Connor in that analysis."

Snapping his fingers, Ty said, "Hang on. Check this out. Kayla Forrester is, or was, Savoy's little sex toy, right?" Glancing down at Jessica's naked body, he shook his head. "And with a woman who looked like her at home. Anyway, he buys this expensive condo for his extracurricular activities with Kayla. Then she cheats on him with Jessup. He finds out about it, so he kills them both in a jealous rage. Then, he finds out his wife is banging some guy behind his back. Maybe Connor. And that really sends him off."

Clay looked skeptically at Ty. "You're suggesting Tony Savoy killed his girlfriend and her lover and then his wife out of jealousy?"

"Yeah, it could've happened that way," Ty said defensively.

"Okay, then why didn't he kill his wife's lover?"

"Uh, well," Ty hesitated. "How about this? Savoy's wife gets a warning, maybe from the security guard, that her husband is on his way up. The lover freaks, grabs his clothes, and runs. Savoy just misses him, but he's a smart guy, a lawyer. He figures out she was screwing some guy."

"So, if it's not Connor, who could it be?" Clay asked. "He was the only visitor logged in on Friday, and there's been none since then."

"Assuming the security guard isn't mixed up in this somehow, maybe it's someone who lives in the building."

Clay nodded again. "That's possible. Include the guard on duty and every tenant on your interview list. Find out if any male residents knew Jessica Savoy. Maybe well enough to get in her pants behind her husband's back." He paused, thinking as he looked around the room. "Let's see, one more thing. Who are you assigning to interview Connor?"

"Probably Malone. With his informants, he has the best chance of finding him quickly."

"Sounds good. Make sure Danny knows finding Connor is a top priority. It's time we had a talk with our former officer."

Chapter 28

The police interview room was a typical institutional structure consisting of four block walls painted a drab white. The only break in the visual monotony was a bright blue metal door and a small window with a two-way mirror that concealed a tiny viewing room. Three cheap plastic chairs and a small metal table completed the décor.

Roy Connor slouched in one of the chairs. Dressed in camo cargo shorts and a green tank top, he sat with arms folded over his chest as he gazed across the table at Danny Malone. Danny's eyes roamed over the numerous tattoos covering Connor's enormous arms, noticing in particular several patches of acne on Connor's shoulders attesting to his heavy steroid use.

Connor glanced around the room, his attention coming to rest on the mirrored window. Pointing, he said, "What have you got, a roomful of people in there watching this little party you're throwing for me? Who's in there?" Frowning, putting a finger to his temple as if trying to solve a complex mathematical problem, he said, "No, wait, lemme guess. Randall. Honchen. Maybe Wilson." Grinning at Danny, he said, "How am I doin' so far?"

When he didn't respond, Connor said, "No hints, huh? That's okay. I still remember how cops think. I haven't been out of the business that long." When Danny still offered no response, Connor growled, "Malone, I never liked you any better than the rest of the assholes here. Keep in mind that I could have told you to pound sand when you asked me to come in, but I didn't. I'm here because it's obvious you people need help solving these brutal murders plaguing our city. Since I left the PD, it's not safe to walk the streets anymore."

Danny opened the folder in front of him. Flipping through the pages, he paused, appearing to read something with interest.

Standing abruptly, Connor leaned over the table. "If you think you're gonna intimidate me with your silence, then you and those assholes in the other room are dumber than I thought."

"Roy," Danny said calmly, "if you'll just have a seat, I have a few questions that I need answers to. Give me what I need, and then you can go back to your, uh, to whatever it is you do."

Connor stared hard at Danny, wondering what Malone meant by that last remark. *Does he suspect I'm dealing drugs?* Sitting down heavily, he crossed his arms, deciding to see where Danny was going.

"First, I'm going to advise you of your rights. I know, I know," he said, holding up his hand to stop Connor before he could interrupt. "You can recite them word for word, but I have to do this, okay?"

"Yeah, you do that," Connor said, leaning back in the chair.

Danny read the constitutional rights from a pre-printed card as Connor stared at the ceiling, giving every indication he was bored. When he finished, Danny asked him if he understood his rights. Connor nodded curtly.

"I have to have a verbal response, Roy. You know the drill."

"Yeah, yeah, fine. I waive my damn rights. I'll even answer your second question before you ask it just to cut down on the time I have to spend listening to you." In a singsong voice, he said, "Having waived my rights, I'm willing to talk to you without an attorney present." Reverting to his normal, deep voice, Connor concluded, "Now, let's get this shit over with."

Danny looked down at his notes. "Who do you work for, Roy?"

"Who I work for has nothing to do with your investigation of a murder-suicide."

Looking up from the document he had been studying, Danny frowned, "How do you know I'm investigating a murder-suicide?"

Roy hesitated, *Shit! Did the media call it that?* Deciding they must have, he responded, "Cute, Malone. You think you'll trip me up by implying no one knows it's a murder-suicide except somebody who was there. But I heard it on TV, just like everybody else."

Danny said, "I wasn't implying anything. I was just curious how you knew. You answered my question, so let's try the first question again. Who do you work for?"

Figuring they probably knew anyway, he couldn't see any danger in answering truthfully. "Tony Savoy. Least I did before he decided to pop his old lady and then himself. I guess that means I'm now unemployed. Why? JBPD got any openings for police officer?" he asked, smirking.

Ignoring the attempt to bait him, Danny asked, "Where were you last Friday between four-thirty and about eight in the evening?"

Looking at the ceiling, Connor put a hand on his chin. "Let's see now. Last Friday, where was I?" he mused, drawing out the words slowly as if trying to remember. Continuing to stare at the ceiling, he asked, "What time Friday was that?"

"Between four-thirty and eight," Danny said evenly.

"Between four-thirty and eight, huh? Well . . . and that was Friday, you said?"

"You know damn well I said Friday!" Danny objected loudly, his composure beginning to crack.

Connor grinned, "Patience there, Mr. Detective. Remember your role. You're supposed to pretend to be my best friend. You know, suck up to me to get me to say something incriminating even if I haven't done anything. I know how the game is played. Remember?"

"Yeah, I remember, Connor. So why don't you just answer the questions without all this bullshit you keep throwing out. Then you can haul your ass out of that chair and out of the building. You're making the place smell bad."

As the two men glared at each other, the door opened suddenly, and Clay strode into the room. "Danny," he said sternly, "leave."

"But–"

"No but. Get the hell out of here. Now!" Clay said, his voice rising.

Danny left the room, slamming the door behind him. Clay kept his eyes on Connor, giving no indication he had noticed Danny's departure.

"Pretty boy Malone. Got his hand bit by the big dog," Roy said, laughing.

"Connor, you're a worthless bag of crap, but that's not news. What is news is a series of homicides in which your name keeps popping up. You've got your own six degrees of separation going here, only it's more like one degree."

Clay's referral to a 'series of homicides' made Connor uneasy. "I don't know what you're talking about."

"Well, let's see," Clay said, ticking off points on his fingers. "Let's start with the most recent and work backward. Tony Savoy and his wife are found dead in their penthouse suite. Initial indications are murder-suicide. Time of death was estimated to be between six p.m. and midnight last Friday. Savoy was your employer. Security records indicate you went to the penthouse at four-thirty-two Friday afternoon, but there's no record of you leaving. That means you appear to have been there when Savoy arrived shortly before six."

"Well, I wasn't."

"You weren't there at all, or you weren't there when Savoy arrived?"

"You know damn well I was there. But only for about five minutes."

"Why wasn't your departure time listed on the security logs?"

Connor raised his eyebrows. "Why are you asking me that? I don't work for the security company. Ask those rent-a-cops if you wanta know. All I can tell you is nobody was at the desk when I left."

Just then, Clay's cell phone vibrated. Glancing at the screen, he saw a text message from Chief Wilson, "Take a break right now!"

"I'll be back in a minute," Clay said, abruptly leaving the room.

Mike Wilson was standing in the hall when Clay walked out, an irate expression on his face. Without a word, he gestured for Clay to follow him into the adjacent interview room. Danny and Ty were standing in the hall, studiously avoiding Clay's eyes.

The chief closed the door and whirled on Clay. "Explain to me exactly why you chose to disobey my direct order," he said coldly.

"Mike, Danny was blowing the interview. Connor got under his skin, and he started arguing with him. If I hadn't stepped in, Connor would have walked. He was that close," Clay said, gesturing with thumb and forefinger half an inch apart.

"Why didn't you use Honchen if you thought things were getting out of hand?"

"I was the only one there when it started going south. I had sent Ty to check on some times from the security logs. Since I was there, I figured I might as well ask him some questions. I kept my cool, Mike. I know how important this investigation is."

Wilson stared hard at Clay, finally nodding curtly. "Okay. Keep going. But," he said, grabbing Clay's arm as he turned to go, "you know what I expect."

"I know, Mike. The six o'clock rule is permanently tattooed on my brain."

Stepping back into the interview room, he saw Connor close his cell phone and slip it into his pocket. "Calling a lawyer, Roy?"

"Trust me, Randall. I don't need a lawyer to deal with you or any of your detectives."

"Okay, then let's get back to it. Why did you go to the Savoy residence?"

Connor shrugged, "To deliver some papers Tony needed."

"But he wasn't there. Why didn't you take them to his office?"

"I was headed out of town, so he told me I could leave them at his house since it was on the way. He said he needed them over the weekend."

"What were the papers?"

Connor smirked, "Confidential lawyer stuff. You understand."

"What were the documents in?"

"They were, uh, in a brown envelope."

"And you say you gave them to Mrs. Savoy?"

"I didn't say that, but, yeah, I gave them to her."

"Funny thing about that. We didn't find any envelope."

Connor shrugged again. "That's not my problem. I gave them to Jessica, Mrs. Savoy. Who knows what she did with them after I left? Maybe she cooked them and tried to serve them to Tony for dinner. Maybe that's why he killed her. Damn! See what y'all missed by never making me a detective?"

Clay made a notation and then continued, "Were you and Mrs. Savoy having an affair?"

The abrupt shift startled Connor. He blinked once, twice, then said in a blustery tone, "What? You're asking me was I tapping Tony's wife?"

"That was the question."

With an innocent look, Connor responded, "Naw, man. I wasn't hittin' that pussy. Not that she wasn't hot, you understand. But I'd never jump my boss's wife behind his back. I have principles."

Clay smiled at Connor's statement. "Let me make sure I've got this straight," he said, checking his notes. "You went to the Savoy residence to deliver some documents. You handed them to Mrs. Savoy and then you left. Right so far?"

"Yep, that's right," Connor sighed, making a show of looking at his watch.

"Did you go inside the residence?"

"Nope. Stood at the door."

"So you never went inside the residence."

"That's what I said."

"Then that means we shouldn't find your prints or DNA inside, right?"

Connor hesitated, knowing where Clay was going. "Not necessarily."

"What do you mean?"

"My prints are probably all over the place. I worked for Tony, so I was there a lot."

"All over the place, huh," Clay said in a thoughtful tone. "Including the master bedroom?"

Connor smiled thinly at Clay. "Still tryin' to hook me up with Mrs. Savoy, aren't you?"

"It's a fair question."

"I don't have any recollection of ever being in Tony's bedroom," Connor said.

Clay made another notation, then, "Who is Kayla Forrester?"

Connor's eyes narrowed, realizing they were getting into dangerous territory. Obviously, they had linked Kayla to Tony. What he didn't know was whether they had connected him to her, also. He considered clamming up, demanding to see his attorney. He wasn't under arrest. He could just get up and walk out, and they couldn't stop him. But he knew any of those choices would make Randall more suspicious than he already was.

"Hello? Roy, you there?" Clay asked, waving his hand in Connor's face.

Snapping back, he growled, "Cut that shit out, Randall. I was trying to remember where I heard the name." Scratching his head, he said, "Isn't she the one that took a nosedive off a balcony a while back?"

Clay nodded. "Come on, Roy. You know exactly who she is."

Connor grinned, "Okay, yeah, she was one of Tony's girlfriends."

"Did you also know the guy who was killed at the same time? Name of William Jessup? Went by the nickname Trey?"

Connor frowned, closing his eyes as if trying to recall, and then said, "Nope. Never heard of him."

Clay watched Connor closely. Connor stared back, giving nothing away. "Any reason your prints would be in that condo?"

"Not a chance, Randall. I've never even been in the building," he lied smoothly. He had worn long sleeves and gloves the entire time he was in the place, so he wasn't worried about leaving any evidence there. Besides, they would have already arrested him if they had found anything to tie him to the killings. "Tell you what, Randall," he said, glancing at his watch again. "I have to go home and work on my résumé, seeing as how I'm now unemployed. But before I go, let me give you my theory about how Tony and his wife ended up dead."

Clay leaned back in the chair, "Okay sure, Roy. Let's hear your theory."

"You have to understand. Tony was a cocksman. He bragged about how he'd screw a rock pile if he thought some pussy was in it. But he was insanely jealous of Jessica. He didn't want her around any man, no matter how old or decrepit. Hell, he'd even get pissed if she talked to a queer. This from a guy who had to get some strange at least every other day or else he claimed he got nut cramps. My guess is she probably got a bellyful and told him she wanted a divorce. He told me he didn't get a pre-nup when they got married. So if she divorced him, she'd get a shitload of money. I think that's what happened. She told him she wanted out, and that pushed him over the edge. Then, of course, once he killed her, he knew he was screwed. Probably figured being a lawyer and all that, he was going to prison for life at a minimum. Consequently, he took the easy way out."

Standing, he said, "I bet if you do a little digging, you might even find old Tony was the one that popped Kayla and that guy, whatever his name was. Maybe they were blackmailing Tony with the threat of snitching him off to Jessica. Who knows? Stranger things have happened. Or maybe Jessica found out about Kayla, and she did the killings. That oughta be enough leads to keep those hotshot detectives of yours busy for the next six months. And with that, I'm outta here," he said, hitching up his shorts and strolling out the door.

Chapter 29

Danny came in, shaking his head. "Can you believe the balls of that guy? He knows we're looking at him, and he still plays with us."

Clay looked up and frowned. "Danny, what the hell's the matter with you?"

"What? What did I do?" he asked defensively.

"You let Connor get to you. You reacted like a rookie cop. Couldn't you tell he was baiting you?"

"I thought I held it in pretty damn well, Commander," Danny said, getting angry.

"You know what? You didn't. And if you don't get a grip, I'll bust you back to patrol," he said, glaring.

Danny stared angrily back at Clay. Then, like a balloon punctured with a pin, he exhaled loudly, slumping into the chair, his eyes downcast. Clay said nothing. Best friend or not, he was growing increasingly irritated with Danny's erratic behavior.

"What's going on?" Clay asked.

"Nothing," Danny answered sullenly.

"Wrong answer. You forget. I've known you since the seventh grade. You've changed. You seldom laugh and cut up any more. It's Rachel, isn't it? You've been this way since she got sick."

A loud sigh was Danny's only response as he continued to stare at the floor.

His voice softening, Clay said, "Talk to me, man. I'm your boss, but I'm your friend, too. You gotta open up and let me help."

"There's nothing you can do," he said, raising his head to look at Clay, his eyes red.

"It's still the money situation, isn't it?"

Danny nodded. "Yeah, it's the money, or the lack of it, I should say. I'm working every extra job I can get, but it's never enough to cover the regular bills and pay for the doctor and her meds. That damn excuse for insurance we've got is about to break us!" he said vehemently.

"They still won't cover Rachel?"

"They keep saying there's no medical evidence to support a diagnosis of Lyme disease. They say she's either got MS or Lupus or she's crazy. Then there's all the rest of the crap that keeps piling on. The bank's threatening to repo her car. We're two payments behind on the mortgage. It's so damn frustrating. I just can't seem to get ahead of the bills," he said with anguish in his voice.

"Well, you have to let your friends help. Dana and I have been offering for months now, but you're too damn proud to accept. You're gonna have to do something, or you'll end up losing your car *and* your house. Then how will you take care of Rachel?"

Danny wiped his eyes with the back of his hand. He stood up, a crooked smile on his face. "Just knowing the offer is there from my best friend is great. And anyway, I heard Fletcher High's new football coach is looking for someone to tutor a few of his linemen in the finer points of math and English. I can dust off the old teaching diploma and dazzle those jocks with my brilliance, you know? Don't worry. I'll get us out of this hole. And I promise I'll get my act together," he said squeezing Clay's shoulder before walking out of the room.

Clay watched as Danny headed down the hall, more worried about his friend than he had been in years.

———————

Within a week, lab tests confirmed Tony Savoy's prints were the only ones on the gun. The report further noted he had fired the gun that killed Jessica as well as himself. The evidence pointed directly at murder-suicide, as Ty and Connor had predicted.

Clay was convinced Connor knew something about the killings, but the evidence to link him was simply not there. He closed the case with reluctance and turned his attention back to the killings of Kayla Forrester and Trey Jessup.

Chapter 30

Several weeks later, at one in the morning, Ty Honchen and his team of detectives moved into their assigned positions. A major cocaine deal was going down in South Beach Park, a large recreational area with swing sets, kiddie slides, and walking trails. They were there based on information Danny had received that a major cocaine deal was about to go down in the park.

Ty crouched behind the slides, radio pressed to his ear to pick up reports from the other detectives hidden at various points around the park. The object of their intense focus was a white RV parked in a space facing South Beach Parkway, a lone man in the driver's seat.

Three Rivers hid behind a large palmetto bush near the basketball courts. Fontana Jones and Rafe Santos were at the opposite end of the parking lot, uncomfortably cramped inside a dilapidated camper mounted on a rusty old pickup. Danny Malone waited beside Ty.

Their target was Ricky Wise, a cocaine dealer known for his vicious temper. A forty-six-year-old skinhead, Wise's criminal career began early, demanding lunch money from his elementary school classmates and beating them up when they refused. By the time he turned twenty, he was in prison for killing a man during a drunken rage.

Twenty-two years later, he walked out of prison covered with jail tattoos and bulked up from pumping iron in the prison yard. He planned to stay out of jail, but not to go straight. In the four years following his release, Wise advanced from small-time street hustling to a successful career pushing large quantities of cocaine.

A CI told Danny the word on the street was that Wise had killed one of his lieutenants several months before for skimming cash during his pickups from street-level dealers. However, with no corpse, police were unable to confirm the rumor.

Team members were growing impatient as they watched the RV. The unknown man had driven into the parking lot shortly after they got into position, and they had tensed, expecting Wise to show up at any moment. After two hours, they were still waiting and watching.

The man had not moved from the driver's seat of the vehicle, although he had made several phone calls. Shortly after three, a black SUV pulled into the lot, stopping two spaces away from the RV.

"Okay, guys," Ty transmitted to his team, "it's show time. Tana, is the video cam rolling?"

"Recording and focused on both vehicles, Ty," she responded.

Kneeling beside his sergeant, Danny said, "Ty, I forgot to tell everyone. Wise is left-handed, so he carries his nine in his left pants pocket."

Honchen quickly transmitted the information to the rest of the team. Three responded, "No problem, if he pulls a gun, I'll double tap his ass, and Mr. Wise will be interviewing for a job in hell five minutes later."

All talking ceased as Ricky Wise stepped out of the SUV, looking in all directions. When he saw the surveillance pickup, he paused, staring intently at it for almost a minute before walking toward it.

Ty called on the radio, his voice anxious, "Rafe, Tana, he's coming your way. Keep your heads down."

"Rafe," Tana whispered, "check the camper door. I can't remember if I locked it."

Santos checked the handle. "It's good. Here, cover up with this tarp," he whispered as he spread the blue plastic cover over himself. Tana quickly did the same and then grew still, her hand gripping her gun.

As the other detectives watched, Wise reached the pickup and looked into the cab. Apparently seeing nothing that alarmed him, he stepped to the side and peered through the camper window, but the dark film covering the glass made it impossible to see anything. He moved to the back of the truck and tried the door to the camper shell. Finding it locked, he tried unsuccessfully to see through the rear window. Finally satisfied, Wise headed back toward the RV.

Tana and Rafe stayed motionless until Ty called, "You're clear." With shared looks of relief, they resumed their surveillance as Wise reached the recreational vehicle and climbed inside.

Danny keyed his radio, "Guys, my CI said Wise never carries the dope on him. He keeps it stashed in a hidden compartment in his car.

When the deal is made, he makes the buyer wait while he gets the stuff so he can't see the location of the compartment. Then, as soon as the exchange is made, he books outta there."

Suddenly, the van's passenger door flew open, and Wise charged out, dragging the driver behind him. Lifting the little man above his head, he slammed him violently to the pavement. "No one fucks with the Wise Man!" he bellowed, driving a size thirteen boot into the man's temple. The crunch of bone was clearly audible to the detectives as they began running toward the two men.

Three Rivers yelled at the drug dealer, drawing his pistol as he ran. Wise turned and charged, smashing into the detective and driving him to the pavement. Rivers landed hard, the back of his head impacting the asphalt with a sickening thud as his gun hit the pavement beside him. Wise reached for the weapon just as Ty barreled into him at a dead run. Although only five-six, his powerful two hundred pounds jolted the big man away from Rivers. With a scream of fury, Wise yanked his gun from his pocket.

"GUN!" Ty shouted, clawing for his pistol as he lunged to his right. Suddenly, the night was filled with the sound of gunfire. Ty fired twice, both rounds hitting Wise in the chest. Simultaneously, the drug dealer squeezed off a shot that struck the pavement and deflected upward, striking Ty's left foot.

Adrenaline pumping, Ty barely felt the impact as he watched, amazed to see Wise still on his feet. *I couldn't have missed from this close!* Pulling the trigger again and again, he pumped more rounds into the man's body. The impact of the heavy bullets spun Wise toward Rafe and Tana, his gun still gripped in his hand. Both detectives fired, their bullets slamming into his chest and abdomen.

The gun battle ended as abruptly as it had begun. Ricky Wise toppled to the pavement, his career in crime brought to a blazing finish.

Chapter 31

After the deafening barrage of gunfire, the eerie quiet that followed was unnerving. Ty sat on the pavement holding his foot as the pain set in, his eyes locked on the body of the drug dealer. Three Rivers lay moaning a short distance away. Rafe, Tana, and Danny kept their guns trained on Wise watching for signs of life.

Finally, the tension broke. Tana called in the shooting and requested supervisors and a rescue unit to respond as she went to check on Three. Rafe pulled Ricky's pistol from his dead hand. Danny discovered the drug buyer dead from the vicious kick delivered by Wise.

Three rolled over and attempted to sit up, prompting a wave of nausea. Making it to his hands and knees, he vomited the pizza he had eaten hours before. "O-h-h, man," he groaned. "My head's killing me."

"No wonder. You've got a big cut back there," Tana told him. "And you've probably got a concussion as hard as your head hit the pavement. Come on, Three. Let's get you over to the grass so you can lie down."

He climbed unsteadily to his feet and allowed Tana to help him over to the grassy area beside the parking lot. There he sank to the ground, curling into a fetal position.

Danny watched as Ty pulled off his boot and poured out blood and a spent bullet. "Damn! It's like a war zone. You okay, Sarge?"

"Yeah," Ty said, gritting his teeth. "But it hurts like a son of a bitch!"

Seeing blood still oozing from the wound, Danny yelled, "Rafe, get the first aid kit out of Ty's car. Hurry!"

"What about the guy in the RV?" Ty asked.

"DOA."

"Okay, you're in charge as senior detective. Make sure the scene is locked down tight until it's processed."

"I'll take care of it," Danny said.

"Wait," Ty said. "I can't put you in charge. You fired your weapon, too."

"No, I didn't."

"You didn't?" Ty asked, confused. "I could have sworn I saw you shooting along with Jones and Santos."

"No. I saw him fall, so I held up. I figured if he still had any fight in him, I'd load him up, but he was dead. That means I'm cool to run things until IA gets here. Then I'll handle the drug investigation while they do their administrative thing. Don't worry about any of this, Ty. I'll make sure everything is done right."

Over the next four hours, as the stars faded and the sun began to send pale yellow rays into the sky, the park remained a busy place. Ty Honchen and Three Rivers were receiving treatment at the ER. The medical examiner claimed the bodies of Ricky Wise and the unidentified Hispanic male for autopsies later in the day.

Clay arrived and took charge of the investigation, assigning detectives to conduct searches of both vehicles. In the RV, they found an open bank bag containing fifteen thousand dollars in cash. A cell phone lay in pieces on the floor, apparently crushed underfoot during the initial confrontation.

The hidden compartment in the SUV where Ricky Wise stashed his dope proved to be a greater challenge. After scouring the interior for almost an hour, the detectives were frustrated. "We've done everything but rip the seats and headliner out," one of them said to Danny as he came up to the SUV.

"You're not thinking like a dope dealer," he said. Danny walked slowly around the SUV, stopping at the front passenger door. Kneeling, he closely examined the undercarriage and then opened the passenger door. Leaning over, he reached under the seat and pulled on the carpet, twisting and tugging until it peeled away, revealing a circular plate about six inches in diameter. He slid his fingernails under the edge of the plate and pulled. It came up easily, revealing Ricky Wise's dope box. Reaching inside, Danny pulled out two plastic bags of cocaine. Gripping the bags by the corners to protect any possible prints, he held them up for the others to see.

"How did you figure out where it was?" Clay asked, coming up to the car.

"I noticed a bump-out in front of the catalytic converter that isn't standard on this vehicle. If you don't know what to look for, it appears to be part of the design of the undercarriage. I could see that it lined up perfectly with the underside of the front passenger seat, so I figured Wise retrofitted the space to conceal the dope," he concluded, slipping the drugs into a large evidence bag.

"Great job, Danny. Head in to the station and get started on the paperwork. As soon as I get the vehicles towed, I'm going to the hospital to check on Ty and Jeremy."

"Clay, you go on. I'll take care of the tows," Danny said.

"You sure?"

"Yeah. I've got to take the money and the dope to the property room anyway. I don't want anyone else in the chain of custody."

As Clay and the detectives left the scene, Danny locked the evidence in his trunk. Fifteen minutes later, the on-scene investigation complete, Danny waited alone for the wreckers. Crime scene tape surrounded the parking lot in a large circle, the two vehicles at the epicenter. The excitement of a police shooting had attracted a large throng of onlookers as well as the media. After several hours with nothing exciting happening, the crowds began to fade away, slowly at first and then rapidly as the on-air talent left.

Danny stood at the door of the RV reliving the traumatic event. *I should have shot Wise as soon as he kicked the guy.* Shaking his head, he climbed inside to take one more look around just in case his fellow detectives missed anything.

The vehicle was small but efficiently designed. Standing with his back to the driver's seat, Danny noted a couch with a foldout table lining the left side. To the right were counters, a tiny sink, a four-burner stove with a mini-microwave above, and a small refrigerator. A queen-size bed extended across the back.

The sun had heated the interior to the point he was sweating. In spite of his desire to retreat to the air-conditioned comfort of his car, Danny forced himself to move slowly, to be thorough. Turning in a circle, he looked for anything out of the ordinary. Several fruitless minutes later, he shrugged. Nothing jumped out at him. Wiping sweat from his face, he was ready to leave.

Hearing a tree branch scrape the roof, he glanced up, his eyes catching an odd-looking crimp in a corner of the vinyl wall panel above the doorframe. He pushed on the panel, feeling it flex inward slightly. Seeing nothing that obviously held the panel in place, Danny ran his fingers along the top of the doorframe.

"Ouch!" he exclaimed, jerking his hand back as a dot of blood appeared on his index finger. Sticking the injured digit in his mouth, he stretched to see what had caused the prick. A thin wire jutted from the underside of the panel. Carefully squeezing it between thumb and forefinger, Danny pulled. The edge of the wall panel began peeling upward. Getting two fingers underneath, he pried harder. The wall panel suddenly came loose, slipping out of his hand and falling to the floor. In the space behind the panel, money poured out. A lot of money. Bundles of bills held together with rubber bands. He stared in amazement at the money scattered at his feet.

Picking up a wad of bills, he thumbed through the stack. They were all hundreds. He grabbed another and fanned that stack. All hundreds, too. Snatching up one after another, he found every bundle contained the same denomination. He estimated fifty bills in each stack, meaning each was worth five thousand dollars. A quick count brought him to the staggering realization that he was standing in more money than he had ever seen in his life.

His mind screamed, *TWO HUNDRED THOUSAND DOLLARS! Oh, man! This is huge!* Grabbing his cell phone, Danny pulled up Clay's number. As his finger touched the SEND button, he paused, his eyes and mind transfixed by the money. *What are you waiting for? Make the damn call.* But, still he hesitated, his personal life suddenly at war with his professional ethics.

He thought of his sweet Rachel, her mind and body decimated from the effects of Lyme disease. The constant struggle to pay for her incredibly expensive treatments. *If I had more money, I could get Rachel the extra help she needs.*

Wait! What the hell am I thinking? I'm a cop!

But there's all those damn bills. And the bank is still threatening to take the car.

Come on, Danny. You enforce the law. You don't break it.

Yeah, but I'm working eighty-hour weeks, and that's still not enough to get us out of the hole.

I'll figure something out. I can take Clay up on his offer of a loan.

NO! If I take his money, it'll change everything between us.

But I need more money to get Rachel the treatment she needs and get us out of this mess. And I won't beg from Clay or anybody else!

Hang on. The dude driving the RV is dead. So's Ricky Wise. The RV's already been searched. This is dope money, so we'll have to file seizure papers to get it turned over to the police department. Who knows what'll happen then? The dead guy's family could claim it's theirs, and some damn liberal judge will probably give it to them. Then they'll just use it to push more dope.

Who'll get hurt if this money never gets turned in? Nobody, that's who! But I can use it for good. For Rachel. She needs this money a helluva lot more than anybody else.

Coming out of his reverie, Danny flipped the phone closed. Quickly now, he pulled open drawers until he found a wad of plastic grocery bags. Stuffing one inside the other to strengthen it, he kneeled on the floor and scooped the bundles of money into the bag. Grabbing the wall panel, anxious now to finish and get away from the van, he slipped it back into place, pushing the wire behind it.

Danny picked up the bag and looked out the window. Seeing no one around, he walked rapidly to his car. Pushing the bag under the driver's seat, he slid behind the wheel, hands slick with sweat, heart pounding.

For several minutes, he stared through the windshield at the RV. The six o'clock rule flitted through his mind for an instant and then was gone. He had made his choice, one that ultimately would send his life into a downward spiral, careening toward disaster.

Chapter 32

The previous day, Connor had met Ricky Wise at a rest stop on I-95 near St. Augustine to negotiate the purchase of a kilo of cocaine. After agreeing on the price, Connor explained to Wise that one of his lieutenants, Luis Reynaldo, would meet him at South Beach Park that night for the exchange. Wise objected to the location as being too open, but Connor convinced him it would work since every cop on duty would be downtown at that time fighting drunks.

Satisfied, Wise climbed out of Connor's truck, leaning back down to stare at him. "Just don't pull any shit with me, Connor. I hate cops. You were a cop, so that means I hate you. The only reason I'm doing this deal with you is because I need some fast cash. If you jack me over, I'll come after you."

"Ricky, don't worry about it. You'll get your money."

"Good. Just don't forget what happens if you screw this deal up," Wise said, walking away.

"Hey, Ricky," Connor called.

Turning, he looked back at Connor, "Yeah?"

"We'll get this deal done. Then, whataya say you and me take a run at each other. See who's the best. Sound good to you?"

Wise looked into Connor's eyes, seeing something he had missed before. They were the eyes of a man with no fear. "Yeah, uh, that's cool. You just be sure you hold up your end tonight," he said with a show of bravado he no longer felt.

At midnight, Connor sat in his RV in a shopping mall lot on Beach Boulevard as he waited for Reynaldo. As soon as the deal was complete, he would head down to south Florida in the vehicle on a combination vacation and business trip. He wore thin leather gloves. If the RV ever fell into the wrong hands, no one would find Roy Connor's fingerprints. He hadn't forgotten Tony Savoy's mantra about careless drug dealers. In his opinion, he had become successful because he always followed that advice.

Watching for Reynaldo's car, he was startled to see him ride up on a beach cruiser. Leaning the bicycle against a light pole, he came around to the side door and climbed in.

"Before you say anything, Jefe, let me explain," he said, seeing the expression on Connor's face. "My car is broke down. I got in it to come, but it wouldn't start. I don't know why. I knew I couldn't be late, so I grabbed my bicycle."

"And just what the hell do you plan on driving to the meet with Wise?" Connor demanded.

"I don't know."

"Then why didn't you call me on the cell phone I gave you."

"I did, but it kept going to voice mail."

Connor pulled his phone out of his pocket, looked at the screen and cursed. "Damn, the battery's dead!" Jerking open the back, Connor pulled out the dead battery and slapped a new one in place. "Alright, there's no time to get another car. I guess you're gonna have to take the RV. Now you listen to me, Luis. I'm taking this van to Miami tomorrow. Just drive it to the meet, do the deal, and bring it back to me in one piece. You comprendo?"

"I got it, boss man. I take good care of it. Like it was my own."

"Dammit! Don't do that! You can't keep your own piece of shit running long enough to do one lousy deal. Treat it like it's mine!"

Connor reached under the driver's seat and pulled out a bank bag, tossing it to Reynaldo. "There's fifteen thousand in the bag. That's a thousand less than I negotiated with that asshole. He needs to learn he can't intimidate me."

Reynaldo looked anxiously at Connor. "Are you sure that's a good idea, Jefe? Ricky Wise is muy loco, man. If he thinks you're shorting him, he will take my head off."

"Don't worry about it. He won't do anything. He's afraid of me," Roy said, remembering the look in Ricky's eyes when he challenged him.

"Well, I don't know. You sure?" he asked in a worried tone.

"I'm sure. Just do what you're told."

"Yeah, okay, boss," Reynaldo with a shrug.

"Be there by one-thirty. He's supposed to show at two, but my guess is he'll be late. Just chill out and wait. He'll come."

"Okay. Uh, could you take my bicycle with you to your house? I can come tomorrow to get it. I'm afraid someone will steal it if I leave it here."

"You're shittin' me, right?" Connor said. "You are if you expect me to put my ass on that piece of crap. You just need to worry about getting this deal done instead of what might happen to that rusty-ass old bike. Now get moving."

As Reynaldo drove away, Connor stared with distaste at the beach cruiser before taking off at a quick jog. It was only three miles to his place, a distance he covered in less than twenty minutes. Entering his condo, Connor grabbed a beer and drank it while standing at the open door of the refrigerator. Wiping his mouth with the back of his hand, he let out a satisfied belch before grabbing a second beer and taking it with him to the bedroom where he took a quick shower.

Five minutes later, toweled off and dressed in clean shorts and a tank top, Connor came out of the bedroom just as the doorbell chimed. He frowned, *Who the hell could that be at this time of night?* Going to the door, he peered through the peephole, his frown changing to a smile. It was his neighbor, a forty-year-old divorcee from the next building who visited Connor when she wanted sex with no emotional attachments to screw things up.

Opening the door, he said, "Hey, Sandy, what's happening?"

"Oh, you know. Same old thing. Empty condo, nothing on TV, horny as hell," she replied, smiling.

Thoughts of Luis Reynaldo and the drug deal flashed through his head, to be replaced after a second or two with memories of previous sexual escapades with the woman.

Connor smiled back at her. "Come on in, sugar. Doctor Connor has just the remedy for what ails you," he said, taking her by the hand and leading her to the bedroom.

Connor was sound asleep when Sandy slipped out of bed and left the condo. At seven when his alarm went off, Connor hit the snooze button and rolled back over. By seven-thirty, he was awake, staring at the ceiling as he relished the night of fantastic sex.

"Damn!" Connor exclaimed, the erotic scenes vanishing as he remembered the drug deal. "What the hell happened to Reynaldo? I told that bastard to call me as soon as the deal was done," he said aloud.

Jumping out of bed, he ran to the living room and checked his cell phone. No calls had come in. With growing alarm, Connor dialed Reynaldo's phone. It rang once before a recording came on indicating the phone was not in service.

Grinding his teeth until they hurt, Connor debated what he should do. Drive to the park? Keep calling, hoping the damn phone would start working? Keep sitting and waiting? By nine, he was ready to break something. Grabbing the remote, he switched on the television and learned why Reynaldo hadn't called. He watched as the announcer talked breathlessly of a shootout at a Jacksonville Beach park between police and drug dealers. The tally was one cop shot, another suffering a concussion, and two drug dealers dead.

Connor stared at the television screen as his brain went into overdrive. He thought of the van and whether someone could trace it to him. As it turned out, he had been smart to wear gloves. The only fingerprints the cops would find were those of Luis Reynaldo.

The vehicle's ownership wouldn't be a problem, either. Originally registered in Arizona, a professional car thief stole the RV and drove it to Georgia where he sold it for a load of weed. The new owner replaced the VIN with one from a similar vehicle that rested at the bottom of a deep Georgia pond. Finally, Connor used a false name when he bought it. Although satisfied he couldn't be tied to the RV, he was still devastated by the loss. The two hundred thousand hidden in the vehicle was crucial to his plans to expand his business to south Florida.

If the cops had found the money, he was screwed. A judge would end up giving it to the police department so they could use it to buy cars and guns and other professional toys. Conversely, if the hiding place was still secure, there had to be a way to get his hands on the money.

Logging onto his computer, he clicked a desktop icon. The hard drive whirred softly as the program loaded. The initial view was dark at first, with only a small crack of light showing in the lower right corner of the screen. Within moments, the screen brightened to reveal the face of a man he knew all too well. The pinhole camera mounted inside the RV wall panel had activated the moment Danny

Malone pulled the wire. In mounting rage, Connor watched as Danny piled the money, *his* money, into the bag and then slid the panel back into place, shutting off the view.

Reversing the video to a point where Danny's face filled the screen, Connor hit PAUSE, staring intently at the image. As he weighed the possibilities this development presented, his anger subsided, and he began to smile.

Chapter 33

A month later, at six in the morning, Danny trudged out to pick up the morning paper. He was not sleeping well. The exhaustion plaguing him previously from working so many hours was nothing compared to the overwhelming fatigue he felt now.

On an intellectual level, he knew the reason. Guilt. Devastating guilt over taking the money. But because he hadn't spent any of it on himself, Danny still believed he had done the right thing. The money meant he no longer needed to work extra-duty jobs, and he had finally caught up the past-due bills.

He hired a massage therapist to work with Rachel three times a week. A dietician chef prepared healthful meals five days a week, freezing extras for the weekends. He was thrilled to see his wife's color improving, and she had even gained back a few pounds. Yes, he was tired. Yes, he felt guilty. But he could deal with that as long as Rachel got well.

As he bent to pick up the paper, he noticed the flag up on his mailbox. He frowned, knowing he hadn't left it up. He looked quickly in both directions, seeing nothing unusual or suspicious. Danny had arrested hundreds of criminals in his career, so he was always alert to potentially dangerous situations. Gripping the mailbox handle, he slowly opened the door, ready to leap back if a threat presented itself.

When nothing happened, he peered inside, seeing a brown envelope. He pulled it out and stared with alarm at the single word scrawled in large capital letters on the face of the envelope: *GOTCHA!*

As he held the envelope, a feeling of dread overcame him, and he shivered in spite of the warm morning. Tucking it under his arm, he scooped up the paper and hurried back to the safety of his house. He flipped on the coffee maker, and the aromatic smell soon filled the room. With a steak knife, he slit open the envelope and looked inside. There were two items, a computer disk and a single sheet of paper. He started to remove them and then stopped. *Careful*, he thought. *I may need to have this printed.*

Retrieving a pair of latex gloves from the laundry room, he carefully pulled both items from the envelope. Seeing no marking on the disk, he set it aside to examine the sheet of paper. It appeared to be standard printer paper, folded over twice. The words printed on the folded side said simply, "Read before you watch the video."

Danny opened the paper and stared at the printed message.

Malone, you recently acquired a pile of money. You stole it from me.

His hands shook, his mind screaming, *Someone knows!* Taking deep breaths to calm himself, he read on.

It's been a month since you took my money, and I'll bet you've been spending it like a wild man. I have absolute proof of what you did, so don't think you can weasel out of it by denying it. It would be simple to turn you in, but then I'd never get my money back. So here's the deal. You keep it. In return, I want something from you. I won't go into it here. Just know that the payback will even things out.

If you decide not to play along, a DVD starring Detective Danny Malone will be sent to the news media. You just know they'll piss in their pants to run a video of a local cop stealing dope money.

And just in case the DVD isn't enough incentive, remember this. I know where you live, and your wife is there by herself all the time. It would be a real shame if something happened to her because her husband is a crooked cop who refuses to keep his end of a bargain.

Anyway, pop some popcorn and enjoy the video. I'll be in touch.

The letter was unsigned. For a long time, Danny sat staring at the words, his thoughts a blur. Finally, he picked up the disk and fed it into the computer. There was no denying it. His face was clearly recognizable.

He brooded over his options. There were none that he could see, certainly none that would keep him out of jail. Stripping off the gloves, he tossed them in the wastebasket beside the desk. Then he leaned forward, putting his head in his hands. He was screwed, no matter which way he turned.

"Honey, are you okay?" a weak voice asked.

Danny jumped as if he had been shot. Spinning around, he saw Rachel leaning against the doorframe, her arms crossed over her chest. He hurried over and took her in his arms, giving her a brief hug and kiss. Then he guided her into the kitchen before she saw the video or, more importantly, the letter.

"I'm okay, darling," he said calmly, in spite of his inner turmoil. "Just a little headache. I probably need my morning shot of caffeine. Can I get you some coffee?"

"Maybe half a cup," she said. "That's about all my stomach can take this morning. Were you watching a video?"

"Wh, What? Oh that?" he stammered. "Just a case I'm working on. No big deal. Now, let me get you that coffee."

Danny made a light breakfast for Rachel and sat watching her while she ate. His love for her knew no bounds. He kept his emotions tightly under control as they talked about her latest treatment and the slow forward progress her body was making. After breakfast, he helped her upstairs and into a hot bath. He then hurried back to the den where he ejected the DVD from the computer and slid it along with the letter back into the envelope.

His thoughts churned. Who was behind this? It was obviously someone who knew him, considering how much personal information the letter contained. The person had to be in the drug business, which showed a lot of balls to complain about somebody else taking dirty money. Danny knew he was wrong, but he had only done it to help Rachel. In his mind, that made it okay.

Chapter 34

Now that the DVD and the threatening letter had been delivered, Connor was eager to go forward with his plan. But to do that, he needed Malone's cell number. Knowing he couldn't simply call the police department and get it, he scrolled through a mental checklist of people who might know the number and be willing to give it up.

He smiled as he remembered the one person who had it and would surely give it to him. Andi LaBelle. Andi had met Connor at the bar where she worked and been immediately attracted to his bad-boy image, coupled with his seemingly responsible job as an investigator for an attorney. While Andi knew he was an ex-cop who had spent time in jail, she had no inkling of the depths of Roy Connor's darker nature.

Months before, she had shared with Connor that she was a confidential informant for Danny Malone. She told him Danny had given her his private cell number to call when she got information on drug dealers. He was intrigued, thinking he might be able to use her at some point to get information from Malone about his drug investigations. Until the dirtbag had stolen his money, Connor had never envisioned the need or desire to call the man directly. Now, he wanted that number desperately.

The following night, Connor paid Andi a visit, bringing a quart of spiced rum, her favorite alcohol. After numerous drinks and a two-hour session in bed, she fell asleep, giving him his chance. Connor eased up on the side of the bed, his back to her as he dug her cell phone out of her purse. Scrolling through the contacts, he found Malone's unlisted cell number. He quietly opened the bedside table, grabbed a pen and a scrap of paper, and wrote down the number, the glow from the phone providing just enough light to see.

As he leaned over to replace the pen, Andi said sleepily, "What's going on?"

Startled, Connor concealed the piece of paper and her phone in his hand, saying over his shoulder, "Nothing, go back to sleep."

She stretched, threw off the covers, and turned on the bedside lamp. "I have to pee," she said. She came around the foot of the bed, her hair tousled from sleep. In spite of his familiarity with every inch of her body, Connor couldn't keep from leering as he tried to slip the phone back into her purse.

She stopped, a quizzical look on her face. "Roy, what are you doing with my phone?"

"I, uh, I was just checking messages at my place," he said.

"But, your phone's right there on the bedside table. And the home phone is right beside it. Why would you get my cell out of my purse?"

Irritated, he snapped, "I don't have to explain myself to you. Just go pee and come back to bed."

His tone set her off. "Excuse me, but I asked a reasonable question, and you just gave me a bullshit answer. I want to know right now what you were doing with my phone. And what's on that piece of paper in your hand?"

Connor glanced down at the note. "Nothing," he said.

"Don't give me that," she said. "You're acting very strange. You get up in the middle of the night, get my phone out of my purse, and then write something down. Did you get a number from my address book?" she asked, crossing her arms over her breasts.

Connor didn't answer, standing and putting on his pants. Andi retrieved the phone from her purse and opened the address book, seeing Danny's name and number pop up. Her head came up, eyes blazing. "What is this? You got Danny Malone's number, didn't you?"

Connor continued to dress, not looking at her.

"You did, didn't you?" she insisted. "Tell me why you want Danny's cell number. It's unlisted, and no one's supposed to have it but his CIs and other cops."

Thinking fast, Connor turned, a plausible explanation forming in his mind. "Look, it's no big deal. I just need to talk to Malone. I was working a case the other day and ran across some information about a drug dealer. I figured since you snitch for him it would be okay for me to call. You know, so I could let him know about the drug stuff."

"How did you hear about a drug dealer?" she asked, her anger temporarily subsiding. "Since your boss killed himself, you said you weren't doing private investigation stuff anymore."

"No, you're wrong," he said. "I said I wouldn't be doing any more PI work for Tony since the stupid bastard killed himself. Not that it's any of your damn business, but I'm starting my own PI firm. I have bills to pay."

"Well," she said skeptically, "okay, but you can't just call Danny on his cell. You need to call the police department and ask for him."

"Naw, I think it would be better if I talked to him privately. You know, just me and him, so no one there knows I'm calling. You didn't forget that I left the PD over some trumped-up crap, did you? I'm an outcast now, especially with Clay Randall still around," he said bitterly.

"You can talk to him privately if I call Danny and set it up. So, come on. Give me the number," Andi said, holding out her hand.

Connor stuffed the paper in his pocket. "I'll see you later, babe."

She caught him as he reached the door, grabbing his arm. "Dammit, Roy!" she yelled. "Don't you dare walk out of here with that number! Give it back!"

Connor glared at her, jerking out of her grasp. "Don't touch me, bitch," he said angrily. Turning back to the door, he reached for the knob.

Andi screamed in anger, pounding him on the back with both fists. Enraged, Connor shoved her. She flew across the room, her head slamming into the wall. Before she could react, he was on her. Wrapping his hands around her throat, he yanked her completely off the floor. Her feet drummed against the wall as she tried to draw a breath.

Leaning in close, his face twisted, Connor yelled, "Bitch, don't ever hit me again!" Seeing her eyes roll back in her head, he released his grip, and she crumpled to the floor. He stood over her, chest heaving. He thought about killing her, but self-preservation stopped him. His fingerprints were everywhere in the apartment, and his DNA was inside her. He thought about leaving her where she lay and just walking out the door. But she might call the cops and report the attack. Then Randall and company would be all over him again.

The attention they focused on him over Tony's death had caused enough trouble. He didn't need any more.

Carrying her to the bed, Connor pulled the covers up to her chin and sat down beside her. Remembering the scrap of paper, he removed it from his pocket and stared at Malone's cell number, committing it to memory. Then he put the paper on the covers by her hand.

Andi began to stir, drawing in her breath sharply when she saw Connor. She tried to move away from him.

"Hey," he said gently. "You feeling alright?" When she didn't answer, he said, "Listen, babe. I'm sorry I lost my temper. I've always been that way. When I was a cop, I'd go off on anybody that touched me." He held up the slip of paper. "Look, here's the number back. I know now I shouldn't have taken it without your permission. I'll call Malone at his office like you said."

"Roy," she croaked, her voice raspy, "please leave."

Connor frowned. "What do you mean? I said I was sorry. And it won't ever happen again."

"I believe you," she said, looking away. "But my throat hurts, and I don't feel well. I'm very tired. I need to sleep."

"That's cool. You do that," he said. Satisfied he had sufficiently charmed her, Connor patted her cheek. "I'll call you later. See how you're feeling. Maybe I'll come by," he grinned, rising to leave. "That good for you?"

"Yeah, good," she said. As soon as the door closed behind Connor, Andi hurried to the kitchen and grabbed a phone book. Before he had gone a block, she was calling a 24-hour service about getting the locks changed.

Chapter 35

Late that afternoon, Danny and Rachel relaxed on their patio with Clay and Dana as they shared a bottle of wine. All except Rachel, that is, who sipped a glass of mineral water. With the medications she took every day, alcohol was not an option.

"When Ty gets here," Danny said, "I'm gonna be all over him for gimping around trying to get people to feel sorry for him."

Clay laughed, "Yeah. Ty said Anne won't cut him any slack. She told him getting shot in the foot didn't qualify as a real injury. She said their kids have gotten worse injuries on the playground."

Rachel managed a tired smile at the banter between Danny and Clay. Dana watched her friend closely, seeing the dark circles under her eyes. She glanced at Clay before saying, "Rachel, you look exhausted. We should go and let you get some rest."

"No, please don't," she protested. "I'm fine, really. It's just the new meds making me a little sleepy."

Danny reached over and gently squeezed her hand. "I told her you'd understand if we cancelled, but she really wanted to see you. She's spent so much time in the bed that she said she was starting to grow roots to the mattress."

"That's right, so don't you dare leave," Rachel laughed softly.

At that moment, the Honchens came around the corner of the house. Ty led the way, manipulating his crutches as if he had been born with them. Anne followed behind carrying a large bowl of potato salad. In a booming voice, he exclaimed, "Tiberius Aurelius Honchen and his favorite wench, Anne, are in the house. Let the celebration begin!"

Anne slapped him on the arm, saying, "I'll make you think favorite wench, Tiberius Aurelius. I'd better be your only wench, or I'll have you put down like the lame old dog you are."

Everyone laughed at the friendly insults they threw at each other. Ty flopped into a chair beside Rachel and gave her arm a squeeze. "How are you doing?" he asked with a smile.

"I'm getting there, Ty. Thanks for coming. I know you must be in a lot of pain," she said.

"Hey, I'll never let a little thing like a bullet get in the way of a party, darlin'." Turning to Anne, he said, "Woman, you made me endure your wild driving all the way over here. The least you can do is get me a beer to settle my nerves."

Before Anne could respond, Danny said, "Ty, you best step lightly around your little wife. We all know she can whip you when you have *two* good feet. You don't stand a chance now, all banged up like that."

As the afternoon slipped into evening, they all enjoyed the easy camaraderie close friendships develop. Danny watched with pleasure as Rachel grew more animated than she had been in weeks. The way she communicated to their friends always amazed him. She seemed to have that rare talent for making people feel better about themselves. It was a gift, he realized. One he knew he didn't have, but one that he cherished in his wife.

After dinner, over coffee and drinks, the conversation shifted to Rachel's ongoing treatments and the high cost of her medications. She said with real enthusiasm, "You won't believe the good fortune that came our way recently."

Danny glanced with alarm at his wife. "Rachel, honey, there's no need to bore them with that."

"What do you mean? It's not boring. It's the best thing that's ever happened to us."

As Danny started to protest again, Clay spoke up. "Yo, Malone. Your beautiful wife wants to share some good news with her friends. Trust me, you might bore us, but she won't."

Danny flashed a smile he didn't feel, nervous about what Rachel would say.

"Tell us the good news, Rachel," Dana encouraged.

"Well, a woman called here about a month ago. She was the executor of the will of a Henry McDougle who died in Ohio. The first thing Danny did was ask her who Henry McDougle was, and the lady said he was a relative."

"You're kidding, right?" Ty asked Danny. "You don't know your own relatives?"

"Well, it's kind of a long–"

Rachel interrupted, "Henry McDougle was Danny's father's second cousin twice removed. Hey, I said that without messing up."

"Ouch, I think I got a brain bleed trying to follow that," Ty said, holding his head in mock pain.

"Anyway," Rachel continued, "the lady said Danny was his only living relative, and he left his whole estate to him. But the best part of all is how much money it was."

"Rachel," Danny said sharply, "the amount doesn't matter. What's important is that we now have enough to cover the medical expenses and take care of the bills that we got behind on."

Clay clapped him on the back, "Hey, man. That's great. It's way past time something good happened for you both."

"Thanks," Danny mumbled. "How about I get some fresh drinks," he said as he headed for the kitchen, hoping Rachel would drop the subject while he was gone.

He had slept little since receiving the package from the drug dealer three days before. It had become more and more difficult to maintain his focus at work. The fear of exposure overshadowed the pleasure he took from seeing Rachel's condition improve.

As he got ice from the freezer, Clay came into the kitchen. "Hey, ole buddy, that's really great news about the inheritance. I mean, what are the odds of that happening?"

"Yeah, it was wild," he responded unenthusiastically.

Clay looked closely at his friend. "Danny, how long have we known each other?"

Confused, Danny asked, "What do you mean?"

"It's a simple question."

"Come on, man. I'm not really in the mood for games."

"My point exactly. You've been more down than I can ever remember, and it's been going on for a while now. I don't get it. With Rachel getting better and the inheritance and all, it sure seems like you ought to be happy. But you're not."

Danny continued to fill the glasses with ice, avoiding eye contact with Clay. *Yeah, my life is fantastic,* he thought. *Except for whoever's trying to blackmail me over the two hundred thousand dollars I stole.*

Keeping his expression blank, he said, "Aw man, you know, it's just, everything's been coming down all at once. I've paid off some bills, but our credit is still screwed up. Then there's all the crap going on at work. Ty getting shot. A dude stabbed with a longhorn steer. Women flying off balconies. Murder-suicides. I tell you, Clay, it's getting crazy."

"You're right, Danny. When you lay it out like that, it does sound like a lot to cope with. But all kidding aside, you have to keep this crap in perspective. After all, your family is what's most important. Don't ever forget that."

Danny nodded, wishing things were as easy as Clay suggested. He knew he had to get it together. Clay was an intelligent and perceptive man. Moping around day after day was only going to cause him to start wondering what else was going on.

"You're right. I just need to remind myself how lucky I really am," he said, forcing a smile. "Hell, I got you as my best bud. What more do I need?"

At that moment, his cell phone vibrated. Glancing down at the screen, he saw an unfamiliar number. Being an undercover drug cop, he was used to getting strange calls at all hours of the day or night. An occupational hazard. For a moment, he thought about sending the call to voicemail. After all, he was off duty and entertaining friends. Then he remembered one of his snitches was supposed to call with information about a dealer.

"Go ahead and take the call," Clay encouraged. "I'll take the drinks to the ladies and the cripple. Anyway, you never know, it might be somebody with information on the longhorn murders."

Thumbing the button as Clay walked back outside, Danny answered, "Malone."

The response almost took his breath away. The deep voice, muffled to conceal the identity of the caller, said "Hello, you thieving son of a bitch. It's time to earn your pay."

Danny's face went white. This was the call he had dreaded since receiving the package. He struggled to bring himself under control before responding.

As the seconds stretched out, Connor said sarcastically, "Hello! I'm not hearing any 'Great to talk to you, how ya doin'?' response from you. C'mon, Detective Malone, talk to me."

"What, who is this? What do you want?" Danny stuttered.

"That's what I like to hear. A man who gets right to the point. You asked who this is. Let's just say for now that's on a need to know basis. But before I tell you what I want, tell me how your wife is doing. Are you using my money to buy her some pills or something?"

"Don't talk about my wife, you bastard," Danny growled through gritted teeth. "And how do you know anything about her anyway?"

"Son, I know everything about you and Rachel. And your friends, too. How's Honchen doing since he got shot? He looks like a pussy going around on those crutches gettin' his old lady to wait on him. And of course, there's the world's biggest asshole, Clay Randall, and that fine-looking woman he's married to. What's her name, Dana? How are they all doing at the Malone's humble abode?"

Danny whirled around, staring through the patio doors to where everyone was sitting. The lights cast a glow sufficient to allow someone on the beach to see them clearly. The man must be watching them. He felt naked. Unprotected. Like getting in a shootout with an empty gun. His wife and friends were outside. Did the man have a gun aimed at them right now? Was he going to start shooting?

Forcing a sense of calm he didn't feel, Danny said, "Look, I don't know how you got my number. I don't usually give it to people who stalk me at my home. Anyway, it's obvious you know I'm a cop, so if you've got information about a crime, I suggest you call the police department and talk to an on-duty officer. I'm off duty trying to enjoy the evening with my friends, and you're screwing it up. I'm hanging up."

"I wouldn't do that if I were you. Remember the DVD."

"I don't know what you're talking about. What DVD?"

"Cut the bullshit, Malone!" Connor yelled. "I'm not playing a game here. Either you start cooperating, or I'll burn you to the ground. Now, here's what I want. You give me information on the drug investigations you're involved in. That includes anybody you're working with or know about. DEA, JSO, Atlantic Beach, I want them all. And I don't care if it's marijuana, coke, speed, LSD, heroin, you name it. If it's dope, I want to know about it."

"You obviously know something about police work," Danny said. "So you have to know I can't give you information like that. I'd get fired and go to jail."

"That's not my problem. I told you what I want, and you're gonna give it to me by midnight tomorrow night, or I'll be sure every TV station between here and Miami gets the DVD. If you doubt me, get ready to spend the next ten years sharing a cell with some big ape that'll make you his favorite bitch."

Danny began to sweat. If he refused, the man would no doubt follow through on his threats. The chief would fire him. He would be arrested, with a trial and certain conviction to follow. The only question would be how many years he would spend locked away. Who would care for Rachel then? With no money coming in and unable to work, she would be out on the street in no time.

The threat to harm Rachel in the letter added to Danny's anxiety. He couldn't live with himself if she got hurt because of him. If he agreed to cooperate, he might be able to limit the damage to his cases. He would give the man minor stuff that wouldn't hurt anything critical. If nothing else, it would buy him time to try to figure out how to get out of the mess he had created.

"Okay, where do we meet, and how will I know you?" Danny asked.

"Be under the Jax Beach pier at midnight tomorrow night. And don't worry about what I look like. I'll find you, trust me. Just be sure you're alone. If I get the slightest hint that you're trying to set me up, I promise I'll make you pay. And I don't mean in cash."

"You don't need to threaten me," Danny said angrily. "The picture is very clear."

"Good. I think that concludes our business, so go back to being the party host."

"One thing," Danny said.

"What's that?" Connor asked smugly.

"If you touch my wife, I'll kill you," he said coldly, breaking the connection.

Chapter 36

After the phone call, Danny pleaded a bad headache, prompting their friends to leave a few minutes later. Rachel was concerned since Danny was almost never sick, but he assured her it was just a tension headache from everything going on at work.

After she went to bed, he stayed up going over his cases, searching for one he could give up without compromising the investigation. By three o'clock, his eyes were bloodshot, and he had developed a real tension headache without finding anything he thought would satisfy the drug dealer's demands.

Frustrated, he shifted his attention to the CIs who worked for him. Within minutes, he rejected each of them from consideration. They were all too valuable. *This is impossible. I'm screwed if I can't come up with something.*

Getting up from his desk, he went to the kitchen and poured his third shot of whiskey within the last hour. Over the past month, his alcohol intake had increased dramatically, although he had been careful to hide it from Rachel. Getting a buzz took the edge off his mounting anxiety, which had increased exponentially since receiving the incriminating DVD. The phone call from the drug dealer had now ramped up his stress even more.

Steeling himself, Danny chugged the alcohol, setting the glass down empty. His eyes burned, and he coughed, trying to be quiet so he wouldn't disturb Rachel. Heading back to the den, he resumed his review of cases and CIs. As the effects of the whiskey took hold, he started feeling better. More relaxed. Almost cheerful. He could do this. He was a smart man. He would feed the guy information that wouldn't hurt any of his cases until he could come up with a plan for getting the guy off his back permanently.

A name suddenly came to him, and he grinned. The alcohol had freed his mind to think outside the box. Leon Nelson was a CI for a Jacksonville Sheriff's Office narcotics detective. A registered sex offender, he had gone to prison for exposing himself to little boys. After serving six years, he returned to Jacksonville. Although there were no more sex crimes arrests, a DUI conviction landed Nelson on probation. The narcotics detective had contacted Danny to tell him the sheriff's office had recently busted Nelson for possession of marijuana. This meant he faced a year in the county jail for the probation violation.

To avoid a trip back to jail, Nelson had begged the JSO detective to let him work off the weed arrest by turning informant. He told the detective he had information on marijuana dealers in Jacksonville Beach, hence the offer to share the man's information. Danny had reluctantly interviewed Nelson, thinking a convicted sex offender was not someone he was particularly interested in taking on as an informant.

After talking to Nelson for a while, Danny became convinced his twisted desire for little boys was still very much alive. The man also exhibited a cocky, self-righteous attitude, as if he were doing Danny a favor by feeding him information. Considering all that, Danny refused to work with the sex offender, a decision the Jacksonville detective could definitely understand.

Nelson's perfect, Danny thought. *He's a useless piece of garbage, and I wouldn't get all worked up if he got his ass kicked big time.* Amused at the mental image of Nelson getting pounded, he rose and walked unsteadily up the stairs. Slipping into bed beside Rachel, he thought about his plan and pronounced it sound. Drifting into an alcohol-induced sleep, he imagined the meeting with the blackmailer. He would give him the information on Leon Nelson, and the bastard would go away and leave him alone.

Connor would prove him more wrong than he could possibly imagine.

Chapter 37

The following evening, Danny checked off work at seven. He picked up Mexican takeout and headed home for a quiet dinner with Rachel. Afterwards, the two of them sat on the couch holding hands as they watched a rerun of one of their favorite action-adventure movies.

When it ended, he told her he had to go back to work. Rachel protested, but he assured her it would only be for a little while. He said a CI had information on a major drug case he was working and couldn't meet him until midnight when he got off work. Disappointed, Rachel kissed him and told him to be careful and hurry back. He left, feeling guilty for lying to her. He just had to keep reminding himself that it was all for her benefit.

At eleven-thirty, Danny rode his beach cruiser into the pier parking lot. He carried a small backpack containing his pistol, police identification, cell phone, and a pint of whiskey wrapped in a towel. As he came to a stop, he checked the area for officers working the downtown beat. They would instantly recognize him, and he would have to lie about why he was there. Seeing none of them, he pushed his bike over the dunes and under the pier.

There was just enough light to see that no one lurked in the shadows. He leaned the bike against a pier support and squatted beside it. Glancing at his watch, Danny saw he still had twenty minutes until the meeting. He took a couple of deep breaths to steady his nerves.

A little shot would be nice right about now, he thought. He pulled out the bottle of whiskey and took a long swallow. Shuddering as the fiery liquid went down his throat, he looked around before taking a second, longer pull.

"Ah-h, that'll do it," he said under his breath, sliding the bottle into the backpack and settling down to wait. The minutes ticked by slowly. As the alcohol began to work, he smiled, his confidence returning. Just before midnight, he saw a figure approaching from the south. He stood up, guessing this must be the drug dealer.

The man stopped several feet away. Smiling, he lifted the leg of his shorts and exposed his erect penis to Danny. "Man, you're beautiful. You wanna party with me?"

It took a second for Danny to realize the pervert was not the blackmailer. Then he went off, "You scumbag! Get the hell away from me!"

The man continued to smile as he tucked himself back into his shorts and walked on by. "Don't knock it 'til you've tried it," he said in a mocking, effeminate voice.

Danny shook his head in disgust. *Un-freakin'-believable. Standing here waiting for a blackmailing drug dealer, and a damn queer propositions me.*

Watching the man as he rounded the far side of the pier, Danny failed to see Connor slip into the shadows behind the adjacent piling. "Got a hot date after our meeting?" Connor asked.

Danny whipped around, looking for the man behind the voice. Connor stepped out from the piling. He was dressed all in black, including a tight fitting hood that covered everything but his eyes and muffled his voice.

In the dim light, he could tell the man was large. "Screw you," he said, upset at being caught off guard.

"Temper, temper, Malone. No need to get all hostile on me."

"No need? Screw you again! You're a damn drug dealer who oughta be in jail."

"And *you* should be there for stealing my money," Connor retorted.

Danny snorted, "Your money? You act like you earned it honestly instead of pushing dope. It's dirty money."

"If it's so dirty, why did you take it?" Connor asked softly.

Flinching inwardly at the truth of Connor's words, Danny blustered, "I had a valid reason."

"Yeah, I bet, asshole. But we're getting off topic. What do you have for me?"

"First, who are you?" Danny asked, thinking the voice sounded familiar.

"I do the asking, and you do the answering. Not the other way around. Again, what do you have?"

Danny checked the beach in both directions, suddenly nervous, knowing he was about to step over another ethical and legal line. "I've got the name of a CI," he said.

"Yeah?" Connor said casually.

"Yeah. His name's Leon Nelson. He's working for a JSO narc. He claims he knows about marijuana dealing at the beach."

"Who's his handler?"

"A detective named Cedric Baker. He's been with JSO narcotics a long time."

"Okay, what else?"

"What do you mean? Isn't that enough?"

"No. You've given me nothing but a name. What the hell do you expect me to do with that?"

"Well, I figured, a man in your position, you'd know the players," Danny retorted sarcastically.

"Okay, I can see you're not taking me serious about turning you in. You better hire a good lawyer, 'cause you're gonna need one," Connor said with feigned anger as he started walking away.

Panicked now, Danny said, "Wait, hang on! I have more information."

Connor took several more steps before stopping and turning. "Don't waste any more of my time, Malone. I got more important things to do than to keep screwing around with you."

Danny pleaded, "Come back. I'll cooperate."

Connor turned slowly, "Okay, one more chance. No more bullshit, or I'll make you pay. You got that?"

"Yeah, yeah, I got it," Danny said, nervous sweat dampening the armpits of his tee shirt. "Man, this is hard."

"That's not my problem, now give."

"Leon Nelson is a registered sex offender. He went to prison for diddling little boys. After he got out, Jacksonville busted him for possession, so he asked to work off the arrest to keep out of jail. He lives on Fourth Avenue, South at Second Street in a duplex on the west side. He drives a piece-of-crap pickup, light green or blue, I think. When he's out looking for dope to buy or trying to dig up information to pass along, he rides a red beach cruiser kinda like mine there," he said gesturing toward his bike leaning against the piling.

Connor nodded, "Okay, that's better. Now, when and where is your next search warrant for dope gonna be?"

Frantic, Danny said, "No, no, no! I can't give you stuff like that."

"That's cool. I'm gone," Connor said, starting to walk off again.

"Wait, damn you! I, I gotta think a second. Just hang on."

"Look, Malone. I know cops like to think of themselves as honorable. But we, uh," he stumbled, "you're just as prone to temptation as everybody else."

In spite of his agitated state, Danny caught the "we" reference. He tried to put the familiar voice together with what he had just heard. It was so close, but he couldn't quite put a face and name together. "Okay, I've got a search warrant scheduled for next Wednesday or Thursday. Some guy's selling crack out the front door of his house on First Street. I've made two buys from him over the past week. There, is that enough?" Danny asked angrily.

"That's cool. For now. We'll talk again soon."

"How long is this gonna go on? I can't keep giving you information forever," he protested.

Danny couldn't see Connor grin behind the mask. "Not forever. Just until I make enough money to retire. And when that happens, I'm gonna climb on top of the tallest building and piss on everybody that walks by."

Danny stared at the man's broad back as he started walking away. Tall. Muscular. A deep voice that had grown more and more familiar to him as he talked. His use of the pronoun "we" like he either was or used to be a cop. His comment about climbing the tallest building and pissing on everybody. A cop had made that same statement on more than one occasion. It had stuck in his mind because it was so out there.

Then it hit him. "Connor!"

He stopped in his tracks, standing completely still for almost ten seconds. Turning, Connor walked back. When he got close, he pulled off the mask, revealing himself to Danny.

"Roy Connor," Danny breathed.

The big man's eyes narrowed as he stepped closer to Danny. "Yeah, it's me, but that doesn't change anything. You're still a dirty cop that stole my money, and you're still gonna give me information. Got it?"

"Yeah, I got it, Roy. You know, you couldn't make it as a cop. I got a feeling you're not gonna make it as a drug dealer, either."

"Oh, I don't know, Malone," he said, grinning. "I'm making a ton of money. I've got a cop in my pocket. Life's good. I'll be in touch now, you hear?" Turning on his heel, he walked away laughing.

Chapter 38

Over the following weeks, Connor called frequently demanding information on investigations, names of CIs, and locations of search warrants. As the pressure increased, so too did Danny's drinking. He began carrying a pint of vodka in a small cooler he kept in the trunk of his unmarked police car. He had always preferred conducting surveillances with a partner. He liked having someone to talk to during those interminable hours spent watching a target as they waited for something to happen. Now, he was careful to arrange surveillances so that he was always alone.

In the privacy of his car, he would stash the cooler behind the passenger seat, the bottle covered by a layer of ice. Every few minutes, he pulled it out and took a sip. Nothing like cold vodka to pass the time on boring stakeouts, he told himself. As the effects of the alcohol kicked in, anxious thoughts about what he had done and how he could stop Connor would begin to ease a little. However, they never went completely away regardless of how much he drank.

Meanwhile, changes in Danny's appearance and behavior were escalating. Clothing and grooming standards for narcotics officers were different from other officers. He had grown a beard at times and let his hair grow to shoulder length, even shaving his head at one point to infiltrate a biker gang. Through it all, however, he had been meticulous about his personal hygiene. But even that was changing now.

Several weeks after his downhill slide began, Clay was taken aback to find Danny asleep at his desk. His long hair hung in greasy clumps, partially concealing his face. His clothes looked like he hadn't changed them in days. The worst part was the overwhelmingly sour smell emanating from his body.

"Hey, Danny," Clay said, tapping him on the shoulder.

"Roy, you bastard. I'll ki . . .," Danny mumbled, drifting back off in mid-sentence.

Clay shook him harder. "Danny, wake up!"

"Huh? Wha, What's going on?" he said, raising his head and blinking slowly. He rubbed his face, yawned, and looked up bleary eyed at his boss.

"Oh hey, Clay. Man, I must have nodded off for a second there. Sorry about that."

Clay frowned. "Danny, I think you'd better come with me."

"Sure. Where are we going?"

"Out," Clay said tersely. "Come on."

"Um, listen, I, uh, I got a couple of cases I'm kinda behind on the paperwork. So if it's okay with you, can we get together later on? Like maybe tomorrow or the next day?"

"Danny, this isn't a request. Get your ass out of your chair. Now!" Clay ordered as he turned and walked out.

Danny followed, muttering, "Damn. Why's he so pissed off?"

Clay walked quickly to the parking lot and got into his car. Danny followed more slowly, flopping into the passenger seat with a grunt.

"Man, it's bright out today," he said, squinting through the windshield.

"Roll your window down," Clay said, brusquely.

"Huh? For what?"

"Never mind," Clay answered, hitting the buttons to lower all four windows.

"Why are you doing that? It's hot out today."

"Because you stink like you ran out of soap a week ago. That's why."

Danny raised his arm and sniffed. "Whoo-whee! You're right, bro," he said, grinning. "When a man can smell himself, he's definitely ripe!"

"What the hell is the matter with you?" Clay asked angrily as he drove off the lot.

"Whataya mean? Nothing's the matter. What's the matter with *you*?"

Clay gripped the wheel tightly, trying to keep his temper in check. Danny's behavior had changed so radically over the past couple of months that he could no longer ignore it. Something was terribly wrong with his friend, and he intended to find out what it was even if it meant pulling rank. He drove in silence until they reached the parking lot of Angie's Subs. Pulling to the far corner of the lot, he parked and turned to Danny.

"Great choice for lunch, dude," Danny said. "I'm havin' Ed Malin's best, the Peruvian Sub. You gettin' your usual Dirty Yellow Gringo on rye?"

"Cut the crap. We're not here for lunch."

Pausing with one foot out of the car, Danny looked over his shoulder. Seeing the scowl on Clay's face, he closed the door. "Okay, it's obvious you're pissed. What's the deal?"

"Danny, you are seriously messed up, and I want to know what's causing it."

With a wary look, Danny responded, "I have absolutely no idea where you're coming from. I'm just trying to do my job. If it's about me falling asleep at my desk, hell, that's easy to explain. I've been working tons of hours for the past month or so on a big marijuana deal that's about ready to bust wide open. I'm just tired. Other than that, I'm lost, buddy. Give me a clue what you're after."

Holding up an index finger, Clay said, "We'll get to this marijuana investigation in a minute. But first, let's start with your appearance."

"What's wrong with the way I look? I'm a dope cop. I dress to fit the people I run with. I haven't forgotten how Mike Wilson went off on me my first day as a detective because he said I was dressed too neat. Remember?"

"Yeah, and I also remember a guy I've known since middle school. A guy obsessed with personal hygiene. You told me one time how you took four showers in one day because you felt sweaty. Well, look in the mirror and tell me what you see right now. Better yet, tell me what you smell. Oh, wait, you already told me, didn't you?" he said sarcastically.

"Look, Clay, I'm playing a role. I'm trying to infiltrate a bunch of homeless guys dealing marijuana on the Boardwalk. So I have to look, act, and, yeah, even smell like a homeless bag of dirt if I'm going to be convincing."

"Okay, let's talk about your investigation. Who's working with you on it?" Clay demanded.

"I, I'm doing this one solo."

"*What*! You're not authorized to conduct a major investigation without backup."

"Come on, man. That's bullshit, and you know it."

Clay's face registered shock. "Tell you what, Danny. Let's you and me go see the chief and you tell him to his face his policy is bullshit!"

"Whoa, hold up, bro. I didn't know that was Wilson's policy. I thought it was just some crap still on the books from when Gordy Cooper was chief."

"And what if it was? It's still a rule, and in case you forgot, we follow rules around here."

"I know, I know," Danny answered impatiently. "But sometimes rules and procedures and shit like that just get in the way of doing what's right, Clay. You know that."

"No, I don't know that, Danny. Breaking rules is not 'doing what's right,' as you say."

"You know what? You're too damn rigid for your own good. You see everything as black and white, but it's not. Almost nothing is, in fact. It's mostly different shades of grey. Sometimes, you have to do things that don't necessarily follow the rules to the letter. You know, for the greater good, that kinda stuff."

"You're talking about situational ethics, Danny, and that's just plain wrong. The ends *don't* justify the means. You're saying it would be perfectly okay for a cop to violate the law to catch a bad guy. That's crazy, and you know it."

"I do know it, and that's not what I'm talking about," Danny said. "It's just that, that sometimes . . . things happen, and people make decisions based on what they think is right at the time, and . . . ," he trailed off.

Clay sensed hidden meaning behind Danny's words. Was he talking about the job? Or was it Rachel? Could he get Danny to open up to him? That was unlikely to happen, he figured, based on months of trying and Danny playing him off every time. For the moment, he put those thoughts aside to deal with the drug investigation.

"Okay, enough of this philosophical discussion. As long as you realize you don't cross the line in this job. Ever. As for your dope investigation, you don't make another move on it without getting some help. Got it?"

"You got it," Danny said in a relieved tone.

"And when we get back to the office, I want to see the reports you've done on the investigation so far."

"Well, I, uh, I've gotten a little behind. I haven't actually started any yet."

"That's unacceptable, and you know it. You're supposed to keep up with your paperwork as you go along," Clay said. "Listen to me, Danny. You're sleeping at your desk in the middle of the day. Your clothes and your body are filthy. When you're off duty and I call you at home, you sound wasted. You've never been a big drinker, so what the hell is going on with you?"

"You're just imagining things. I'm fine," he said.

"No, I'm not imagining anything, and you're not fine," Clay objected. "And while we're talking, who is Roy?"

Danny frowned, "Who? Roy? What are you talking about?" he asked, looking away as he shifted in the seat.

"When I found you asleep, I shook you, and you mumbled something like, 'Roy, you bastard, I'll–,' and then it sounded like you were about to say the word 'kill' before you drifted back off."

Clay watched closely for a reaction. As the seconds stretched out, he began to suspect a dose of Danny's patented bullshit was coming.

"Clay," Danny said, a slight tremor in his voice, "I can't imagine who Roy would be. Unless maybe it's one of the transients I've run across on this weed case."

"Was it Roy Connor you were dreaming about?" Clay asked on impulse.

Danny's nostrils flared, "Wh, What? Who'd you say? Roy Connor?"

"Yeah, Roy Connor, Danny," Clay said, getting angry again. "You damn well know what I said. Now answer my question."

Tucking his greasy hair behind his ears before speaking, Danny said, "Yeah, I know you said Roy Connor. I was just screwin' with you. And to answer your question, no, I wasn't dreaming about that prick."

Seeing the wide-eyed, innocent look in his eyes, Clay nodded. "Well, maybe you should spend less time immersed in your drug persona and more time taking care of yourself. You're a physical wreck in addition to smelling like a garbage dump in August."

Tapping Clay on the shoulder, Danny replied, laughing, "Hey, what can I say. I never do anything half assed. It's warp speed all the way, baby!"

"Seriously, Danny, you really need to watch your drinking. Before you realize it, you're going to have a real problem. You already have enough headaches taking care of Rachel."

"Come on, Clay. Lay off the big brother stuff. I'm taking care of business. I'm cool."

"I don't know about that," Clay said with a raised eyebrow. "Anybody who thinks the hobo look is cool has some serious style issues."

Chapter 39

Danny became more conscious of his personal hygiene after the argument with Clay. To cover his lies about the paperwork, he created several reports with vague information about homeless people dealing dope. And Clay's disapproval of his drinking habits convinced him he needed to cut back on his alcohol consumption. That and the fact he was starting to have blackout spells during the heavier drinking binges.

Several weeks before, he left home at midnight after drinking a fifth of vodka. In the midst of an alcohol blackout, he somehow managed to drive his detective car all the way to St. Augustine. Leaving the vehicle parked illegally in a fire zone, he tried to climb the outer walls of Castillo de San Marcos fort, a national monument built in the 17th century. Several feet up, he slipped and fell, fortunately landing in the middle of a freshly mulched flowerbed.

The collision with the ground brought Danny to his senses. He stared in confusion at the thick shell and mortar wall of the fort. "Where the hell am I?" he asked.

"In deep shit if you don't get the hell away from my stuff," a deep voice answered.

Danny looked groggily over his shoulder, seeing a disheveled old man standing there. "What stuff?"

"My backpack that you're layin' on," the homeless man said.

"Sorry, dude, I didn't notice," Danny said, getting unsteadily to his feet. "No kidding, where am I?"

The man shook his head in disgust, "What is your problem? You're in St. Augustine."

Danny's eyes widened in surprise. "Really? Damn, how'd I get here?"

"You flew here. How the hell do I know? Just get away from my stuff before I kick your ass."

Danny was just aware enough to realize he didn't want a physical confrontation with the man. He staggered off toward the road, eventually finding his car. Still drunk, but now awake, he headed back home, driving ten miles an hour under the posted speed. As he turned into his driveway, he congratulated himself on making it home without encountering an arrest-happy cop.

For weeks after, he tried unsuccessfully to remember why he felt the need to climb the wall of an old fort. Finally, he realized he had to stop drinking or face the real possibility he might die in one of his blackout drives. Cutting out the alcohol was both good and bad. He was more alert, both at home and at work, and that pleased both his wife and his boss. Unfortunately, sobriety brought with it the clamoring voice of his conscience, once again given free rein to hammer him for his transgressions.

A week after Clay's criticism about his appearance, Connor called demanding information about a possible confidential informant. This time, Danny balked. "I can't talk about that. It's sensitive."

"Don't give me that crap, Malone," Connor said. "Why do I have to keep reminding you about your obligation? The drill is, I ask, and you tell. Those are the rules. So I'll ask one more time, and I want a straight up answer. Is Todd Skinner a snitch?"

Skinner was indeed a CI, a very valuable one. Unlikely as it seemed at the time, Bobby Hawkins had actually done some real police work, busting the nineteen-year-old for possession of a small amount of PCP. Worried about going to prison, Skinner asked to work for Hawkins as an informant. In only three months, he passed along enough solid information for Danny, serving as Bobby's liaison, to make five arrests and take several thousand tabs of the drug off the street.

Working with Bobby Hawkins was a pain in the ass, but Danny had grown to like Todd and hoped the kid would use the opportunity to clean up his life. But now? What choice did he have but to give Connor what he wanted? Danny said quietly into the phone, "He's a CI, but he's not mine. He's working for Bobby Hawkins."

"Hawkins? That idiot doesn't have enough sense to unzip before he takes a piss, much less work a CI."

"Well, that's who Todd is working for. Listen, Connor, he's a good kid who fell in with the wrong crowd. He's trying hard to straighten out his life, so just leave him alone."

"Don't get your pecker all bent outta shape, Malone. I was just curious. I'd heard he got busted, so I figured he was probably working off his drug arrest. How good is his information, by the way?"

"I'm not saying anything else about Todd Skinner. Except that he's never dropped your name."

"No reason for him to," Connor said with a sarcastic laugh. "I'm just a poor, struggling PI trying to scrape by."

"Yeah, right. You're a lot of things, Connor, but honest ain't one of them," Danny said, hanging up.

Chapter 40

Danny was unaware that Todd Skinner had been one of Connor's drug runners for more than a year. Since Skinner's arrest, Connor had grown increasingly concerned that he was snitching. Now that Malone had confirmed it, he was pissed at himself for not doing something sooner. He should have known the cops would be able to turn an immature kid like him. His only surprise was that a loser like Bobby Hawkins was the one to do it.

In spite of Malone's assurances, Connor assumed Skinner had given him up. For all he knew, someone might be putting a case together right then. So, Skinner was a liability that had to be removed. Malone would immediately suspect him, but the sweet thing about it was that he couldn't say anything without his own crimes coming to light.

Connor went to the bedroom and opened a chest at the foot of the bed, tossing clothes aside until he found a small metal box. From it, he removed a tiny listening device that could be hidden easily just about anywhere. He called Skinner and arranged to meet him at the gym he frequented.

Two nights later, Connor arrived around nine and began his usual lifting routine. After an intense back workout, he began a series of exercises designed to increase the size of his already-considerable arms. Watching his technique in the mirror, he saw Skinner come in the door and start his way. Pretending he didn't notice, Connor busied himself with the weights.

"Hey, boss man, you wanted to see me?" Todd asked, plopping down on a weight bench. He gawked at Connor's twenty-two inch arms effortlessly curling eighty-pound dumbbells. "Impressive set of guns you got there."

Connor didn't respond, instead focusing intently on each bicep as he moved the weights slowly up and down. Finishing the set, he dropped the dumbbells and flexed for several seconds. With a final, admiring look, Connor grabbed a towel and wiped sweat from his face.

He pretended to see Skinner for the first time. "Hey, kid, when did you get here?"

"Just now. Listen, can you show me some exercises I can do to get big like you?"

"Later. Right now, we have business to discuss."

Turning on his heel, Connor headed out the door with Todd tagging closely behind. At ten o'clock at night, there were only a few people walking to their cars from a nearby restaurant, none within hearing range.

As they climbed into Connor's new car, Todd said, "Man, what a sweet ride."

"Yeah, it'll do. Pay attention now. I have something I want you to do."

"Sure, anything you need, I'm your man."

"I've been watching you. You're doing okay since you got out of jail. Speaking of that, what's happening with your little legal problem?"

"Oh, it's goin' good. My lawyer says he thinks he can get it dropped to a misdemeanor possession charge and get me credit for time served while I was in the county jail. If that happens, I'll be done with it. He said my previous clean record was a big plus."

Connor smiled, "That's great. You know, I've been impressed with you. You've been straight all the way down the line with the dope and the money. So I've decided to promote you in my organization."

"Really?" Todd asked, wide-eyed.

"Yeah, really. Of course, that means you'll be taking on more responsibility. For starters, you'll be supervising four other dealers. Think you can handle it?"

"Oh, man, can I? Absolutely!"

"Okay, then here's a little bonus for you. Just my way of saying thanks," Connor said, pulling a small packet from his workout shorts and slipping it to Skinner. The kid peeked at it, startled to see what he guessed was at least a half-ounce of cocaine.

"You do what you want with that," Connor said with a friendly smile. "Give it to a friend. Sell it, and keep the money for yourself. Whatever you want. Is that cool?"

"Oh, wow, that's maximum cool!" Todd said enthusiastically.

"One rule, though. Don't use it yourself. I want my lieutenants clean and clearheaded at all times. You keep yourself straight, and you'll go to the top with me. You good with that?"

"You bet, boss!" Todd said with a big grin.

"Okay, so here's your first supervisory assignment. One of our guys is skimming, and I can't have that. You with me?"

Todd responded, "I'm with you. Who would be stupid enough to do that?"

"Joey Horn."

"Horn? Damn, I can't believe it. Okay, what do you want me to do?"

"Well, I was thinking. If he got busted, he might start naming names, you know what I'm saying? Instead of keeping his mouth shut like you did."

Todd nodded, his mouth suddenly dry.

"So, he has to go."

"Go? Li, Like, how?" Todd stuttered.

"Go, as in depart from this life," Connor said, staring intently at Skinner.

"I, I, I don't know what to say."

"Alright, come on, Todd. Calm down. I'm not asking you to do it. I just need you to lure him somewhere, and I'll take it from there. Think you can do that?"

Connor watched in solemn amusement as Skinner's inner turmoil played across his face. "Damn, Roy, I've never done anything like that. I mean, can't we just like beat him up or something?"

"Nah, that'd just piss him off and make him run to the cops for sure. Tell you what, don't worry about it, kid. You're obviously not ready for this."

"No, I, I can maybe do it. I appreciate what you've done for me, and I don't wanta screw things up between us," Todd quickly added.

Smiling, Connor reassured him, "We're cool, kid. You're still gonna get your bump up. And more money, too. Can't beat that, huh?"

"No, uh, you sure can't beat that," Skinner replied, his eyes blinking rapidly.

"Okay, son, now get outta here. I got some hot pussy waiting for me. I'll be in touch."

As Todd started to get out, Connor grabbed his arm. "About Horn and our little discussion."

"Yeah?"

"That was totally confidential, you know what I'm saying?"

"Uh, yeah, absolutely! Confidential," Todd said, shutting the door and jogging across the parking lot to his car.

Connor watched until he cranked up the engine and drove away. Reaching into the center console, he took out a small black box and plugged in the DC power cord. He turned on the unit and sat back to listen to the bug he had concealed in the kid's car the night before. The first sound he picked up was Todd ranting to himself, his voice so clear Connor could have been sitting beside him in the car.

"Damn, what have I got myself into?" he raved. "The guy's crazy! Wantin' me to help him kill Joey Horn? I must have been outta my mind to sign on with that maniac!"

For several minutes, all Connor could hear was the sound of the engine and wind noise as Todd continued to drive. Finally, it grew quiet, and Connor heard a series of beeps as Skinner made a call.

"Come on, pick up! . . . Hey, Bobby, I didn't think you were gonna answer. . . . Yeah, it's Todd. Listen man, we gotta talk. . . . Yeah, I know you're working. I'm telling you, man, this is some bad shit I just heard. . . . No, this can't wait until tomorrow! . . . Right, okay, where? . . . Angie's Subs? . . . I don't know, man. That's kinda like too wide open. What about the cemetery across the street? . . . Okay, come in off Second Avenue and turn left. . . . Yeah, okay. How long? . . . That's cool. I'll be there."

As the call ended, Connor wheeled out of the parking lot, a grim look on his face. Within two minutes, he was in position a block west of Warren Smith Cemetery in the driveway of an empty house sporting a sagging For Sale sign in the yard. He quickly pulled a pair of black pants and a long-sleeved black tee shirt over his workout clothes. Reaching under the front seat, he grabbed his nine-millimeter pistol with a silencer attached to the barrel. Sliding the gun into the waistband of his pants, he eased out of the car and sprinted across the street.

Entering the grounds of the well-kept cemetery, Connor worked his way through the gravesites to a position that would give him the best sightline. Crouching behind a double headstone, he settled down to wait.

Chapter 41

Earlier that day, as the evening watch briefing ended, Bobby Hawkins hurried across the squad room to greet his partner for the night. Summer Hayes was a rookie officer beginning her third week on the job. After serving four years in the military, she was excited to be starting this new chapter in her life.

Bobby was excited, too, although for a very different reason. Twenty-four years old, Summer Hayes was drop-dead gorgeous. She was tall, slender, with dark brown hair, and pale blue eyes that seemed to look right through you. Summer knew she was attractive, but she wanted to earn the admiration of her fellow officers based on her abilities rather than her looks.

Having previously rejected his sleazy advances, Summer's female co-workers quickly gave her an education on Bobby Hawkins. Because Bobby was not a field training officer, she had so far avoided having to share a patrol car with him. Unfortunately, her FTO called in sick at the last minute, resulting in her temporary assignment as Bobby's partner.

"Hi, there beautiful, I'm Bobby Hawkins," he said, breath reeking of wintergreen mints. "And may I say that I absolutely love your name . . . Summer Hayes," he said slowly, giving it a vaguely obscene roll off his tongue. "It reminds me of summer days . . . Wait! Summer Hayes. Summer days. Cool play on your name, huh? Anyway, those summer days lying on the beach with a beautiful girl beside me comes to mind. She's wearing a tiny yellow bikini. *Um-um-um*," he said, rolling his eyes in ecstasy at what Summer guessed was more likely an Internet fantasy than reality. "So, I guess you know the sergeant assigned me to be your escort for the evening."

My escort? Is this guy for real? she wondered.

"And we're gonna have a great time, you and me," Bobby continued. "I'll show you how things are really done instead of that crap you've been getting from your FTOs. Then, after work, I'll take you someplace that serves adult beverages and share some training tips I've picked up in my career. What do you say, Summer Hayes?"

"Thanks for the invitation, Officer Hawkins, but I–"

"Please," he interrupted, "Officer Hawkins sounds so formal. It's Bobby. Just Bobby."

"Officer, uh, Bobby, thanks, but I've got other plans."

"Hey, no prob. But remember that you are now the proud owner of a genuine, limited edition Bobby Hawkins rain check, to be cashed in whenever you feel the need for scintillating companionship," he said with a grin.

"Thanks, Bobby. I guess we better get on the street before the sergeant gets mad," she said as she gathered up her gear and walked quickly toward the parking lot. *This is going to be a very long night.*

Shortly after ten o'clock, Summer was finishing a burglary report on the in-car computer while Bobby talked to a woman on his cell. Winking at Summer, he said, "So whataya say, Brittany. Go out with me, and you'll be wined and dined and celebrated like nothing you ever experienced before, and . . . hang on, I've got another call coming in."

Without waiting for a reply, Bobby immediately clicked over. His shoulders visibly sagged when he heard Todd Skinner's voice. After arranging to meet him, he switched back to Brittany, only to discover she had disconnected. Shrugging, he dropped the cell phone in the drink holder.

Glancing at Summer, he said, "One of my boys is ranting about wanting to meet me. Probably needs his Bobby Hawkins fix."

Although curious about the call, Summer just nodded, hoping to discourage conversation until she finished her report. Finally, she spoke, "You said one of your boys needed to meet you. Is he a confidential informant?"

"Yeah, he's one of my CIs. That's what we call a confidential informant in poh-lice jargon," Bobby said with a grin. "Why?"

"I just assumed from your conversation that's who you were talking to. I've heard some officers say they don't want anyone else around when they meet with their informants. If you need to drop me at HQ, I can finish the burglary report while you're gone."

"Naw, it's no problem," he said, reaching over to pat her leg as he negotiated a turn onto Beach Boulevard. Sensing the move, Summer quickly swiveled the laptop computer on its mount, and

Bobby found himself patting the keyboard instead, causing the computer to beep loudly.

Clearly embarrassed, he tried to recover, "Sorry about that. I was trying to call up the vehicle registration screen to check on that car we just passed. But no big deal. I'm sure it's not stolen."

Summer stifled a grin. His pathetic effort to be cool was laughable, but she silently vowed he would get a baton across his knuckles if he tried to touch her again.

"Yeah," he went on. "I'll introduce you to him, and if he doesn't like it, that's tough. He didn't tell me what his problem was, but he sounded all hinked up. The boy's probably high on something, and he's just being paranoid. By the way, are you doing anything tomorrow night? I was wondering because I'm having a little party at my house for a few close friends."

Will this guy ever give up? In the past five hours, he's used more sleazy come-ons than I heard my whole time in the Army. I can't take much more of this. Deciding a lie was her best defense under the circumstances, she said, "Bobby, you're a nice guy and all, but I'm seeing someone right now. I hope you understand."

"That's cool, but that's also no reason why you can't see me, too. Besides, once you've been with Bobby Hawkins, dating any other guy would be like going to a fancy steakhouse and ordering a hot dog instead of the prime rib. You know what I mean?"

In the darkened interior of the patrol car, Bobby couldn't see Summer roll her eyes. *The man hears nothing but the sound of his own giant ego.* As they approached the light at Penman Road, Summer tried to shift the conversation to a safer topic. "Did your CI say where he would be?"

"Yeah, we're supposed to meet at the cemetery. We'll go in off Second Avenue, and he said he'd be parked a little ways down on the left." Turning in, Bobby spotted Todd's car parked facing them. He rolled to a stop fifteen feet away and climbed out of the police car. "Let's go, Officer Hayes. I told you I'd show you some real police work. Watch and learn as I demonstrate the right way to handle a squirrelly snitch."

"Shouldn't we check out on the radio with our location?" Summer asked.

Bobby snorted, "And what would we say we were doing in the cemetery, checking a suspicious grave? Come on, Summer. That's a typical rookie mistake. We're meeting a snitch. Nobody else needs to know."

She got out, embarrassed at showing her ignorance and angry at Bobby for his condescending attitude. As she slid her mini-flashlight into the holder on her utility belt, Summer was surprised to see that Bobby didn't carry a flashlight. She thought. *Maybe my rookie mistake isn't as bad as his officer safety screw up.*

As they approached the vehicle, the interior light came on briefly, revealing an obviously-frightened Todd Skinner. "Bobby, thanks for coming, man. I'm totally freaked."

Bobby smiled, "Chill out, Todd. The good guys are here now." Looking over his shoulder at Summer, he said, "This is my partner, Summer Hayes. She's a rookie I'm instructing in the finer points of law enforcement."

Summer nodded at Skinner as she visualized shooting Bobby with her TASER one time for each wiseass comment he had made since the shift started. But she figured the battery would die before she worked her way through the first two hours.

"So, what's the deal, my man?" Bobby asked cheerfully.

Todd looked around at the hundreds of headstones, pale shades of gray and white in the darkness. Streetlights from the surrounding roads reached only a short distance into the grounds, leaving the three of them in deep shadow.

"I, uh, I gotta tell you something, and it's probably gonna piss you off," Todd said hesitantly.

Bobby's flippant attitude cooled slightly. "What's that?"

"Well, I haven't exactly told you everything."

"About what?" Bobby said.

"About, uh, other stuff I've been doing."

"Damn, Skinner!" he said, raising his voice. "Quit dragging this out. What the hell are you talking about?"

In a breathless rush, he said, "I work for the biggest coke dealer in Jacksonville and I was working for him when I got busted and I've never stopped and he got my bond posted to get me out of jail and while I've been giving you information I've still been working for him."

Bobby glared at Skinner. "What were you thinking? You know damn well you're supposed to stay straight. If the judge finds out you're back dealing dope, he'll ship your ass to prison for about ten years!"

Skinner hung his head. "I know, Bobby. It's just, I needed the money, you know? Anyway, that's not the worst part."

"What could be worse than this?" Bobby demanded.

"Before I tell you, you gotta promise you'll give me protection. The guy is crazy. I was talking to him like a half hour ago, and he was telling me how he was gonna promote me in his organization and put me over other street dealers. Then he tells me one of them is stealin' money or dope, I don't remember which. And he says this guy has to be taken out. He said he wanted me to lure him somewhere so he could kill him. I almost shit my pants when he said that. He musta seen how freaked I was because he told me I didn't have to do it after all. I'm telling you, if he knows I gave him up, I'm dead!"

"Todd, you got a bad case of overactive imagination. That kind of stuff doesn't happen here. Miami? Probably. Jacksonville? Maybe. Not in little Jax Beach, though. No way."

Looking back with a wink at Summer, he said, "Tell you what. You want protection? You got protection, Todd. We'll put you in the Witness Protection from Crazy Drug Dealers Program," he said.

Todd frowned, "Is there really a program like that?"

"Course there is. What, you think I'd screw with you? Now tell me who this guy is," Bobby insisted.

Todd turned in a complete circle, staring hard at the nearby headstones and the indistinct, ghostly shadows in the distance. Shivering in the mild night air, he slowly turned back to face the two officers.

Chapter 42

While Bobby talked to Skinner, Connor quietly crawled up behind the two officers, kneeling beside the right front bumper of the patrol car. The position was perfect; Bobby's body completely blocked Todd's view of him.

Slowly raising the gun, he sighted in on Bobby's head. *I could pull the trigger, and he'd never know who killed him.* As he fantasized shooting Bobby, he realized Skinner was about to drop his name. Leaning slightly to his right, he could just see the kid's face in the dim light. Shifting his aim toward Skinner, he began to squeeze the trigger slowly.

In the glow from the adjacent streetlights, Todd suddenly caught a glimpse of Connor aiming a gun at him over Bobby's shoulder. Pointing, he shouted, "Bobby, look out! Con–"

Suddenly, a small hole appeared in Skinner's forehead. A split second later, the back of his head exploded, splattering blood and gore across the hood of his car. He collapsed, twitched once and was still.

Hearing the muted sound of the gunshot, Bobby clawed for his weapon as he turned to face the threat. Before he could pull his gun, Connor fired twice. The ballistic vest Bobby wore stopped the rounds from penetrating his chest, but the blunt force knocked him down, temporarily stunning him.

Connor shifted his gun toward the female cop, who had yet to react. In the dim light, he could see the confusion on her face as she tried to process what was happening. Hawkins was down, but he would recover soon enough to be a threat.

While he had no argument with the woman, she was still a cop armed with a gun. He aimed for the middle of her back, intending to incapacitate her long enough to escape. However, she bent over toward Bobby just as he pulled the trigger. Instead of hitting her vest, the bullet struck Summer in the head. Racing over to her, Connor saw blood seeping from her left ear. *Shit! I killed a fuckin' cop!*

This wasn't going the way he planned. He had meant to kill only Skinner and then slip away into the darkness, knowing by the time the two cops figured out what happened, he would be far away. Now everything was screwed up.

Connor heard a loud wheeze behind him. Turning, he saw Bobby's head tilt slowly in his direction. Shifting to kneel beside him, Connor saw the injured cop's eyes widen as he recognized the danger. Fumbling with the holster release, Bobby frantically tried to free his pistol. Connor stood quickly, pinning his hand under his boot.

Blinking his eyes at the man looming over him, recognition brought a groan, "Connor!"

"Why did you have to come here tonight? You're usually sleeping behind a building by now. Instead, you had to act like a real cop for once," Connor snarled.

"You killed my CI, you bastard," Bobby said with difficulty, still unable to draw a deep breath. Looking at Summer, lying a few feet away, he groaned, "And you killed my partner, too!"

Bobby fought to free his gun hand, but Connor was too strong. Unable to reach his gun, he grabbed for the radio mic with his other hand. Connor ripped the radio off Bobby's utility belt, turning it off and throwing it away. "You're not calling anybody, Hawkins," he said.

Connor considered what he should do. If he left now, Hawkins would call for help. Then he wouldn't get far before some asshole cop spotted him and tried to make a name for himself. On the other hand, if Hawkins was in no condition to make the call, his chances of escaping increased dramatically, especially since there would be no witnesses.

He knew what he had to do, but still he hesitated. He loathed Bobby Hawkins, but there was still a tiny part of him that felt the urge to help a fellow officer in trouble. He was somewhat surprised and disgusted by his feelings. The man Roy Connor had become would stop at nothing in pursuit of money and power. Now, here he was feeling sorry for these two cops.

Run now and take my chances, he thought *Or kill Hawkins so there are no witnesses.*

But now there was a problem with the second option, one he had not anticipated. An inner voice, the frayed remnants of his conscience, was demanding attention, telling him to render first aid, call Rescue, surrender and accept whatever punishment awaited him.

Connor started to lift his boot from Bobby's hand. Then he stopped. *What was I thinking? This guy is all that stands between me and freedom.*

"You probably won't believe it, but I never intended to kill a cop," Connor said softly. Pressing the gun against Bobby's forehead, he pulled the trigger without hesitation. Bobby Hawkins died instantly.

Without a backward glance at his bloody handiwork, Connor took off running.

Chapter 43

The first sensation Summer felt was pain. A throbbing ache in her head that pulsed with every heartbeat. Gently, she touched the area above her ear and came away with blood on her hand. Groaning, she rolled over slowly to keep the pain from worsening.

Summer saw Bobby Hawkins sprawled on his back. She tried to get to her feet, realizing quickly that was a bad idea. Fighting nausea, her head feeling as if it weighed more than her whole body, she crawled to where her partner lay. "Bobby," she said, weakly, "are you okay?"

When he didn't respond, she fumbled for her flashlight and thumbed the switch. Bright light flared, revealing a ghastly sight. The pressure of the bullet as it plowed through his head had caused both eyes to swell and blood to trickle from his ears, nose and mouth. Turning the light toward Todd Skinner, she saw grievous damage to his head, also.

Unable to take her eyes off the carnage, Summer punched the Signal 34 emergency button on her portable radio. The dispatcher immediately responded and asked if she was seventy-seven, the code meaning, 'are you okay?' She reached for the radio mic to answer, but it had come loose from her shirt when she hit the ground. Noticing a car going slowly past the cemetery, Summer flashed her light trying to get the driver's attention. The car stopped suddenly. *Thank God. Someone to help me,* she thought.

Finally locating the mic, she yelled, "Officer down! Officer Hawkins is down! He's dead!" Remembering that Bobby had insisted they not give their location when they arrived, she added, "We're in the cemetery! Beach at Penman!"

Straining to see in the darkness, Summer saw a figure approaching fast. As she shone her flashlight in that direction, the beam exposed a man pointing a gun at her. Suddenly, damp earth exploded as a bullet plowed into the ground inches in front of her face. She reacted without thinking, lunging to her left and scrambling toward the safety of the patrol car as rounds peppered the ground all around her. Yanking her pistol, she fired wildly in the direction of the shooter. Reaching the car, she used the front wheel for protection as the shots kept coming, puncturing both tires on the driver's side.

Summer stuck her gun around the edge of the car and fired several more rounds, simultaneously screaming into the radio, "SHOTS FIRED! I'M BEING SHOT AT!" Dropping the mic, she crouched low, swiveling her head back and forth. Her mind screamed, *Where is he? Is he coming around the front? What about the back of the car? Oh, my God. What if he dives over the hood and shoots me in the head?* Her heart pounded in her ears. Her head ached viciously. Squeezing the pistol tightly in both hands, she strained to listen for sounds of the killer's approach. It was quiet. Deathly quiet.

Seconds passed, and then she heard the roar of an engine. Bracing herself on the hood of the car, she watched as the vehicle careened onto Penman and raced away north. Keying the radio, she spoke with a calmness she didn't feel, "Suspect vehicle fleeing north on Penman. Small, light colored, two-door, unknown make. White male suspect, bald, dark clothing, armed with a pistol."

The radio erupted with noise as every officer on duty tried to get through. Summer's eyes drifted to where Bobby Hawkins lay, his childish come-ons forgotten. Hot tears burned as she stifled a sob. Feeling dizzy again, she slid to the ground, leaning back against the fender. Black spots swirled at the edges of her vision. *Fight it,* she commanded. Sticking her knuckle in her mouth, she bit down hard, the sharp pain driving the darkness back.

Pressing her hand to the side of her head, she climbed to her feet and walked slowly over to her partner. Kneeling beside his body, she touched his arm. In a voice choked with emotion, Summer whispered, "You didn't deserve this, Officer Hawkins . . . Bobby. And I promise . . . the man who did it won't get away."

Chapter 44

Connor fought to control his fear and anger as he raced away from the cemetery. "I can't believe she's alive!" he ranted, slamming his fist against the steering wheel. Had she seen his face? Maybe even recognized him? He didn't know, and that complicated things. His only option was to run, but he needed cash and he had to dump the car on the off chance the female cop got a good look at it. But right now, he needed a place to hide until things cooled down.

Approaching the intersection at Atlantic Boulevard, Connor saw the red and blue lights of several police cars coming toward him at a high rate of speed. His pulse jumped at the realization they were responding to the shooting. Whipping into the nearest driveway, he killed the lights and slumped low in the seat. Seconds later, a Neptune Beach police car passed, siren screaming, followed a block behind by two Atlantic Beach cars.

Nervous sweat rolled down his face as he waited to see if they would turn around. Relieved as the echo of their sirens faded, he backed out, a plan of escape forming in his mind. Andi LaBelle lived in Mayport a few minutes away. He would ditch the car there and take hers.

Ten minutes later, Connor turned into Andi's driveway, immediately killing his lights. A lamp was burning in her bedroom; otherwise, the house was dark. Pulling around the corner, he parked next to her ten-year-old SUV. Shutting off the engine, Connor thought about their fight when she caught him getting Danny Malone's private number from her cell phone. He hadn't seen her since that night and wondered if she was still pissed at him for choking her. Not that he cared.

Going to the back door, he tried to insert the key she had given him months before, but it wouldn't fit. After several tries, he cursed, "Damn bitch must have changed the locks on me." He ran to the bedroom window and knocked on the frame. "Andi, hey, Andi. It's me. Roy." After several seconds with no response, he knocked again, louder this time. "Andi, you in there?"

He watched as a shadow approached the window. Andi peeked through the blinds. When she recognized Connor, she said under her breath, "Oh, shit. Roy Connor." Raising the blinds, she spoke through the screen, "Roy, it's late. I was about to go to bed."

"Andi, I need help. Come open the back door. My key won't work," he said, ducking down suddenly as a car passed by on the street.

"What's going on, Roy?" Andi asked, a tremor in her voice.

"I'll tell you inside. Open the back door," he ordered, walking away.

Andi dropped the blind and stood for a moment, hugging her arms tightly to her chest. Glancing at her phone, she said, "Don't even think about calling 9-1-1. The cops would never get here in time."

Reluctantly, she went to the door and unlocked it. Connor stepped quickly inside, shutting and relocking the door. Without a word, he went to her bedroom and switched off the light, plunging the house into darkness.

"What is the matter with you?" she asked, her voice betraying her anxiety.

Still not speaking, Connor went to the living room and peered through the curtains at the street. Finally satisfied, he came back to the kitchen. Andi flipped on the overhead light, revealing Connor drenched in sweat.

"Turn off the damn light!" he demanded.

She immediately hit the switch. "Roy, what's wrong? What happened?"

"I, uh . . . ," he stopped, so rattled he couldn't think of a cover story. Wiping his face with the back of his hand, he struggled to get himself under control. "Look, it's none of your damn business what's wrong. I just need your car."

"My car? No way," she said. "I need it for work."

"I'll leave you mine to drive. It's a helluva lot better ride than that piece of crap you drive anyway."

Andi frowned. "But why do you need my car? Did you do something? Are the police looking for you, Roy?"

"Let's just say I might be accused of something, and I don't want to be here when . . . ," he faltered.

"When what?"

"Never mind. Just give me the damn keys," he said harshly.

Shaking her head, Andi said, "I'm not giving you my car unless you tell me why you need it. And I'm not getting involved in whatever is going on."

Connor walked menacingly toward her, his eyes narrowing. Everything had gone to shit all of a sudden, and this stupid bitch thought she was going to stand in his way? Not likely. Reaching out with lightning speed, he yanked her off her feet and slammed her to the floor. Andi's head struck the side of the kitchen table, opening a gash over her eye.

Connor leaned over her prone body, his face a mask of rage. "Tell me where the keys are right now, bitch," he snarled.

Dazed, blood pouring down her face, she staggered to her feet, clinging to the table to keep from falling. She pointed at her purse on the counter by the door. Connor upended the bag, digging through the contents until he found the keys. Opening the door to leave, he suddenly stopped, turning to look back at Andi. Her head was down, the cut above her eye dripping blood onto the floor.

"Come here," he said, his voice softening slightly.

Without speaking, Andi crossed the kitchen to where Connor stood. He flipped the light switch over the range and studied the cut over her eye. "It's just a scratch," he said. "Anything around the eyes always bleeds like a mother."

Pulling paper towels from the rack, he wet them in the sink. Andi stood mute, her eyes closed as he cleaned her face and neck of blood. Finished, he put his hands on her shoulders. "I wish you hadn't made me do that. But I need your car, and I don't have time for bullshit."

Guiding her to the table, Connor gently pushed her down into a chair. He kneeled in front of her, engulfing her small hands in his. "I want you to listen close to what I'm gonna say."

When she didn't look at him, Connor put his hand under her chin and raised her head. Andi avoided his eyes as he continued, "If you're asked, I've been here since seven o'clock. We ate dinner and then . . . did you see a movie tonight?"

She shook her head.

"Okay, it's probably better if we don't start making up crap about watching something that wasn't even on. Here's what we did. We ate dinner and then sat around and talked a while. Then we went to bed where we stayed all night. Simple. No way to prove it didn't happen that way. Alright, you clear on what we did tonight?"

She nodded, dropping her eyes to the table.

"Tell me. I want to hear you say it so I know you've got it down."

In a monotone, she responded, "You got here around seven. We ate and then talked until we went to bed."

"Where we stayed all night. Don't forget that part," Roy insisted.

In the same lifeless tone, she repeated, "Where we stayed all night."

"That's good. Okay," he said, standing abruptly, "I'm gone. I've got some things I gotta take care of, and then I'm hittin' the road."

Andi looked up. "You're leaving town?"

"Yeah, soon as I pack a few things." He stood there going through a quick mental checklist of the stuff he would need. "Shit," he muttered. "I just remembered I've got no cash on me. You have any?"

She pointed at the wallet Connor had dumped on the table. "There may be twenty or thirty dollars in there. Take it."

"Damn, woman, how far you think I'll get on that? The west side of Jacksonville? I need big bucks," he said angrily as he took the money and stuffed it into his pocket. Pressing the paper towels to the cut over her eye, Andi said nothing.

Tense, lost in thought, Connor tried to decide what to do. He thought of Danny Malone and wondered if there was some way he could use him. Then it hit him. Malone might be the key to his escape. Without another word, he rushed out the door.

Andi waited until she heard the engine crank on her old car. Then she lunged for the back door, locking it and jamming a chair under the knob. Jerking open a kitchen drawer, she grabbed a large butcher knife and ran to her bedroom, locking herself inside. She wrestled the dresser in front of the door and climbed into bed. Pulling the covers up to her chin, she gripped the big knife tightly as she stared at the door.

"If that bastard comes at me again, I'm gonna make him pay," she said fiercely.

Chapter 45

Within an hour, the area inside and outside the cemetery was a chaotic mix of police, curious onlookers, and media. Cops strung yellow and black "Police-Do Not Enter" tape around the scene as evidence techs erected screens around the bodies of Bobby Hawkins and Todd Skinner.

Many of Bobby's fellow cops, along with officers from surrounding departments, stood guard at the perimeter to prevent any unauthorized person from entering and possibly destroying evidence. Some of the officers walked around in a daze, struggling emotionally with the loss of one of their own. Others vented their anger by shouting at the crowds and media people who tried to slip past the tape barricade.

As the Detective Commander, Clay was in charge of the investigation, while Chief Wilson handled the media and ensured Clay had whatever resources he needed. Rescue transported Summer Hayes to the emergency room, and Three Rivers was en route to interview her.

Clay's face twisted as he watched an evidence technician shoot crime scene photos of Bobby Hawkins. Although he had never respected Bobby as a cop, he was shocked and angered by his death at the hands of an unknown killer.

As the ET took close-up photos of the chest area, Clay noticed what appeared to be two small tears on Bobby's uniform shirt. Leaning over the technician's shoulder for a closer look, he saw they were bullet holes. "Can you tell if the rounds penetrated the vest?" he asked the ET.

"If I had to guess, I'd say no, Commander. But I can't say for sure until the ME strips the vest off."

Clay's eyes roamed over the body, looking for any clue that would point his detectives toward a suspect. He blinked at what he saw on the back of Bobby's right hand, which still loosely gripped the butt of his pistol. Dried mud clung to the skin in four wavy, parallel lines, clearly indicating the sole of a shoe or boot.

"Son of a bitch," he said softly. "Bobby was trying to draw his gun, and the killer stepped on his hand to stop him."

Clay heard a voice behind him, "Oh no!"

He turned and saw Danny Malone standing beside the body of Todd Skinner, bending over as he took deep, wheezing breaths.

"Danny, hey man, you okay?" Clay asked, going over and putting a hand on his shoulder.

Danny didn't answer, continuing to stare in horror at the body. Then he staggered over to Bobby Hawkins, where the look of revulsion deepened. Putting a hand over his mouth, he ran, weaving between headstones until he was beyond the crime scene. Falling to his knees, he vomited explosively.

Clay grabbed a bottle of water from an officer and hurried over to his friend. "Here, take this," he said, touching Danny's arm with the bottle.

"Thanks, man," he said softly.

"You okay?" Clay asked, helping him to his feet.

"Sorry. Hope I didn't screw up the crime scene," he said, swaying unsteadily as he took several swallows of water.

"No harm done. It's a shitty thing for all of us to have to deal with," Clay said, gesturing toward the scene.

"Yeah," Danny said, looking away.

Clay stared at Danny, seeing a haggard look on his face in the reflected glow of the spotlights illuminating the death scene. "Bro, this is some bad stuff, and I need you focused. You have to put your feelings aside. Can you do that?" he asked, squeezing Danny's shoulder reassuringly.

Massaging his temples, Danny answered, "Yeah, I'm okay."

"Good," Clay said. "How about rousting your CIs and see if anyone has a line on our shooter?"

Voice shaking, Danny asked, "What have we got for physical and vehicle descriptions?"

"White male, tall, bald-headed, wearing dark clothing. Small sports car, light-colored, maybe beige or white. Hayes couldn't be more specific than that."

Clay saw a look of revulsion cross his friend's face. "Okay, I'm on it," Danny said harshly as he walked away. Stopping beside the bodies, he looked first at Todd Skinner and then at Bobby Hawkins, his hands shoved in his pockets. Glancing over his shoulder, he saw Clay staring at him. With a curt nod, he hurried to his car.

Danny had to get away from the cemetery, from the grisly results of his betrayal of everything he stood for. His hatred for Connor burned white-hot. At the same time, he felt an overwhelming sense of shame for his role in two murders. He couldn't change what happened, but he could damn sure do something about Roy Connor. As he slammed the door of his unmarked police car, his cell phone rang. The screen showed "Unknown Caller."

"Malone," Danny snapped.

"We gotta talk," Connor said.

His eyes narrowed as he recognized the voice. "You cop-killing bastard!" he yelled. "Where are you?"

"I don't know what you're talking about. I didn't kill anybody," Connor said evenly.

"You're a lying piece of shit! You better turn yourself in with a bunch of lawyers all around because I'll kill you if I find you first!" Danny shouted, so angry he began to hyperventilate.

"You got all that out of your system? You ready to talk sensible now?" Connor asked.

Holding the phone away from his ear a moment, Danny forced himself to calm down, to focus. "You killed a cop," he said.

"So?" Connor responded. "Nobody could stand the son of a bitch anyway. I did y'all a favor."

"A favor?" Danny said, his voice rising again. "You kill a police officer and call it a favor because of the man's personality? What kind of animal are you?"

"Careful, Malone. You're in no position to criticize me."

"Screw you! I'm done with this! I'm going to Clay and tell him everything. I don't care what happens to me."

"Oh, I think you might when they charge you with murder."

"What are you talking about? I didn't kill anybody. *You* did!"

"You didn't pull the trigger, but you sure as hell set it up when you told me Skinner was a snitch. That might be enough to get you the needle in this state."

Startled, Danny didn't immediately respond. He considered the possibility that Connor could be right. If he was lucky, he might get a lifetime trip to prison. If he wasn't, he could find himself strapped to a gurney with deadly chemicals flowing through his veins.

As the silence lengthened, Connor spoke, "Good. Got your attention, didn't I, asshole?"

Danny's anger flared, overcoming his apprehension. "At this point, I don't give a shit!" he said heatedly.

"Don't give me that crap! You care plenty. So here's the deal. I need two things from you. One, I gotta have money to get out of here. My money you stole. And two, I want you to point the investigation at someone else. Pick anybody, I don't care who. Tell your buddy Randall you got a call from a snitch that identified some guy as the shooter. Randall can then round up a posse and go beat down the guy's door. If I'm lucky, one of your cops will get jumpy and kill him, and that'll be the end of it. Even if that doesn't happen, by the time they figure out he didn't do it, I'll be far away."

Danny's outrage knew no bounds. "Connor, you don't have the slightest trace of humanity in your body. You were a police officer once. It's bad enough that you could kill a cop. But then to casually suggest pinning it on some innocent person? You're a despicable piece of shit!"

"Fuck you, Malone! And don't give me that crap about an innocent person. Nobody's innocent! Everybody's got an angle. You included. So, I want my money back, and I want you to push the story I told you, just like I said. You do exactly that, and everything will be cool. I'll be out of your shitty life, and you can go back to being a crooked cop with somebody else's money."

Danny desperately wished he had the ability to blast a .45 caliber bullet through the phone to take Connor's head off on the other end. With that vision still in his head, he growled, "I don't know what I'm going to do. About anything."

"What do you mean? You *better* know!"

"I'll think about it, Connor," Danny said, disconnecting the call.

Chapter 46

Sitting on his couch, Connor glared at the phone, furious that Malone had dared to challenge him. He immediately dialed his number again, getting a "Not in Service" message.

"Son of a bitch!" he exploded, throwing the phone against the wall where it shattered into pieces. Breathing hard, he stood up, shrugging his shoulders in an effort to relieve the tension. He felt no remorse at killing Skinner. The kid was a snitch who tried to play it both ways. *Screw him. He deserved it.*

Bobby Hawkins was a different matter. Connor felt weird about killing him. Was it because he had once been a cop himself? Remembering that sense of camaraderie, that feeling of brotherhood? He didn't know. He just knew he damn sure didn't like feeling this way. Then there was Malone's sudden rebellion. From the time he was a teenager, enduring regular beatings from his alcoholic father, Connor had sworn he would never again let anyone control his fate. Now he worried that Malone was doing exactly that. *If the bastard runs his mouth to Randall and agrees to testify against me, he'll probably get off easy. And I'll be the one taking the trip to death row.*

Ever since Tony Savoy's lecture about stupid drug dealers, Connor had worked on an exit strategy, a plan of escape if he got wind he was about to be arrested. While he wasn't certain Malone would roll over on him, he couldn't wait to find out. He would have to run without getting his money back from the asshole. But he swore to himself that he would come back when things died down. Then he would get it. And the price Malone would pay for all the trouble he caused would be his life.

Going to his bedroom closet, he ripped up the carpet covering a floor-mounted safe. Spinning the dials hurriedly, he twice entered the wrong code. Cursing loudly, finally getting it right on the third try, Connor ripped open the door and removed a bank bag. His anxiety increased as he unzipped the bag and dumped out the money. It took only seconds to count. *Eighteen hundred dollars. Shit!*

Closing his eyes, Connor rubbed the back of his neck. *You dumb bastard. You thought you put together a foolproof escape plan. Half a mil in cash in your safe deposit box set aside in case you need to run far and fast. But you forgot one important detail. How can you do that when the banks are closed? The money's no good if you can't access it.*

Reaching back into the safe, he retrieved a bundle of documents that included a counterfeit passport, driver's license, and social security card. *They'll be good enough to get across the border into Mexico, but I gotta have a lot more cash than this once I'm there.*

He stared at the floor, lost in thought. Then it came to him. He knew exactly how to get the money he needed. Pulling a suitcase off the shelf, he threw the cash and documents inside. Snatching shirts and jeans off their hangers, he dropped them on top. From a dresser drawer, he took a black ski mask and shoved it in his back pocket. A pre-paid cell phone and a set of lock picks from the nightstand drawer went into another pocket.

Trembling now in his haste to leave, Connor grabbed the final piece of equipment he needed, the stun gun. He ran to the parking lot, tossed the suitcase in the back of Andi's SUV, and raced through the complex to the exit. Heading to the beach, he took Butler Boulevard to stay as far away as possible from the activity in the cemetery.

Within minutes, he cruised slowly through a neighborhood of well-kept homes fronting the ocean. He checked for vehicles at a particular house as he drove by. Seeing none, he turned around and pulled into the driveway, killing the engine. He quickly slipped around to the ocean-side patio, pausing to pull on the ski mask before going to work with the lock picks. Within seconds, he was in.

Standing in the den, Connor listened to the house. It was quiet, the only sound a soft clunk as the icemaker dropped new cubes into the tray. He had been in the house years before. Closing his eyes, he searched his memory for the location of the master bedroom. Upstairs, last door on the right.

Going to the stairwell, Connor pulled a lock-blade knife from his pocket and opened it. He began to climb, staying close to the wall to minimize any creaking sounds his weight might cause. He paused to listen once again at the top of the stairs before going down the hall to the master bedroom.

The door was open a couple of inches, a dim light from inside spilling into the hallway. He hesitated, unsure what to do. Putting his ear to the opening, he listened intently. Hearing the sound of snoring, he smiled. Connor pushed open the door gently and stepped into the room. He could see a figure in the bed facing toward the window. The other side of the bed was empty, as he expected.

A lamp was on a low setting, providing just enough light for Connor to scan the room for anything that could be used as a weapon. There was nothing. He went to the side of the bed, standing over the sleeping form. Something, possibly the slight shifting of air caused by his movement, awakened her, and she opened her eyes. In the faint light, she could see a large figure looming over her. A figure with no face, only darkness where eyes, nose, and mouth should be. She squeezed her eyes shut for a moment, as if not convinced what she was seeing was real. When she opened them again, the figure was still there.

Connor touched the point of the knife to her neck, at the same time putting his hand over her mouth. "Hello, Rachel. Are you awake?" he asked.

Rachel Malone came fully awake, trying to pull away until she felt a sudden pain on the side of her neck.

"Don't move!" he said harshly. "It's a very sharp knife you're feeling, and I'll use it if you don't cooperate. If you understand, nod your head."

Eyes wild with fear, heart pounding, Rachel nodded, trying to keep the knifepoint from penetrating her skin.

"Okay, good girl. Now, you and I are going for a little ride. If you fail to do exactly what I say at all times, I'll make you beg me to kill you. Nod if you understand that."

Rachel dipped her head slowly again as tears started to flow.

"I'm going to take my hand away, but don't make a sound, or you know what will happen."

She began to sob, the sound muffled by his hand.

"Stop crying! I said be quiet! Don't be a whiny bitch like your husband!" Connor snarled, pulling the knife away. When she didn't react, he took his hand off her mouth and pulled her to her feet. "Get dressed. We're leaving."

Tears still glistening in her eyes, Rachel pleaded, "Why are you doing this to me?"

"Ask your husband. He knows."

She frowned, "What do you mean? He knows what?"

"That's not important. Just understand that if he does what I tell him to do, you'll be fine. If he doesn't, well . . . ," Connor answered, leaving the threat unsaid. "Now, cut the questions and get dressed."

Rachel stared hard at the masked man, a startled look on her face. "I know that voice. Roy Connor? Is that you?"

In response, Connor yanked off the mask, a wild look in his eyes. "Yeah, it's me. And I'm not going to tell you again to get some damn clothes on!"

Trembling, Rachel pulled shorts and a tee shirt from the dresser drawer and then stopped, looking at Connor. "Please turn around so I can get dressed."

"You don't have anything I haven't seen in a hundred other women. Besides, you're not my type. You're like a skeleton with skin."

Rachel flushed, "I've been sick for a long time. I've–"

"Yeah, yeah, I know. Big fucking deal."

Glaring, Rachel turned her back to him and slipped on her clothes. Going to the closet to retrieve her sandals, she saw the open door to her bedroom. In desperation, she ran for it, barreling into the hallway and heading for the stairs. But in her weakened state, she was no match for Connor. He caught her before she reached the stairwell, grabbing her arm and yanking her off her feet. Her head hit the floor, driving spikes of pain through her skull.

"Stupid bitch!" he raged.

Snatching her up, Connor threw her over his shoulder and headed downstairs to the garage. Using duct tape he found on Danny's workbench, he bound her hands and feet before adding a strip across her mouth.

Two minutes later, he drove away with his living, breathing insurance policy stuffed on the floorboard behind the driver's seat. Now it was simply a matter of making a phone call to initiate the final part of his plan.

Chapter 47

Danny felt lost. There was no one to turn to for advice, for support, for sympathy. The obvious choice under other circumstances would be Clay, his best friend, the man he trusted with his life. Clay Randall was that rare person who always seemed to know the right thing to do, a talent Danny realized he did not have. His tendency to act without thinking had gotten him into trouble more times than he could count. However, the stupid stunts he pulled in the past were immature child's play compared to now. No, there was no way he could tell Clay what he had done. He would never understand.

Racked with guilt, head in his hands, he jumped when his cell phone rang. Looking at the number, he saw Andi LaBelle's name. He thought of ignoring it but instead listlessly picked up. "Hey, Andi."

"Danny, I need to talk to you right away," she said breathlessly.

"Now's really not a good time," he responded in a subdued voice.

"Danny, listen to me! I just turned on the TV and heard about a shooting in Jax Beach, and–"

"Yeah, we're working a double homicide involving a police officer. Andi, I don't have time, and I really can't talk about the circumstances. It's–"

"I know who did it," she interrupted.

"What? What did you say?" he asked, bolting to his feet.

"Roy Connor. I think Roy Connor did it, Danny!"

"How the hell would you know that?" he demanded.

"He came here apparently right after it happened and left his car behind my house. He said he couldn't drive it because he thought the cops might be looking for it, so he took mine."

"You still drive that old brown SUV?" Danny asked, opening his notepad and grabbing a pen.

"Yeah. It's pretty much junk, but it's all I can afford."

"Do you know the license number?"

"Yeah, it's a personalized plate, 'DANCER' like, you know, a dancer?"

"Yeah, got it."

"Danny, he . . . ," she hesitated, "he knocked me around when I told him he couldn't take my car. Then he told me to tell anyone who asked that he was here since seven o'clock. That we had dinner and talked and then went to bed. I, I'm really scared. I've always known he had a temper, but bad enough to kill somebody? He was a cop for years. I don't understand how he could do something like that."

"How long ago did he leave, and did he say where he was going?"

"He's been gone about an hour, and all he said was that he had to get out of town."

"Damn, I need to find him. Okay, if you think of anything else, call me. I'll get back with you later to get your statement as soon as things slow down a little."

"Wait, Danny. Before you go, there's one more thing," she said. "He said he needed money and got mad when I didn't have hardly any to give him. He took what I had and then he stood there. All of a sudden, his eyes lit up like he had just remembered something, and he took off. As soon as he was out the door, I barricaded it. I'm sitting here right now with a butcher knife in my hand. I swear I'll kill him if he comes back, Danny."

Not if I find him first, he thought, grimly. Danny knew the reason for Connor's unusual reaction at Andi's place, but he wasn't about to share it. "Okay, Andi. Listen, you've been a big help. Now, I want you to stay away from his car. Don't touch it. I'll get someone out there in a little while to process it. There may be DNA evidence in it that'll tie him to the murders. Talk to you soon," he said.

The phone call from Connor played again in Danny's mind. The bastard needed money, and where better to get it than from the man who took it in the first place. Danny had to get control of the situation before Connor killed someone else, maybe another cop or two. Maybe him. He knew there was only one way to guarantee an end to Connor's murderous rampage. And that was also his only chance to escape the nightmare he had created.

His cell rang again as he contemplated adding murder to his own list of crimes. Danny couldn't imagine as he answered that things were about to get much worse.

Chapter 48

"Malone," Danny answered.

"I need my money, asshole."

"Screw you, Connor! I'm not giving you a damn thing."

"Oh, I'm not talking about you giving me anything. I'm talking about a trade for my money."

"You couldn't possibly have anything I want, except maybe your life. Tell you what. You kill yourself, and I'll donate your filthy money to a worthy cause!"

"Yeah, right," Connor said sarcastically. "And I bet the worthy cause would be the Danny Malone benefit fund."

"I've never used a penny of that money on myself! It was all for my wife."

"Funny you should mention your wife. How is Rachel doing these days?"

"Don't say her name," Danny growled through clenched teeth.

"Oh, I think you're gonna find I've done more than say her name, Malone."

Danny hesitated, cold dread gripping his heart. "What do you mean?"

"I mean, Detective Malone, that maybe you should go home and conduct a welfare check on the woman who lives there. I'll call you back, say, in fifteen minutes," Connor said, hanging up.

In a panic, Danny floored it, arriving at his house in less than five minutes. Slamming on the brakes, he leaped from the car and ran for the door. Fumbling with the keys, his hands shaking badly, he finally got it unlocked.

He went in low and fast, the barrel of his gun following his gaze as he scanned in all directions. The house was quiet; nothing appeared out of place. He was beginning to question whether Connor was lying to him when he saw the rear patio door standing open several inches. Fighting panic, he stepped quietly across the room, gun held tightly in both hands. He stooped to examine the latch, seeing clearly visible scratch marks. *The son of a bitch broke into my house,* his mind screamed.

Turning, Danny saw the garage light shining through the partially open door. He hurried across the room, a growing sense of urgency overriding his need for caution. Charging into the garage, prepared to fire if Connor was there, Danny cursed to find it empty. Turning to leave, he saw a half-empty roll of duct tape on the floor. It had been full yesterday. His imagination ran wild as he visualized Connor wrapping tape around Rachel's head to smother her.

Fear seized him. He ran, bellowing her name. Taking the stairs three at a time, he raced down the hall to their bedroom. Throwing open the door, afraid of what he would find, Danny let out a gut-wrenching howl. Staring at the empty bed, he was unable to wrap his mind around Connor's monstrous act. Until that moment, he had assumed the murders of Bobby Hawkins and Todd Skinner were the worst things he had ever experienced. He knew now he was wrong.

He slumped to the floor, anguish overcoming him. Connor had taken Rachel, and there was no way the madman would let her go unharmed. Even if he gave back all the money. As the full impact of what he had set in motion became clear, Danny curled into a fetal position, arms wrapped tightly around his body, sobbing hysterically. He had only tried to help the woman he loved, and now he was going to lose her. Everything he valued in life was slipping away, and he felt powerless to stop it. Without Rachel, there was nothing left.

Minutes passed before Danny was able to regain control. Wiping his nose on the sleeve of his shirt, he went downstairs to the garage. Kneeling in front of his upright tool chest, he opened the bottom drawer, pulling out various tools and throwing them aside, where they hit the concrete floor with a clang.

Grabbing a metal box from the drawer, Danny set it on the workbench. He raised the lid and stared at the banded stacks of hundred-dollar bills that filled the box. Forty thousand dollars stared back at him. Danny scowled as he visualized the hiding place of the remaining hundred and thirty thousand dollars. Another in a long line of stupid, impulsive decisions.

He jumped as his phone rang. Knowing it had to be Connor, hoping he might have a shred of decency left and would spare Rachel, he answered, "Please don't hurt her, Roy."

"Good to hear some humility in your voice, Malone," Connor said.

"I don't care what happens to me. Is Rachel okay?"

"She's fine, and she'll stay that way as long as you do exactly what you're told."

"I will. Just tell me what you want," Danny said.

"Are you stupid, Malone? How many times I gotta tell you? I WANT MY MONEY!" Connor screamed.

Danny said, "Okay, okay, calm down, Roy. I'll give you your money. But I don't have all of it. I've spent about thirty thousand on my wife's medical bills. And I'm looking at forty right in front of me. The rest is, uh, someplace that'll take me a day or two to get. Tomorrow, maybe. The day after, for sure."

"You gotta be outta your mind if you think I'm taking forty thousand with an IOU for the rest."

"I can't help it, Roy. The money is, is hidden at . . . well, just somewhere that makes it very difficult to get to right now. Please, take the forty thousand, and I promise I'll have the rest for you soon. I just need a little time to figure out how to get it without, uh, anybody finding out."

"Where is it, at Randall's house?"

"N, No, it's not."

"You're lying to me. What's the deal? Is Randall in on this with you?"

"Clay doesn't know anything about this!" Danny exclaimed. "I hid it there, I mean . . . ," he stammered.

"Okay, now that we've established the money is at Randall's house, I want you to get it. I don't care what bullshit story you make up. Just get it, you understand?"

"Come on, Roy. I told you that's impossible right now."

"I'm sick of your excuses, Malone. Get the money now, or I'll let you listen to your wife's dying screams over this phone!" Connor roared.

In a panic, Danny tried to buy time. "Alright, I'll do it. I'll do it. Just don't hurt her."

"Get the money and meet me in thirty minutes at the Sandcastle Plaza."

"Wait, Roy. I can't get there that fast. The money's not easy to reach, and I've got to come up with some excuse to tell . . . to tell Dana. Give me an hour, and I promise I'll be there."

"Okay, one hour! Sandcastle Plaza parking lot. You get there one minute late, and she's dead!" he snapped, hanging up.

It was true. Danny had hidden the bulk of the cash at Clay's house while attending a cookout. Making an excuse to go to his car, Danny retrieved an identical metal box containing the cash. Slipping into Clay's garage, he used a stepladder to reach a row of cabinets mounted on the wall near the twelve-foot ceiling. Clay had previously told him the cabinets contained miscellaneous papers, old toys, and books from his childhood. He hid the metal box behind cartons of old tax records.

Danny hadn't wanted all of the money at his house, afraid Rachel would be upset if she discovered he had not deposited the "inheritance" windfall in the bank. His reasoning for using Clay's house had seemed logical at the time. Now, not so much, as he realized he might have put his best friend and his family in danger.

Focusing on Connor's demands, Danny's mind churned. He had an hour to come up with a plan. Staring at the money, thinking hard, an idea popped into his head. Running upstairs to his bedroom, he rummaged through the closet until he found a nylon bag containing his tactical gear. Pushing aside knee and elbow pads, a ballistic helmet, and a TASER, he grabbed a flat-black, cylindrical device from the utility vest.

Racing back to the garage, Danny dumped the money out of the box. He placed the device inside and closed the lid. It wouldn't work; the box was too deep for what he planned. He thought a moment, his eyes on the bundles of money. Removing the device, Danny began piling stacks of hundreds into the box. After building up a one-inch layer, he repositioned the device on its side with the safety handle facing up. This time, the lid pressed down against the handle with sufficient force.

Rooting through a junk drawer in the kitchen, he found a roll of string and cut off a strip about twelve inches long. Tying one end of the string around the pin that held the handle in place, he stretched the other end outside the box. He lowered the lid until it began depressing the handle. This was the tricky part. It was all about the timing. At the exact moment he pulled the string to release the safety pin, he had to slam the lid closed. If it worked right, the next person to open the box would receive a nasty surprise.

Danny's nerves were jumping. He had only one shot to get it right. Holding the string in his right hand as he kept the lid partially closed with his left, he realized he was sweating profusely. *You can do this,* he told himself. Counting down silently, *three . . . two . . . one,* he yanked the pin out of the handle and slammed the lid in one motion. Holding his breath, he counted up to five. The box was quiet.

Danny let his breath out with a *whoosh*. The trap was now set. He hurriedly changed into dark clothing and strapped on his pistol. Carefully picking up the box to keep from jostling the contents, he ran out the door.

Five minutes later, he pulled into the parking lot at the Sandcastle Plaza and settled back nervously to wait.

Chapter 49

Light rain dotted the windshield of Danny's unmarked police car as he waited in the parking lot. Hands damp with nervous sweat, he imagined all the ways this could play out, most of them ending in disaster. Mental and physical exhaustion threatened to overwhelm him. Lowering his head, he rubbed his face vigorously. *Come on, Danny. You gotta keep it together.* He took deep breaths to calm emotions that bounced from intense rage to deep despair. Glancing at the box on the floor, he thought, *If this doesn't work . . . Stop! Don't go there. It has to work!*

Just then, Andi LaBelle's brown SUV turned into the shopping center, coming to a stop a short distance away. Wheeling out of the adjacent parking lot, Danny slid to a stop behind the vehicle. He touched the butt of his pistol to reassure himself it was still there. Jumping out, he tucked the box under his arm like a running back protecting the football.

Danny tried to see through the back and side windows as he approached, but the dark tinting only reflected his own image. Reaching the driver's window, he glared at Connor with a look of intense hatred. "Where's my wife?" he asked harshly.

Connor answered calmly, "You bring the money?"

"Yeah. Now tell me where Rachel is," he demanded.

"In the back," Connor gestured with his thumb.

Danny put his face to the tinted window and squinted. Rachel's head was jammed against the passenger door. He could see black tape binding her hands and feet, another strip covering her mouth. Her eyes appeared desperate with fear.

He grabbed the door handle and yanked. "It's locked. Open the damn door!"

"Give me the money first," Connor said.

Danny passed the box to Connor and stepped back, closing his eyes and pressing his hands against his ears. Connor ignored him as he opened the latch and lifted the lid.

"What th–," he yelled, slamming his eyes shut just in time to avoid the blinding effects of a one-million-candlepower flash-bang grenade. However, his reaction wasn't fast enough to prevent the powerful, 175-decibel concussion from breaking his eardrum and peppering his face with bits of burning money. Connor screamed, pressing his hands to his head.

Danny stared with grim satisfaction at the sight of the mighty Roy Connor writhing in pain. "Well, you got your money back. Are you happy now, prick?" Danny taunted, jerking open the driver's door and reaching for the passenger door lock. Just as his fingers found the lever, Connor slammed an elbow into the side of his head.

"You bastard, I'll kill you!" Connor screamed.

Danny staggered back, dazed, reaching for his weapon. As Connor fumbled for his own pistol, he saw Danny's gun already coming up. He stomped the accelerator to the floor, causing the SUV to fishtail on the wet pavement. Frantically, Danny grabbed the window frame as the tires suddenly gained traction and the vehicle surged forward.

Struggling to hold on with one hand, Danny raised his gun. But before he could pull the trigger, Connor smashed his fist into Danny's jaw, at the same time twisting the steering wheel hard to the right. Stunned, he felt his grip failing. Feet dragging the pavement, Danny panicked, dropping the gun and grabbing the window frame with both hands. As the speed increased, Connor swerved toward a light pole. Seeing it coming, Danny let go, grunting loudly as his body struck the rain-soaked pavement. Sliding out of control, he slammed into the base of the metal pole, his leg taking the brunt of the impact.

Precious seconds passed as he lay on his back, his leg racked with pain. Finally, he rolled slowly onto his side, raising his head in time to see the SUV barreling onto the street. Danny roared in anger and frustration. Gritting his teeth, he struggled to his feet. Dizzy, he willed himself to stay conscious. He took several halting steps and found he could walk. Barely. Limping back toward his car, he found his gun lying against a curb, deeply scratched but apparently still functional.

Danny made it to his car where he collapsed behind the wheel just as a new shockwave of pain hammered his leg. His mind demanded that he rest, if only for a few minutes. But he ignored it. *I won't wait! I can't! I have to save Rachel.*

Whipping the car around in a tight U-turn, he raced toward the exit. As he neared the shopping center's retention pond, he abruptly slammed on the brakes. His heart was pounding so hard he thought it would explode. Reaching inside his shirt, he gripped the heavy gold badge hanging from a chain around his neck. The metal felt cold in his hand. Alien.

Danny scowled as he remembered the tremendous pride he had felt the first day he pinned on his badge, a cop's tangible symbol of honor and integrity. He thought again of the fateful decision he had made that started this terrible series of events. *The day I took that money, I dishonored what this badge stands for. And because of it, I'm going to lose everything!*

Looking at his hand, Danny was surprised to see he was gripping the badge hard enough to leave a perfect imprint on his palm. He yanked the chain, breaking it. Hurling the badge into the pond, he never heard the splash as he roared onto the street in pursuit of Connor.

Chapter 50

Racing away from the Sandcastle Plaza, Connor bellowed in pain from the effects of the stun grenade going off almost under his nose. "If that motherfucker's not already dead, I'll kill him for this!" he yelled over his shoulder at Rachel. "Do you hear me, bitch? He's a dead man!" He squeezed the steering wheel with a death grip as visions of torturing Danny until he begged to die filled his head.

Connor pulled the SUV into an apartment complex near the ocean and tuned off the lights. Glancing down at the box where it had fallen, he could see bundles of hundred dollar bills still smoldering. He carefully removed the still-hot grenade and tossed it out the window. The faint glow of fire still licked at the money as he savagely beat it out with his fist.

Looking over his shoulder at Rachel, her terror-filled eyes stared back at him. He reached out and roughly jerked the tape off her mouth, tearing the tender skin on her lips. She whimpered but said nothing. Leaning over inches from her face, he said, "I'm going to get my money, and you're going to help me."

"Wh, What? I don't understand," she said in a weak voice.

"Don't pull that shit on me," Connor said. "You know exactly what I'm talking about."

Rachel shook her head forcefully, frowning, "What happened to my husband?"

"If he's lucky, his ass is dead back there on that parking lot. If he's not, I'll make him wish he was."

Crying again, she started to object, "Danny would never do anything like that. He's good, and honest, and decent, and–"

"Give me a fucking break. He's dirty and you know it."

"I, I don't know what you're talking about," she said, her body quivering in fear. "Can you please just let me go?"

"Yeah, I'll let you go. After I get what's mine."

"But I don't understand!" she wailed.

The sound of her whining was ratcheting up the pain in his ear to the point that he wanted to smash her face to a pulp. As he drew back his big fist, she made no effort to turn away. He paused, *Maybe the bitch really is out of it.*

Trying a different tactic, he spoke in a softer voice, "Listen to me. I'm going to cut you loose. When I do, climb over the seat and sit beside me. Do you understand?"

After a moment in which she seemed to be processing what he said, Rachel nodded. Connor cut the tape from her wrists and ankles and helped her climb into the front seat beside him.

"Okay, pay attention here," Connor said, waiting until she looked directly at him. "Here's the drill. You're gonna call Randall's house and tell his wife that you're too scared to be alone. You'll ask her to let you come over. Are you with me so far?"

"Yes, I think so," Rachel answered, touching her torn lip gently.

"Alright. When we get there, you go up to the front door, and I'll be off to the side. When she opens the door, I'll take it from there. And don't try to warn her. If you do, I'll get very mad at you, and you don't want that to happen, do you?" Connor said, unable to keep the menace from his voice.

"No, I don't want that."

"Okay, good. Now, do you know her phone number?"

Rachel looked down at her hands, her brow furrowed as if she were trying to think. "I, I used to know it. But . . ."

"That's okay. I'll dial it," Connor said, punching in the number and handing the cell phone to Rachel. Before releasing his grip on the phone, he cautioned her, "Don't forget. You cooperate, and everything will be fine. When you talk, hold the phone out so I can hear what she's saying."

Dana answered on the third ring.

"Dana, it's Rachel."

"Rachel," she said, concern in her voice, "what's wrong?"

"I, uh, could I come over? I, I'm a little shaky."

"Of course. You don't sound like you have any business driving. I'll come get you."

Rachel looked at Connor, obviously confused by Dana's offer. He mouthed for her to tell Dana that she was fine and could drive herself.

"Rachel, are you still there?" Dana asked.

"Yes, I'm here. I'll be there in a few minutes."

"Well, if you're sure you're okay to drive . . ."

"Okay, I'll see you soon."

Connor took the phone from Rachel and disconnected. "That was good," he said. "When we get to her house, walk slow so I can get in position. Then when she opens the door, you get outta my way in case I have to deal with that damn Rottweiler of theirs."

"Please don't hurt Taz," she said anxiously.

"Don't worry about it. I like dogs. In fact, I like them better than most people, but I won't let him bite me. If he tries, I'll use this on him," he said, raising his shirt to show her the gun he had used so recently. "Sit back now and be quiet."

Connor drove the short distance to Ocean Drive, parking down the street from the Randall's beach house. He told Rachel to get out and start walking slowly. She did as he ordered, stopping several times to look around uncertainly as if trying to remember where she was going. Connor ran ahead, keeping to the shadows. Reaching the house, he stepped quietly onto the porch and stood to the side of the front door as he watched Rachel approach. Lights glowed dimly around the edges of plantation shutters covering the living room windows. As she climbed the three short steps onto the porch, the door opened.

"Rachel, I was so worried about you," Dana said, hurrying out the door. Seeing movement out of the corner of her eye, she began to turn, but Connor was too fast. He wrapped a thick forearm around her neck and squeezed hard.

"Don't make a sound, bitch, or I'll pop your neck like a twig," he hissed, the side of his head pressed tight against her temple. Dana struggled to break the stranglehold that was cutting off her air, her hands clawing desperately at his arm.

"Get inside the house, Rachel," he ordered as he dragged Dana through the front door.

Rachel screamed, "Let her go! She can't breathe!"

Connor loosened his grip slightly and turned his head to look. He was surprised to see Dana's face had turned an unhealthy shade of purple. Letting her go, she slumped to the floor.

Rachel ran to her, lifting Dana and cradling her in her arms. Suddenly lucid, she glared at Connor, "You're an animal, Roy Connor!"

"I don't give a shit what you think. I want what's mine, and I'll have it, or people will die. Now, get her up so I can ask her some questions."

Dana started coming around, blinking and coughing as she rubbed her throat. When her eyes met Connor's, the fear he saw reflected was what he wanted. He needed the two women to be so afraid of him they would do whatever he demanded without thinking.

"Get up! Both of you!" he commanded.

As they rose shakily, a low growl came from the hallway behind Connor. Spinning, he saw Taz charging him, his toenails clicking loudly on the floor. Connor snatched a vase off a sofa table and bashed Taz in the head in mid-leap, shattering the vase and opening a gash between the dog's ears. Taz hit the floor with a thump and lay still.

Dana and Rachel cried out as Connor scooped up the dog, jerked open a closet door and threw him inside. Then he shoved the heavy sofa table against the door to ensure the animal couldn't escape.

"Why are you doing this, Roy?" Dana wheezed, her throat aching.

"I see you still remember me after all these years, Dana. Actually, I'm just here to get my money."

"What are you talking about? What money?"

"The money her husband stole from me," he said, pointing at Rachel.

Dana looked at Rachel. "Danny stole money from him?"

"I don't understand. What money?" Rachel asked with a confused look.

"Ignore her," Connor said. "She's floating in and out of reality."

"Considering what you're doing, I don't blame her," Dana said heatedly.

Ignoring her comment, Connor said, "Pay attention to me, not her. Danny Malone stole a shitload of money from me, and I'm here to get it back. When I do, I'm gone, and y'all can go back to your pathetic little lives."

"But . . . Danny's a police officer," Dana said. "He wouldn't steal money from anybody."

Connor laughed bitterly, "He would and he did. He's a damn thief and a crooked cop."

"Danny is not a bad man! Not like you!" Rachel protested angrily.

He glared at Rachel. "Where do you think he got the money to pay all your doctor bills and shit? Didn't you ever wonder why? I'll tell you why! Because he stole it from me!"

"He did not! He got an inheritance," Rachel said. "From a dead relative."

"Inheritance, my ass," Connor snarled.

"But," Dana interrupted, "I still don't understand why you're here. Danny hasn't given us any money."

"He told me he hid it somewhere in your house. He claims your husband doesn't know it's here, but I'm not buying it. Clay Randall is as big a crook as Danny Malone."

"He is not, and you know it!" Dana exclaimed.

"That's enough of this bullshit! I want my money! Now! Or somebody's gonna die!"

"You're not a killer," Dana said.

"No? Bobby Hawkins and his snitch might argue that point. That is, if they were still alive," he said menacingly.

Dana looked at Rachel, whose shock mirrored her own. "You . . . you killed Bobby?" she asked, her voice cracking.

"Yeah, I did. So I've got nothing to lose by taking out a few more if I don't get my money."

Dana's eyes welled up with tears. Turning to Rachel, they held each other in a tight embrace. Connor watched coldly, his mind going over his options. Time was flashing by, and Randall could show up at any time. Even Malone might join the party, that is, if he survived his tumble in the parking lot. Staring hard at the two women, Connor looked for the lie. For a facial tic or other sign that they knew about the money. He saw nothing there. He decided they must be telling the truth.

But he had to be sure. Pointing his gun at them, he demanded, "Tell me where my money is, or tell me which one of you wants it first."

"Mommy?" a small voice called from above.

Connor whirled, pointing the gun at the sound of the voice. Little Cat was standing at the top of the stairs, her baby blanket held against her face with the end dragging the floor behind her.

Dana screamed at Connor, "DON'T point that gun at my daughter!"

He lowered the gun as he looked at Dana. "Go get her and bring her down here. And if you try anything stupid, I won't hesitate to hurt her, too."

Without looking at Connor, Dana hurried up the stairs, scooping Cat up in her arms and squeezing her tightly.

"Mommy, is he a bad man?" Cat asked.

"Don't be scared, honey. It's okay," she whispered.

"But, Mommy, Daddy said–"

"Hush, now. Don't talk. Let Mommy and Aunt Rachel handle this. Okay?"

"Okay," Cat said, putting her head on her mother's shoulder.

She came slowly down the stairs, holding Cat protectively to her breast. When she reached the bottom, Dana shifted Cat to her other shoulder to put her body between Connor and her daughter. She said, "Roy, no one knows anything about any money that Danny may have hidden here. If you need money, I've got about five hundred dollars in my wallet. Take that, and leave."

"Not likely," he laughed. "Not when there's over a hundred thousand here somewhere." He realized any further attempts to get information from either woman would be a waste of time. And time was growing critical. His only choice was to search the house himself.

"Okay, let's go. Upstairs," he demanded, gesturing for Dana to lead the way. Connor kept the pistol trained on the women as they climbed.

Stopping, Dana asked, "Where are you taking us?"

"What's on the third floor?"

"A game room, the library, and my studio, plus a half bath." Dana answered.

"Okay, Get in the bathroom, and be quick about it," he said, nudging Rachel with the barrel of the pistol as she lagged behind Dana. Reaching the tiny bathroom, Connor shut them inside. "Don't make a sound," he said through the door. "And don't try to get out, or your kid will be the first one I come after," he said, wedging a nearby chair under the knob. The chair's rubber-tipped feet gripped the carpet firmly, ensuring they wouldn't be able to force their way out.

Connor searched the third floor quickly but thoroughly. He dumped out the contents of drawers, rooted through cabinets, ripped books off shelves, and overturned furniture as he searched every conceivable location where Danny might have hidden the money. When he came up empty, he hurried to the second floor to continue his frenzied quest.

Chapter 51

Danny's leg ached brutally, but he tried to block it out. His only thought was to save his wife. Driving north in the direction Connor had fled, he grabbed his cell and hit the speed dial for Clay. After two rings, he heard, "Commander Randall."

"Clay, I need help!" Danny exclaimed.

Clay's hand tightened on the phone at the fear and desperation in Danny's voice. "What's going on?"

"I don't have time to go into details. Just trust me on this, okay?"

"Sure, okay. Talk to me, man," Clay said.

"Roy Connor is the killer. He shot Hawkins and Hayes and my CI. And now he's kidnapped Rachel. I just tried to rescue her, but he got away. And–"

"Wait, wait! What did you say? Roy Connor is our killer? And what was that about Rachel? There's a lot of wind noise in the background."

"Shit, Clay! Quit asking so many questions!" Danny snapped. "Connor kidnapped Rachel, and I'm almost sure he's headed to your house."

"My house? But why?" he asked, incredulously.

"I'm running out of time! Just get to your house! And hurry!" Danny yelled.

Clay looked around to see officers staring at him. Heading toward his car, he said, "Danny, I don't understand what's going on, but I'm on the way. And when I get there, you be ready to tell me why the hell your wife and my family are involved in this, this, whatever the hell it is!" he shouted, slamming his phone shut.

Reaching his car, he yelled at Honchen, "Ty, I have to go home!"

Honchen walked toward Clay's car, a look of concern on his face. "What's going on? You need any help?"

"I don't know right now. I'll call if I do. In the meantime, you're in charge," he said, slamming the door and roaring off.

———

Danny parked his car behind Andi's SUV. He knew Clay expected him to wait until he arrived, but that wasn't going to happen. Gun in hand, he approached the SUV and looked inside, hopeful that Rachel was still there. She wasn't. The metal box lay on its side on the floorboard, burnt hundred-dollar bills scattered all around. With a grimace, he kept going.

It was a risk going after Connor alone, but he had no choice. Every second he waited could mean the difference between Rachel living or dying. But he had a second motive, too. He had to kill him before Connor could tell Rachel her husband was a thief. Even if the asshole had already told her, though, he would claim Connor was lying to cover himself. And with the man dead, he couldn't dispute Danny's version.

Eyes peeled for movement, he sprinted to the side of the house. After a pause to catch his breath, he raised up high enough to peek between the window frame and the plantation shutters. Through the tiny gap, he could see a large sofa table jammed against the entryway closet. *Are they in there? Or is it a setup? Maybe Connor's hiding around the corner waiting for me to run to the closet.* He shrugged. It didn't matter. He was going in anyway.

Creeping onto the porch, Danny quietly depressed the door latch, finding it unlocked. Gripping his pistol tightly, he hesitated only long enough to review his initial strategy once he got inside. Satisfied, he hit the door hard with his shoulder. The door flew in, striking the wall with a loud bang. Coming in low, he dived to his left and took cover behind a large leather sectional. He anticipated Connor charging into the living room to investigate the noise, which would then give him a clear shot at the man. Danny waited nervously for the reaction that didn't come. The house sat silently, as if holding its breath in anticipation of some terrible event about to begin.

A minute passed, the only sound Danny's rapid breathing. With Clay on the way, he couldn't wait any longer for Connor to make a move. Standing in a half crouch, Danny saw the broken vase and blood on the hardwood floor. *Please God, don't let that be Rachel's,* he begged silently. He stared intently at the closet door as if trying to see what, or who, was inside.

He started toward the door, stopping abruptly as he looked over his shoulder at the darkened dining room. *The closet will have to wait. I've got to make sure he's not behind me.* He checked the dining room, kitchen, and breakfast nook. All were clear. Through the kitchen window, landscape lights revealed an empty patio.

Danny retraced his steps through the living room to stand once again in front of the closet. He tapped softly on the door. Getting no response, he cautiously pulled it open. He was startled at the sight of Taz lying unmoving on the floor, blood covering his head and congealing on the floor. He could see the dog's chest rising and falling and hear his labored breathing. *Thank God, he's not dead.* Danny debated what he should do, finally deciding Taz would be safer in the closet if bullets started flying. Closing the door gently, he looked around the living room. He had been in the house less than three minutes, although it seemed much longer. As the seconds passed without any response from Connor, his anxiety grew. He wiped his sweaty palms one at a time on his pants, ready to shoot if Conner suddenly appeared.

Rachel, I'm so sorry for what I've done, he agonized. *I was only trying to help you. And now look what's happened. I've put your life in danger along with Dana and Cat.* Feeling the tension in his neck and shoulders, he forced his mind back on task. Find Connor. Kill him.

The garage was next. Danny scowled as he realized he had forgotten a flashlight. He could have thrown open the door and shined the light in first, possibly revealing Connor before he could react. There was no time to get one now.

He racked his brain trying to remember the location of the light switch in Clay's garage. *Right or left? Come on, use your head,* he chided himself. *The doorknob is on the right, the door opens in, so the light switch must be on the right.* Switching the gun to his left hand, Danny shoved open the door, at the same time slapping the wall with his free hand where he guessed the switch plate was located.

The lights came on, revealing Dana's convertible on the far side of the three-car garage. As he stepped through the doorway, Connor slammed into him from his hiding place behind the door, hammering the butt of his gun against Danny's head and knocking him unconscious.

Chapter 52

Driving at high speed toward his house, Clay mentally replayed the bizarre conversation with Danny. Roy Connor killing Bobby Hawkins and the snitch and wounding Summer Hayes. Connor kidnapping Rachel. And to top it off, Connor was supposedly heading to *his* house for some unknown reason. It all sounded completely crazy. However, if it were true, his wife and daughter were in grave danger.

Rolling to a stop behind Danny's obviously empty car, Clay thought angrily, *Dammit, I told him to wait!* He struggled to control his emotions. *Calm down. Don't jump to conclusions. Maybe he went closer to try to spot Connor.* But he quickly dismissed that idea. Danny's track record of recklessness almost guaranteed he had already gone inside, giving no thought to the consequences. *Danny's out of his mind if he thinks he can take Connor by himself. And he's putting my family at even greater risk!*

Clay ran to the rear patio where exterior stairs led to the second and third floors. Dana had argued against building the staircase, saying it ruined the aesthetics of the ocean view. Over her objections, he had insisted on the stairs as an alternative escape route in case of a fire. He paused at the bottom step, left hand on the railing as he scanned the upper floors. The patio door at the top of the stairs opened into an east/west hallway that ran the length of the third floor. He could see light shining through the glass door. Alert to any sound or movement, he began to climb.

The second floor was dark. Clay quietly checked the patio door and found it secure. If Dana and Cat had come that way, he reasoned, it would have been unlocked. He kept going up, planning to start his search on the top floor and work his way down. Clay wanted the high ground in the event shooting started.

Reaching the third floor deck, he stood to the side of the door and took a quick look down the hallway. No one was visible. He could see a chair jammed under the doorknob of the bathroom. The space was small, containing only a toilet and sink that left little room for more than one person. Was it a trick, or had Connor caged someone in there? Maybe Taz?

Clay tested the patio door, finding it locked, also. *They must still be inside*, he thought. Unlocking the door with his house key, he stepped into Dana's studio, listening intently. Hearing nothing, he went across the large room to a point where he could see down the stairwell. There was just enough light to ensure no one crouched there.

He cleared the game room and library, frowning at the disorder Connor had caused. Returning to the bathroom, he put his ear to the door and listened. He thought he heard someone whispering. Then he heard a voice clearly that made his heart race.

"Mommy, why do we have to stay in here?"

"Hush, sweetie," Clay heard Dana tell Cat softly. "It's going to be okay. Daddy will be here soon."

Clay's eyes welled up at the sound of their voices. *They're safe.* Casting a look over his shoulder at the stairwell, he put his lips close to the door and whispered, "Dana, it's me. If you can hear me, don't say anything. Just stick a finger under the door."

He couldn't help smiling in spite of the tension as Cat's little fingers appeared at the bottom of the door, wiggling like tiny white worms. "Okay," he continued. "I'm going to move the chair and open the door. It's important that no one makes a sound. Wiggle a finger so I know you understand."

After a moment, Cat repeated her finger wave. Clay lifted the chair away quietly and pulled the door open. Dana rushed into his arms, burying her face in his chest as she sobbed silently. Clay stroked her hair, whispering, "Everything's going to be okay."

As he held his wife, Clay felt his daughter latch onto his leg. Looking down, he saw her staring up at him, eyes wide with fear. Keeping one arm around Dana, he scooped her up and hugged her tightly.

Whispering to Dana, he asked, "Did Connor do this?"

She nodded, "He's crazy. He threatened to kill us if we didn't tell him where his money is supposedly hidden in our house. He claims Danny stole it from him. He also said he killed Bobby–"

"Money?" Clay whispered with a look of surprise. "I know about Bobby, but Danny didn't say anything about any money hidden here. Anyway, we can talk about this later. For now, I need you to take Cat and get out."

"Rachel is here, too."

Clay was startled. He had forgotten about her in the excitement. Looking over Dana's shoulder, he saw Rachel sitting on the toilet seat, hands covering her face. He glanced at Dana, mouthing, "What's wrong?"

She pulled him to the side, putting her lips to his ear as she whispered, "The stress of all this has aggravated her Lyme disease. She's having trouble understanding what's happening, and it's also affecting her motor skills."

"Can you get both of them down the outside stairs?"

Dana nodded, a fierce look in her eyes. "Don't worry about us. Just stop that bastard Connor."

"Is Danny here in the house?" Clay asked.

"I don't know. I heard a loud noise a little while ago before you got here. It sounded like a door banging open. But as far as I know, no one's come back up here since Connor locked us in the bathroom."

"What about Taz?" he asked.

Dana shook her head, a look of dismay crossing her face. "Connor hit him in the head with a vase and threw him in the closet. I, I don't know . . ."

With a grim look, Clay said, "Okay, get the phone from your studio. Take Cat and Rachel and go down the back stairs. My car is just down the street. Get in it and lock the doors," he said, handing her his keys. "Then call 9-1-1 and tell them I need the SWAT Team here ASAP."

Dana's eyes filled with tears. "Clay, I'm so afraid. Please wait until you get some help."

"I can't," he said drawing her to him. "I have to find Danny before he does something stupid and gets himself hurt. Now, you have to go."

Stepping into the bathroom, he pulled Rachel to a standing position. "Rachel, you need to leave with Dana. Do you understand?" he asked softly but firmly, his hands on her shoulders.

"Danny? Where's Danny?" she asked, her eyes opening wide.

Clay looked at his wife for help, afraid Rachel would become hysterical. Dana stepped into the tiny bathroom and took her arm. "Rachel, I think I heard Danny outside on the patio. Let's go find him. Okay?"

She peered at Dana, her eyes only partially focused. "Outside?"

"Yes, honey, outside. Come with me," she said, gently pulling Rachel forward. She went without resistance as Dana lifted Cat and turned toward the door.

"Dana," Clay said, touching her arm. She looked back at her husband, openly crying now. Clay gently brushed away the tears and smiled, "Remember that I love you with all my heart and soul. Today, tomorrow, and forever."

Her lips quivering, Dana fought for control. Nodding, unable to speak, she turned and walked away. As they slipped out the door, Cat raised her head to look at her daddy, her dark eyes solemn as she waved a tiny hand goodbye.

Chapter 53

Connor took great pleasure at the sight of Danny Malone hitting the hard concrete floor. He snatched a coil of rope hanging from a wall hook and quickly tied Danny's wrists together with one end. A heavy punching bag hung from the twelve-foot ceiling near the front of the garage. Grabbing a stepladder, Connor positioned it beside the bag. Taking the other end of the rope, he climbed up and released the chain holding the bag from the mounting hardware. As it fell to the floor, he looped the rope through the eyebolt and jumped down.

Heaving on the rope, Connor hoisted Danny's body into an upright position. He then looped the other end of the rope around a large vise mounted on the workbench, Connor stepped back to admire his work. Still unconscious, Danny's head lolled forward as blood dripped to the floor from a large gash on his head.

Connor was glad that Malone had survived and followed him here. It would make things much easier, having torn apart the upper floors without finding the money. Now, he just had to convince Malone it would go easier on him if he told him where to look. He grabbed a handful of Danny's hair and jerked his head up. His eyes were closed, his breathing ragged. Connor slapped his face hard, twice.

"Wake up, you little weasel," Connor said. "We have to talk." Releasing his grip, Danny's head dropped forward.

"Shit," he muttered. Hurrying to the kitchen, Connor rooted through cabinets until he found a plastic water pitcher. Filling it at the sink, he ran back to the garage and splashed the full pitcher in Danny's face. That did the trick.

Danny sputtered, shaking his head to get the water out of his eyes. He looked around, trying to understand what was happening. Seeing Dana's car, he knew he was still in Clay's garage. Gradually, he became aware of his pounding head. His shoulders and upper arms were on fire, and his wrists and hands were growing numb.

The toes of his boots barely touched the floor, as if he were a dancer frozen in mid-pirouette.

He looked at Connor, his eyes immediately zeroing in on the stun gun in his hand. He knew what the man wanted. If it weren't for his desperate situation, Danny could have laughed at the irony. The money Connor so urgently sought was only a few feet from where he stood. Unfortunately, giving it to him wouldn't matter since Connor obviously planned to kill him anyway. No witnesses meant the ex-cop stood a very good chance of getting away with murder. Multiple murders at that. And Danny was under no illusion as to what Connor was capable of doing to Rachel, Dana, and Cat. That is, if he hadn't already done it.

"Talk to me, Malone. Tell me where my money is."

Danny calculated his chances. Strung up like a deer waiting to be field dressed, the odds were not in his favor. Even if he could somehow free himself, he still faced a man who outweighed him by a hundred pounds or more. Also, Connor was armed with the stun gun and probably a pistol in his pocket. Danny figured his only hope was to keep him talking long enough for Clay to get there.

"Roy, I'm arresting you for the murders of Bobby Hawkins and his CI," Danny said. "Drop your weapons and get on the floor."

In response, Connor drove his fist hard into Danny's ribs, causing a loud *oomph* and a grimace of pain. He snarled, "That's for getting cocky with me, asshole!"

Before Danny could recover, Connor hit him in the jaw, eliciting a sharp groan this time. "And that's for busting my eardrum with your little booby trap."

Spitting blood and part of a broken tooth out of his mouth, Danny smiled through the pain wracking his body, "Roy, I can't tell you anything."

"Oh, you can, and you will," he answered softly. "Especially if I apply this device the same place I did to that tall, skinny doper."

Danny frowned, and then he caught the significance. "Are you talking about the guy with the horn through his chest? Jessup?"

"Was that his name?" Connor asked coldly.

"So, you, you also threw the woman off the balcony?"

"Right again," Connor said calmly. "And I'm sure you're wondering why I shared this with you."

"Because you don't plan on leaving any witnesses when you go," Danny said.

"That's right, asshole," Connor replied. "And now that true confession is over, let's get down to business. Tell me where you stashed my money, or I'll drive stun your balls 'til they explode. Which one's it gonna be?" he asked, jamming the business end of the stun gun viciously into Danny's groin.

Danny grunted as this newest pain joined the others battering his body. He wheezed, "It's not here anymore. I put it somewhere else."

"Bullshit! Tell me now, or kiss your balls goodbye," he demanded.

Danny pleaded, "I swear! It's not here!"

Connor pulled the trigger; Danny's reaction was instantaneous. He screamed in agony, bucking and jerking as he tried to pull away. Connor held the device in place for almost ten seconds before letting up.

"You bastard! Stop. Don't do it again," he begged, tears running down his face.

Connor stood watching him, expressionless. "Tell me where it is, and I'll stop. Lie to me again, and I'll jam this baby up your ass and light it off."

"No, please, I'll tell you," he sobbed. "It's in the cabinets on the wall behind you."

Connor looked up. "Which cabinet?" he demanded.

"The middle one . . . it's, it's behind some cardboard boxes in a metal box like . . . like the one . . . that I gave you before."

"Yeah, and if you booby-trapped this one, too, I'll take you apart an inch at a time!" he yelled, jerking Danny's head up as he glared at him.

"No, it's . . . okay. It's . . ." he said, passing out from the pain.

Connor shoved the stun gun in his waistband beside the pistol before sliding the stepladder over to the cabinets. Looking first at Danny and then at the workbench, he appeared to come to a decision. He pulled a gas can from under the workbench, removing the cap and checking the level. Almost full. Connor upended the can over Danny's head, quickly soaking his body in the highly flammable liquid. Dropping the empty container, Connor started up the ladder.

Chapter 54

"Freeze, Connor!" a loud voice behind him commanded.

Connor turned, one foot on the garage floor, the other on the first rung of the ladder. "Randall, you picked an inconvenient time to show up," he growled, his right hand slowly dropping toward his waist.

"Move your hand another inch toward that gun and you're dead," Clay said softly.

"Hey, hey, be cool, man," Connor said, raising both hands in the air. "I'm cooperating. Just don't shoot."

Clay could see the butt of the stun gun as well as the semi-automatic pistol side by side in his waistband. "Okay, Roy. Here's what I want you to do," he said, his gun pointed at Connor's chest. "Very slowly and very carefully, I want you to use the thumb and forefinger of your left hand to pull that gun out by the butt. Then I want you to toss it away. Understand when I say your left hand and not your gun hand?"

"Sure, sure, I'm with you, Randall. Just don't let your finger get twitchy on that trigger," Connor said. Lowering his left hand slowly as instructed, he pulled the pistol from his waistband, letting it dangle between his thumb and forefinger.

"See, I know how to follow directions. Look, here it goes," he said, flipping the gun up in the air.

Clay's eyes involuntarily shifted to the gun arcing toward the ceiling. Connor used the distraction to draw the stun gun, shoving it against Danny's neck as he ducked behind him.

"Drop it!" Clay shouted, the dismay at his mistake obvious.

"I'd be careful where you point that thing, Randall," Connor said. "I'm not sure a bullet will start a fire, but I guarantee this little baby will turn your asshole buddy into a signal flare if I pull the trigger."

Clay said, "You're not stupid, Connor. You'll turn yourself into a crispy critter right along with Danny."

"Not a chance. By the time Malone gets to cooking good, I'll be gone."

"I guess I was wrong about you being stupid. If you pull that trigger, I'll empty this gun in your ass. Then I'll reload and keep shooting until I run out of bullets. Don't for one second think I won't."

For the first time, Connor wavered. If he used the stun gun, there was no guarantee he could get away from Malone in time to avoid catching fire himself. In fact, he could feel the gasoline soaking through his shirt from where his body pressed against Danny's back.

Connor cursed silently at losing his advantage. Somehow, he had to get his hands on Randall's gun or his own. Glancing toward the car, he saw his pistol under the rear bumper.

Clay saw the look. "Don't even think about it, Roy."

Connor's eyes narrowed as the old familiar rage began to boil inside. He was outgunned and apparently outmaneuvered. He tried a desperate ploy, hoping Randall's ego would give him the opening he needed.

"Randall, you've always thought you were a tough guy, so let's you and me get it on right here, right now. No pistols. No stun guns. You whip me, and I'll go quietly. If I win, I get a head start running. You man enough to take me on?"

"You're insane, Connor! What kind of macho bullshit is that?"

"What's the matter? You afraid of me?" Connor taunted.

"The day I'm afraid of a piece of shit like you is the day I turn in my badge. Now toss that stun gun and prone out on the floor. That's the only deal I'm offering you."

Connor glared at Clay for a long moment as he weighed his chances. Then his shoulders slumped. "Okay, damn you, I give up," he scowled, flipping the device away and getting on the floor.

"Put your hands on top of your head and interlock your fingers. Cross your feet at the ankles. You know the drill," Clay commanded.

Connor did as he was told, making no comment.

"If you so much as twitch, you're dead."

"I ain't goin' anywhere, Randall," Connor said evenly.

Watching him carefully, Clay pulled out his tactical knife and stepped over to Danny. "Hey, man, you okay?" he asked softly, never taking his eyes off Connor.

Danny slowly raised his head, face twisted in pain. He whispered, "All things considered, I'd say no."

"I'm going to get you down," Clay said. "Do you think you can stand up?"

"Yeah . . . Maybe . . . Hell, I don't know. Let's find out."

As soon as the rope released, Danny sagged to the floor with a groan. Cutting the remaining strands of rope, Clay helped him to his feet.

"I need to cuff him," Clay said. "Can you hold my gun on him?"

Danny tried to flex his fingers, but they were numb and unresponsive. He shook his head.

"Okay, I'll handle it," Clay said. "Stay back from him. The gas on you is still wet. I don't want any chance of a spark lighting you up."

"No problem. My fireworks license expired, anyway," Danny said, slumping heavily against the workbench.

Clay went back to Connor, taking his handcuffs out as he approached. "Roy, pay attention to what I'm saying. I don't want any confusion on your part that would cause me to shoot you. Because you know I will. Right?"

"Yeah, let's just get this over with," Connor responded.

Clay kneeled beside Connor's hip, holstering his pistol and shifting the cuffs to his right hand. He firmly grasped Connor's interlocked fingers with his left hand while bringing the cuffs up to lock on his wrists.

As he had done when Jessica Savoy tried the same maneuver, Connor bucked violently upward at the touch of metal on his wrist. His powerful legs swept around, striking Clay in the back and knocking him to the floor.

Leaping to his feet, Connor delivered a vicious kick to Clay's upper thigh, temporarily paralyzing the nerve and rendering his leg useless. Clay struggled to pull his gun from the hip holster, but Connor was too fast. Grabbing the holster, he ripped it off Clay's belt. In a split second, the tables had turned. Connor was now in control.

For several moments, no one moved. Connor breathed hard from the exertion while Clay grimaced at the pain in his leg. Danny, too weak to help, leaned against the workbench aiming a string of curses at Connor.

"Shut up!" he growled, pointing Clay's gun at Danny.

Ignoring Connor, Danny hoisted himself upright and limped slowly toward Clay. Connor slammed his fist into his chest, sending him sprawling on his back. Watching Danny wheezing, trying to draw a breath, Connor was satisfied he was no threat. He turned back to Clay, who was trying to get up.

"It looks like I'm gonna have to kill you both so I can get my money in peace," he said, pointing the gun at Clay. "Any last thoughts you'd like to offer?" he asked sarcastically.

Clay stared directly into Connor's eyes, saying nothing.

"No brilliant words from the commander, huh? That's okay. I'm tired of your bullshit, anyway. So long, asshole," Connor said as he raised the gun to Clay's head.

With a bellow of anguish and rage, Danny snatched up the stun gun and leaped at Connor, jamming it into the man's back as he pulled the trigger. The spark from the device ignited the gasoline soaking both men's clothing. Connor screamed as electricity coursed through his body, combining with searing flames that rapidly covered him.

Clay watched in sheer horror as his best friend held onto both the stun gun and Connor, pulling the trigger again and again and again to keep the current flowing. They staggered around the garage in a dance of death, charred bits of clothing falling into the puddles of gasoline and quickly spreading flames to the walls and ceiling.

As the smoke and fire grew more intense, Clay searched wildly for a fire extinguisher. In desperation, he grabbed a tarp from under the workbench, but it was too late. Both men collapsed to the floor with Danny's arms still locked in a death grip around Connor's chest.

Connor's screams grew weaker as the flames enveloped his head, finally stopping altogether. Through it all, Danny never made a sound.

Chapter 55

One week later, Clay and Dana stood in the driveway surveying the damage to their home. The fire had destroyed the garage and caused extensive smoke and water damage throughout the three-story structure. Dana squeezed Clay's arm as she looked with dismay at the destruction. "It's a total loss, isn't it?" she asked.

"I don't know. Maybe," Clay said in a subdued voice. "We won't know for sure until the adjuster does his thing. It doesn't really matter anyway. It's just a house. But . . ." he stopped unable to continue. His heart ached. When Connor had pointed the gun, his own gun, at his head, he was convinced he was about to die. Then Danny had made the ultimate sacrifice to save his friend. The gratitude he felt for Danny's heroic and selfless act was beyond measure. Yet he blamed himself for creating the very situation that led to his death. *If I hadn't dropped my guard with Connor, Danny would still be alive instead of lying in a freshly dug grave,* he thought.

Dana turned to look at her husband, seeing the sorrow on his face. "How are you doing?"

He smiled sadly. "Not so good. It's like . . . like losing my brother. Danny was always doing and saying crazy stuff, but he was a good man. I could never have asked for a better, more loyal friend. I miss him so much," he said, his voice breaking.

"I know it hurts. It's horrible to lose someone you care about. And especially the way it happened. It will take time to get over this, but there are also a lot of people who care about you who will help," she said softly, touching his arm.

Clay said, "You know, I couldn't have made it this far without you."

She smiled, "That's my job, Clay. I take care of you when you need it. You take care of me when I need it. It's nice how that works out, isn't it?"

He smiled back, giving her a hug as he kissed the top of her head. "I guess we need to find somewhere to live while they decide whether this place can be salvaged."

"Clay," she said hesitantly.

"Yeah?" he responded, his attention on the damaged house.

"What Connor said about Danny stealing money from him . . ."

Clay looked sharply at her. "He was a lying piece of shit! Danny had his quirks, but he was an honest cop. I'd bet my life on it."

"I know, and I believe that with all my heart," she said. "But your guys found out that Connor was a big drug dealer, and now they're speculating on the news that maybe Danny was somehow involved with him."

"A reporter was running his mouth about it the other night," Clay said hotly. "If Rachel asks my advice, I'll tell her to hire an attorney and sue their ass. Danny was a hero, period, and he doesn't deserve this. And neither does Rachel."

"I agree," Dana persisted. "But haven't you wondered why Connor kidnapped Rachel and why he kept saying Danny hid his money here? In our house?"

"Sure, I've asked myself those questions a million times, and I can't come up with an answer. Connor was a vicious killer and a total head case. So maybe the man snapped after killing a cop. Or maybe he invented the whole thing to try to get back at me for sending him to jail years ago. I don't know. But what I *do* know is that Danny was one of the good guys."

Clay felt his pulse pounding in his temples. With all that had happened, his emotional temperature was near boiling. And thinking about Roy Connor, much less talking about him, was pushing him closer to the edge. He hated the way he felt. He needed a break.

Turning to look at Dana's rental car, he could just see the top of Cat's head in her car seat. "Is she still asleep?"

"Yeah, she nodded off right after we got here," Dana said. "I'll have to wake her up when we get to Beaches Animal Clinic. When Dr. Daniel called earlier and said Taz was ready to go, she was so excited she wanted to go get him right then."

"Well, you better run on over there before they close. I'll see you at Rachel's in a little while," he said, walking her to the car and opening the door.

"What are you going to do?" Dana asked.

"I want to check in the garage to try to find my tactical knife. It slipped out of my pocket during the fight. You know, Danny gave it to me for my birthday, and, well, it's, you know, special to me," he said.

"I understand perfectly, honey," Dana smiled. She reached up and caressed the side of his face gently. "I love you, Clay Randall. You said Danny was one of the good guys. Well, you're definitely one of them, too."

Clay watched as Dana drove off, then turned and slowly made his way up the driveway. Stopping at the entrance to the garage, the terrible events of that night played out again as he looked at the spot where his friend died. Questions kept running through his mind, questions with no clear answers. And the only person who could tell him was gone forever. He stared hard at the blackened concrete floor as if the key rested just under the heavy layer of soot, ready to reveal itself if only he looked long and hard enough.

Slipping on a pair of leather gloves, Clay stepped cautiously through debris still damp from hundreds of gallons of water pumped into the burning house. Reaching the area he thought his knife might be, he searched under boxes containing partially burnt Christmas and Halloween decorations, old tax records, and toys from Dana's childhood she was saving for little Cat. But no knife.

As he debated giving up the search, he noticed a metal box lying upside down. It was partially hidden under a still-soggy copy of a novel called *Body Toll* written by a former police chief he met years before. Tossing the book aside, he stared for a moment at the box, puzzled. *I've never seen this before. I wonder if it belongs to Dana.*

Heat from the fire had blistered the paint and warped the box's frame. *Whatever's in there is probably ashes now,* he guessed. Carrying it to the remains of his workbench, Clay tried without success to open it. He found a screwdriver that survived the flames unscathed and jammed the point into a corner of the lid. Slowly, it came open with a squeal of tortured metal.

Staring at the contents, he couldn't believe his eyes. The box contained hundred dollar bills. More than he had ever seen at one time, although every bill was heavily damaged. "Oh, no, Danny. Tell me you didn't do it," he said in an anguished voice. As hard as it was to believe, Connor had told the truth. He was staring at the evidence.

Sifting through the remains of the dope money, Clay flashed back on Danny's odd behavior. *The inheritance from the relative he never knew. Obviously a lie to explain how he suddenly came into a large sum of money. And the heavy drinking. He was apparently trying to drown his guilt in the bottle.*

Their heated discussion about ethics came back to him. Danny had angrily defended his position that decisions had to be based upon circumstances, that nothing was simply black and white. At the time, Clay had dismissed all of it as stress and worry over Rachel's condition. He now understood the real reason.

Those thoughts flew through Clay's mind in a matter of seconds. Then he asked himself the most important question of all, *What am I going to do?*

If he revealed the truth, Danny's reputation would be destroyed. And what about Rachel? How would she cope with the certain knowledge that her husband was at best indirectly responsible for two murders, one of those a fellow police officer? The mental anguish would inevitably aggravate her symptoms and reduce the chances she would ever fully recover.

On the other hand, what if he decided not to turn in the evidence? Say he destroyed it, and then someone found out what he'd done. What then?

Life was full of choices. Most were simple, in Clay's estimation. Obey the law. Be honest. Treat people fairly. Then there were choices that didn't fit the normal pattern. Was it right to take something that didn't belong to you if no one would ever know? What if your motivation was to help a loved one rather than yourself? But wasn't character doing the same thing in private that you would do with the whole world watching? Unfortunately, some questions had no easy answers; some choices didn't lend themselves to a simplistic right versus wrong standard.

Clay now faced his very own six o'clock rule. Should he turn in the evidence and allow the investigation to go wherever it led? Or should he destroy it and ensure Rachel the comfort and closure she so desperately needed?

He stared at the contents in the box. At the charred remnants of Danny's reputation. Closing the lid gently, Clay walked slowly to his car, his head down. Tossing the box on the seat, he climbed behind the wheel. For long minutes, he sat motionless, his thoughts swirling.

Finally, after one last glance at the box, Clay made his decision. With a look of resolve, he drove away.

THE END

John 15:13

AFTERWORD

While some in the medical community still doubt its existence, Lyme disease is an all too tragic reality for its many sufferers. It became personal for the author after a family friend was diagnosed with late-stage Lyme disease. While writing *The Six O'clock Rule*, he decided to create the character, Rachel Malone, in hopes of raising awareness of the terrible illness.

The author encourages his readers to learn more by visiting one of the numerous websites dedicated to educating the public about Lyme disease.